D0259139

South London teenager **Terry Ronald** had dreams of becoming a writer until music, his other passion in life, steered him in a slightly different direction. He began his recording career in 1990 when he was signed to MCA Records with a top-ten single around Europe, 'Calm The Rage', and an acclaimed album, *Roma*. As a songwriter, producer and vocal arranger he has since had success with some of the biggest names in pop, including Girls Aloud and Sophie Ellis-Bextor. More recently Terry has co-written songs for the BBC TV musical comedy series *Beautiful People*, working with a cast that included Elaine Paige and Meera Syal.

Terry's varied experience with vocal production means that he is often called upon for television programmes and music events alike, which have included the Brit Awards, Eurovision and, in 2007, *The X Factor*, which he joined as a guest judge alongside Dannii Minogue. Terry has been part of the creative teams on two West End shows: *Rent Remixed*, starring Denise Van Outen and Jessie Wallace, and *The Hurly Burly Show*, which reopens at the Garrick Theatre in March 2011.

During the summer of 2009, Terry finally set aside time to start work on the book he'd always dreamed of writing. The result is his début novel, *Becoming Nancy*. Terry still lives in South-east London with his husband, Mark.

Although *Becoming Nancy* is inspired by some of the experiences and emotions I had as a teenager, the characters and many of the events in the story are fictitious. I was hugely inspired by the environment in which I grew up, and by my family in particular. The actions and the events described in this story, however, do not in any way reflect those of my own family.

BECOMING NANCY

Terry Ronald

BANTAM PRESS

LONDON • TORONTO • SYDNEY • AUCKLAND • JOHANNESBURG

TRANSWORLD PUBLISHERS
61–63 Uxbridge Road, London W5 5SA
A Random House Group Company
www.rbooks.co.uk

First published in Great Britain
in 2011 by Bantam Press
an imprint of Transworld Publishers

'(I'm Always Touched By Your) Presence Dear' written by Gary Valentine.
Published by Jiru Music Inc/Monster Island Music/Chrysalis Music © 1977.
'The Logical Song'. Words and Music by Rick Davies and Roger Hodgson.
Copyright © 1979 ALMO MUSIC CORP. and DELICATE MUSIC. All Rights
Controlled and Administered by ALMO MUSIC CORP. All Rights Reserved.
Used by Permission. *Reprinted by permission of Hal Leonard Corporation.*
'In The Flesh' words and music by Deborah Harry and Christopher Stein
© Artemis Muziekuitgeverij B.V. (Bum/Ste) and Jiru Music Inc. All rights
administered by Warner Chappell Music Ltd.
'Gangsters' (Dammers/Hall/Planter/Golding/Bradbury/Staples/Byers)
© 1979 Plangent Visions Music Limited.
'On My Radio' © 1979 Davies. Reproduced by kind permission of
Fairwood Music (UK) Ltd.
'Kid' words and music by Chrissie Hynde © 1979, reproduced by
permission of EMI Music Publishing Ltd, London W8 5SW.
'Am I Ever Gonna Fall in Love in New York City' words by Jack
Robinson & Vivienne Savoie/Music by James Bolden © 1977 Robin Song
Music. Reproduced by permission of Peermusic Ltd.
'Voulez Vous' by Anderson/Ulvaeus quoted by permission
of Bocu Music Ltd.

A CIP catalogue record for this book
is available from the British Library.

ISBN 9780593067734

Addresses for Random House Group Ltd companies outside the UK
can be found at: www.randomhouse.co.uk
The Random House Group Ltd Reg. No. 954009

The Random House Group Limited supports The Forest Stewardship
Council (FSC), the leading international forest certification organisation.
All our titles that are printed on Greenpeace approved FSC certified
paper carry the FSC logo. Our paper procurement policy can be found at
www.rbooks.co.uk/environment

Typeset in 11/15pt Palatino by Falcon Oast Graphic Art Ltd.
Printed in the UK by CPI Mackays, Chatham, ME5 8TD

2 4 6 8 10 9 7 5 3 1

Mixed Sources
Product group from well-managed
forests and other controlled sources
www.fsc.org Cert no. TT-COC-2139
© 1996 Forest Stewardship Council
FSC

For Sparky

Acknowledgements

Love and thanks to the people who helped make this book possible.

Pat Lomax, who took a chance on me and changed my life. Thank you doesn't cover it. Sarah 'turn it into a novel and we'll talk' Emsley, who went to bat for me. Cat Cobain, who helped me make 'Nancy' so much better than I ever dreamed it could be. Larry Finlay, Claire Ward, Judith Welsh, Madeline Toy and the team at Transworld for having me. Hillary Shaw, who has kept me safe for so long, and who is the most stylish woman I know. Angela, Jodie, Nikki and Grace at Shaw Thing management. To my entire remarkable family and recently acquired in-laws, especially Mum and Aunt Rose, who saved my life; my sister, Tina, and my Dad who is always there for me. My other family: Michael, Lawrence, Emma and Jo (who interfered as usual). Let's have one more chorus of 'Stoney End?' Also Kenny (we really did meet Abba), Tina and Angela: come on the old girls! Dannii and Ian: long-time musical musketeers, and Daniel, for crying in all the right places. My beautiful New Yorkers, and all my friends in Blighty and Oz. Dee and Sherry, for sending Christmas when we really needed it. Mitch and Baby Dylan Terry, for the experience. Tim Edwards, for priceless help and assurance that I wasn't wasting my fucking time. Joanna Sterling and the Meridian Writers gang for wholehearted support. The divine Kathy Lette, for telling me to go for it.

To Mark, whom I love very much.

This book is for any kid who ever lay on their bed staring up at a poster of Debbie Harry . . . and dreamed of what might be!

Terry

Contents

One

Very Nearly New

September 1979

It's well gone six by the time I sit back down at Mum and Dad's very nearly new, smoked-glass kitchen table with a tumbler of milk and a mint Yo-Yo. I'm still shaken to the core. I'm finally, and unenthusiastically, confronting page thirty-eight of my sociology text-book and I'm disillusioned, but not altogether shocked, to discover that it's no less dreary than it had been the last time I sat down and looked at it. I shove it to one side, again. I just can't focus. I'm too excited, I suppose, or is it fraught? I'm not really sure, but I've chewed the collar of my school shirt till it's soaked. I'm restless. I can't think straight and my mind's all full of the day. I have at least four chapters to read tonight, but so much has happened that concentration just seems futile.

Should I pop some music on, perhaps? Yes, that'll calm me down: help me relax. The house is far too quiet – that's the issue, that's why I'm fidgety and can't focus on my bloody homework. Only it's not. I spring up again and saunter over to the flash new space-age radio-cassette player, which, inexplicably, has had its serial number crudely scratched off and is sitting next to the smart, and also very nearly new, portable colour television set, which came without a box or any sort of brochure or instructions. They're both sitting on top of the recently acquired dishwasher that, rather interestingly, came with a few dirty cups and plates already inside. In fact I'd venture that almost everything in Mum and Dad's freshly overhauled and extended kitchen-diner is nearly new.

I put in a tape and sit back down. Music: that's better. Calm again. The whipcrack of the singer's voice comes at me as I lean back in the chair and push my sociology folder and the tatty textbook far out of my eyeline.

'Was it destiny?
I don't know yet.
Was it just by chance?
Could it be kismet?
Something in my consciousness told me you'd appear.
Now, I'm always touched by your presence, dear.'

I'm moved. Jarred, in fact, by what I deem to be one of Deborah Harry's most sublime and insightful lyrical moments: a sliver of rock genius, if you will. It's as if she's speaking just to me, right at this moment. My best friend from school, Frances Bassey, informed me – somewhat spitefully, I felt – this afternoon, out-side the metalwork room after fifth period, that Debbie had not penned this particular verse herself per se: it had been Blondie's mop-haired bass player, Gary Valentine, who had actually written it. Nevertheless, I thought, it had been Debbie, *not* Gary, who had delivered it, clad in a yellow woollen cowl-necked T-shirt dress, and corresponding thigh-high pirate boots, on *The Old Grey Whistle Test* last year, and that's what chalked up points on my scoreboard.

'David! David!'

A rather shrill pitch rudely invades my thoughts, but I pretend I haven't heard anything and go back to them.

'All right, you monkeys!' Debbie had purred at the start of the song, speaking through those superb teeth, like only Debbie does, bobbing her peroxide head and pouting that mouth as she sang, like only Debbie does, an amber stage light flashing over her shoulder as she hollered – with that smart, blissful, New York twang – the line, *'It's really not cheating, ye know?'* Who gave a flying fuck, I pointed out to Frances, if Gary Valentine had written the words, or in fact the New fucking Testament, for the ensuing two minutes and twenty-six seconds? It was Debbie's presence one was ultimately touched by.

'David, I know you can hear me down there, so don't pretend you can't.'

What on earth does she want? I decide to answer, but only half-heartedly.

'Yes, dear?'

I get up and rewind the cassette, seemingly unable to let the song, with all its apparent lyrical significance, sink and fade to nothing, and I start it again from the very top, turning the volume up loud. Then I sit back in my chair, and I ask myself, for what must be the two hundredth time today, could it possibly be true? Is it in any way feasible? And if it is true, what the hell am I going to do about it? But no answer comes – only Debbie. Oh! What simple truth she brings me now: what elation and insight she offers my poor, bewildered teenage heart. Yes, I know I'm being dramatic, I know! But it's a big thing, it really is. And never, as far as I'm concerned, has a song spoken so poignantly to a boy so unsettled.

'David, you're not deaf; so why don't you come when I call you?'

Just as Debbie is about to lift me into the rapture that is my absolute favourite part of the song – the bit where she sings: *'Floating past the evidence of possibilities; we could navigate together psychic frequencies'* – I become aware of an altogether different sort of presence hovering over my right shoulder. I knew it; she wants something.

'David, could you not hear me? Yes, of course you bloody could. Now would you mind very much getting off your fuckin' arse and running over Liptons? I want twenty Superkings and a Vitbe.'

My mother. She can be ever so common at times.

'Could I not go in a minute, Kath? I'm in the middle of my sociology homework,' I say, not looking up. 'I've got to rustle up an essay about venereal disease and what shoes one should wear if one should happen to catch it.'

I snigger at my own joke, then beat my pencil on the table to the last few bars of the song, singing along as if she weren't even in the room and I was entirely adrift in the music. *'I am always touched by your presence, dear, dear, dear, dear . . .'* And then, finally, I look up at Mother with the most syrupy and insincere grin I can assemble.

'Dear!'

She's smiling back at me, but is clearly unmoved, so I drop my head again, hoping she'll get fed up and trot off to beleaguer my sister, Chrissy. No such joy.

'Come on, smart arse!' she laughs. 'Don't push it! You've been sitting there for over an hour now and I've not even seen you pick up a sodding biro yet, so you can go right now. And don't call me Kath, you cheeky git, or dear for that matter. It's vulgar.'

I slump down on the smoked glass of the nearly new kitchen table as Mum, still glamorous in her work suit, hunches expectantly over me, brandishing a couple of dog-eared pound notes. I'm fairly certain that I detect a whiff of Trebor mint so I suspect she's been on the Blue Nun since she got home from work; no wonder she wants a fag.

'All right,' I say, nodding wearily, and then I grab for the cash, my mother pecking me on the forehead and affording me an absurd grin before she turns and heads for the lounge to watch the back end of *Nationwide*. Lifting my school blazer from the seatback, I sniff at it, wincing at the smell of rain-damp cloth fused with sweat. Then, returning to my main preoccupation of the day, I ask myself: how can I really be sure? I have no idea what it feels like, so how could I possibly know? But again, there is no answer.

'I'd put your blazer on if I were you, David. It's spitting,' Mum hollers from halfway up the passage.

'Well, you're not me, Mother, are you?' I mutter. 'So that's that conundrum sorted.'

I pull on the jacket anyway, and then I gather my sociology stuff from the table to take to my room, Mother shrieking, once more, from even further along the hall, 'And stick all your homework upstairs; your father'll be home in a minute. Last thing I need's him griping about the sodding mess. And get a bottle of Cresta or something if you've got enough change. You and Chrissy can have that with your tea: I got some veal and ham pie from Wallis's.'

'All right!'

I mean, should I have the sensation of being hit by something? Or of being blessed in some way by something marvellously celestial? I just don't know. I scan the kitchen momentarily. Mum was right. Dad would, without doubt, rebuke anyone and everyone who was in earshot if the esteemed and costly 'new kitchen' fell anything short of pristine splendour. Of late, in fact, leaving a cupboard door ajar, or setting a cup down upon any surface that lacked the augmentation of one of Eddie's 'Pigeons of Great Britain' coasters, was a crime punishable by execution, it seemed, or at least a strident and lengthy ear-bashing, often culminating in a sharp clip round the ear. Disarray hadn't really seemed to agitate my father prior to 'new kitchen'. The scullery had been tatty, at best, and the decrepit Formica table in 'old kitchen' had become a dumping ground for back issues of *Family Circle*, bits of fishing tackle and boxes of whatever knocked-off goods Dad had been selling that week. There was a cosy familiarity about 'old kitchen'. You knew where you were.

Since they'd knocked through, however, to construct and erect the magnificence that was 'new kitchen', Eddie Starr had insisted that his family all rise to the occasion; so thereafter, the *TV Times* went straight in the sideboard and the aforementioned fenced goods took up residence in the back of the pigeon loft. The upside of this, however, is that now our entire three-storey house is chock-full of the very latest gadgets, most of them courtesy of Eddie's tepid and rather small-time underworld connections. In fact, the work surfaces in our kitchen often put me in mind of the conveyor belt on *The Generation Game*, laden with prizes. We've recently acquired, for example, a new improved Breville snack and sandwich toaster, a SodaStream, which apparently turns dull, ordinary tap water into an exciting fizzy and flavoured beverage, *and* a Videostar video recorder – and I'm pretty certain that we're the only semi-detached on Chesterfield Street to have one of those!

Dad had ranted to me only last week, when he sadistically coerced me into helping him muck out his pigeons, 'You got to change with the times, David. It's no good standin' still like some of the miserable bastards I have to listen to while I'm driving me taxi, fuckin' moanin' about this and that changing.'

'Yes, Dad,' I'd said, heaving at the smell of pigeon shit and holding a yellow Marigold up to my nose. 'I'm sure you're right.'

'I'm embracing the eighties, I am,' he said, even though the decade was still a good four months away. 'I'm fed up with livin' in an untidy shit'ole! Fed up with it!'

And I watched with some fascination as he prised a crusty lump of pigeon poop out of his thick wavy black hair.

'Yes, Dad,' I said.

He'd even employed a cleaner, Moira, to come three times a week to keep things spick and span, evidently deeming Mum to be entirely incapable of holding down a job whilst concurrently retaining an adequate standard of hygiene in the family home. Mum *did* have a full-time job, too – and had had for years – at Freemans catalogue. This had been rather wonderful for the duration of our childhood, especially around Christmas time as my sister Chrissy and I pawed through the silky pages of shiny new toys, but, frankly, a bane once one hit puberty and had to endure endless packs of ill-fitting Space 1999 nylon underwear from the staff shop. On the plus side, though, Mother had managed to procure me a signed photograph of Lulu modelling a shrimp-coloured safari suit when she'd come to cut the ribbon on the new office a few years back.

Truth be told, however, Mum has never been the most fastidious of cleaners, and her employment at Freemans was just the pretext she required to slack off from the dusting. So Chrissy, me *and* Mum herself had hailed the arrival of Moira the cleaner with a great deal of enthusiasm, despite the fact that a plethora of wigs and hairpieces rendered the woman almost impossible to identify from one day to the next. Blonde one morning, titian the next: the only way we knew it was her on most days was because of her slightly overgenerous employment of dark rouge and the terrible perfume she wore.

Moira came on Mondays, Wednesdays and Fridays most weeks, and, to be honest, when I came home from school the first time she'd been I thought we'd been burgled. It turned out she'd just tidied things away, which was a revelation to all of us, especially Mum. She was nice, in a busty, brusque, straightforward sort of way, and Chrissy and I liked her because she swore lots and didn't mind if we did the same. The major boon in having Moira, though, as far as we were all concerned, was that Eddie's once customary and oft-heard cry of 'Look at the fucking state of this shithouse!' seemed little more than farflung nostalgia these days.

Anyway, I shall do Mum's bidding for the time being and toddle off to Liptons. I'm certainly not going to let her wanton grocery demands, or, indeed, the spectre of my father's manic tidiness, impair my mood. I'm happy today. Elated. Slightly confused, it must be said, and eerily nervous, but good and happy nonetheless. After I've changed into my best blue jeans and a Blondie T-shirt, I head for the front door, swinging it open.

'Back in a jiff,' I yell at no one in particular.

I stride out on to Chesterfield Street, slamming the door of number twenty-two behind me. Unexpectedly, the rain-washed landscape does not appear as it had this morning. Am I imagining it, or does the air smell somehow sweeter and fresher this evening? Is the front lawn that little bit greener? So many questions today and very few answers thus far. I turn out of our front garden and pass Mrs Stirzaker next door. I don't know if it's just me, but she actually looks rather cheery tonight as she clumps the living shit out of her unruly daughter, Stella, and I'm pretty sure I catch her winking at me. Across the street, glum Mr Archibald is smiling and waving over at me, as well – word has it he's not cracked a smile since the Coronation so I'm definitely not going mad, there's something in the air. Perhaps they can tell. Perhaps it is true and it shows. But how will I know? When will I know for sure?

Chesterfield Street, I think, is one of the nicer roads in East Dulwich, because it's that bit wider and it has lots of trees. It's just houses, no shops, and you can walk from one end of it to the other in about three and a half minutes. Of course, a lot of the roads in the area look very alike: Victorian semis with very shipshape front gardens. It's not what you'd call deprived or anything – not like some parts of south-east London – nor is it especially posh. It's just ordinary. But I like our street: it's cheery, and the people keep their houses nice and sponge their cars down regularly. Well, most people. When I pass by my nan's house, which is only two doors along from ours, I detect the familiar but ever-divine aroma of her special thick mince and macaroni cooking. She's made it every Wednesday for donkey's years.

We've always lived two doors down from my nan, which was ace when me and Chrissy were kids as we had two immense houses to tear around in instead of just one, and we loved being so close to her and my grandad. For some strange reason, and completely out of the blue, I find myself thinking about the people who lived in between our two houses years ago, Joan and Bette. They had a hairdresser's on the main road, Lordship Lane, and they took care of their old dad, Bernie. I remember Joan and Bette always looking very 'fifties', with crimson lipstick, stalwartly lacquered, film-star hair and smart grey high-waisted slacks; Bernie had those sea-captain's whiskers, and gave Chrissy and me Merry Maid chocolate toffees. We'd all be out in our back gardens on bright Saturday mornings: me, waiting for my grandad to take me shopping in the high street; Joan and Bette, fussing over their roses; Bernie, sitting in a deckchair puffing on his pipe. I think of all that as I pass by tonight – I don't usually. Maybe it's because the bouquet of my nan's thick mince and macaroni is even more mouth-watering than usual. Or perhaps it isn't, but it seems that way. Everything seems enhanced this evening. Right, somehow. Just what the doctor ordered. I think I know the reason for this and I should keep it a secret: it's both superb and terrifying all at once. But I really need to think about it, process it. The thing is . . . today, for the very first time . . . I think I might have fallen in love! I think I might have accidentally, and very carelessly, fallen in love with the captain of the fifth-year football team.

Two

Casting Aspersions

It had all started this morning when Frances Bassey and I dashed out of the teeming rain and all but barrelled into the lower assembly hall of Dog Kennel Road Secondary Modern with a romp of thirty-five or so other expectant pupils, all keyed up to hear the definitive cast list for the school's autumn production of Lionel Bart's musical version of Charles Dickens' *Oliver Twist*. The final round of auditions had been held on Monday, the first day of the new autumn term, and I'd been surprised, stunned in fact, at just how many kids had decided to thrust themselves forth as prospective performers: I suspect that a good half of them only wanted to be involved because of the number of lessons one can potentially abscond from during the latter stages of rehearsals, especially if one had landed a principal role, which I dearly hoped I had. Besides that, every pupil from the fourth year up was expected, nay compelled, to take part in at least one after-school activity, and the only other half-decent option (if you didn't count football, rugby or some other filthy sport, which I bloody well don't) was the organizing and running of the reliably dreadful bi-monthly inter-school disco. Mr Peacock, our nice Head of English, had formed an American college-style debating society at the beginning of last year for students who, like me, were more inspired by words and intelligent discussion than dashing around a muddy field. I must say I'd been very enthusiastic about *that* at first, but, as it turned out, it was very scantily attended and ended up with just me and a girl from the Upper Sixth in thick glasses shouting at one another in the library about which one of Charlie's Angels, we felt, had the most intellectual wherewithal and which one wore the nicest tops. So that was the end of that.

Anyway, there we all were, sopping wet and keen as mustard in the cavernous old Victorian school hall, noisily dragging petrol-blue plastic chairs across the gleaming polished parquet and vying for a spot next to one of the bulky old-fashioned radiators so we might dry ourselves. Frances Bassey and me pulled our chairs as near to the foot of the stage as we could, both anxious to discover who had been chosen for all the most coveted roles after Monday's auditions, and find out precisely how the autumn production was going to take shape this year.

Now, I must point out to you that there is a fair amount of pressure this term for the school's drama department to 'get it right', as it were, particularly after last Easter's debacle when Marcia Tubbert – one of the Lower Sixth girls – was picked to play the lead in the spring play. Marcia was renowned for being a violent playground bully, not to mention a bigoted and highly accomplished shoplifter who had been banned from virtually every Asian mini-mart in the vicinity of the school. These particulars – along with her self-tattooed knuckles – did not make her an especially popular choice for the part of Joan of Arc in the Dog Kennel Road school's seemingly brave but ultimately foolhardy rendering of George Bernard Shaw's *St Joan*. On opening night, pandemonium had ensued when, in the audience, several parents of Marcia's past victims started hollering things at the stage during the trial scene. 'I've got a pack of Swan Vesta in my handbag if you're stuck for something to light the fire', one disgruntled mother called out, rattling a box of matches. 'Chuck a bit of white spirit on her, she'll go up a damn sight quicker,' somebody else had suggested rowdily – that sort of affair.

When, at the theoretically gripping climax of the production, poor Joan is led away to be burnt at the stake, there was virtual rapture from the audience and a standing ovation for the guards that carted her off. So Miss Jibbs, who had been, by and large, in charge of all things dramatic within the school, was consequently asked if she would kindly set aside her somewhat radical plans to have a crack at *Hedda Gabler – the Rock Opera* for the time being, in favour of fresh blood. Hence the significance of this term's upcoming theatrical extravaganza.

Hamish McClarnon, our drama teacher, who is,

exotically, both Scottish and a homosexual, breezed into the hall waving a lilac ring binder and yelling, 'OK! OK! Calm yourselves, calm yourselves, my young and nascent thespians! Simmer down, now.'

Moist adolescence shook off the rain and hurriedly settled as Hamish, nattily clad as always, took to the stage with a bound and held aloft the all-important cast sheet, poised, flamboyantly, to read aloud. Frances tossed me an excited sideways glance as she ripped the see-through rain bonnet off her brand-new wet-look curls.

'I bet you're going to get one of the main parts,' she said breathlessly, 'what with your lovely singing voice.'

I shrugged my shoulders, but I was hoping against hope: it was all I could think about, to be honest.

'Who knows?' I said nonchalantly. 'I'm not really that fussed either way.'

Then Hamish addressed the hall again, his grand tone hushing the kids like it always did.

'Now! I have te say, it were tough this year. *Oliver!* is not an easy show te cast, particularly with the shortage of girls we have here in the school.'

Ours is an all-boys' school, essentially, though merged with a neighbouring girls' school at sixth-form level. Even then, the so-called fairer sex are fairly thin on the ground, as most of the young ladies of Camberwell High (an establishment my Auntie Val had recently described as 'full of scabby whores') have failed to cotton on to the benefits of further education – principally, one suspected, because a glittering career in smoking outside the Wimpy Bar and shoplifting talcum powder gift sets from Jones & Higgins undoubtedly beckoned.

'So!' Hamish went on, discarding a chunky lemon polo neck, 'I've had to be creative with the casting as ye can imagine, due mainly to the fact that none of the girls seem to be able te carry a tune in a pink bucket.'

'Oy, sir! I can bloody sing!' yelled Frances, sticking her hand in the air. 'My mum says I've the look of a young Gladys Knight.'

'Yes, well, pardon me, Frances,' Hamish snapped back, 'but having the look of a young Gladys is not quite the same as having the voice of a young Gladys, is it? Te be honest, hen, the first time I heard ye sing I thought someone had run over the school ferret. No, I'm afraid I can't offer you any major role, darlin'.'

Frances put her hand in her lap and turned out her bottom lip comically – she does make me giggle. I think that's why she's always been my very best friend: she makes me laugh, and she's never backwards in coming forwards. I decided to shout up.

'Sir! She's the prettiest girl in the Lower Sixth. I hope it's not cos she's black!'

Mr McClarnon looked cross and slammed his ring binder down on top of the piano. 'Shut it, Starr!' he said. 'Half the kids in the school are black, and some o' them can sing. I'm basing ma decision on what's best for the play – not on race, and not even on sex as it turns out. Now, do ye want te hear this cast list or not?'

We all fell silent as Mr McClarnon took a seat, crossed his legs, and began to read the list aloud; then squeals of delight pricked the air as he announced the names of students and their allotted parts in the production: Mr Bumble, Oliver, Mrs Sowerberry, Toby Crackit. One by one he reeled them off.

'Sonia Barker!' Hamish cried, running his heavily ringed hand through his thick ginger wedge-cut hair. 'Now, I'm going to offer you the part of Bet. What do you think te that, dear?'

Sonia, a shrivelled, unkempt girl perched behind Frances and me, lifted her copiously mascaraed eyes off her copy of *Smash Hits* only momentarily.

'Yes, sir!' she sighed, looking as miserable as sin.

'I can definitely visualize you as a fifteen-year-old Georgian streetwalker, dear,' Hamish told her. 'But whether you can rally yourself sufficiently te hold down four or five choruses of "Oom Pah Pah" is yet to be discovered. However, I'm throwing prudence te the wind, all things considered, on this spectacular, so we'll give you a whirl, hen.'

'Yes, sir!' Sonia sighed again, returning to her magazine.

'You see, I could have done that part,' Frances hissed at me. 'She's only here so she can bunk off double maths, and she looks like Patti Smith's mother.'

I nodded, only half listening, as Hamish continued.

'David Starr!'

I sat bolt upright and prayed quietly to myself: Fagin. I had to get Fagin. There weren't many parts left, and I was almost sixteen and far too lanky for the Artful Dodger, surely. And I couldn't possibly have been shoved in the chorus, could I? No. No. The degradation of that would be too much to bear. Too much! I'd not even be able to set foot in the school again, let alone on to the stage. I held my breath.

'David, I thought your audition piece was very, very good on the whole,' Hamish smiled, 'though I must say, I did wonder if Kate Bush's "Wuthering Heights" might have been a tad overambitious, particularly with the dance routine. Nonetheless, you've a stunning wee voice, and after much thought I've decided that you're the only one here who can do the part justice.'

Yes? Yes?

'So, David, you'll be playing the part of Nancy!'

'Oh!'

Well, I hadn't been expecting that.

'How brilliant!' Frances yelped. 'How completely and utterly brilliant.'

'Yes,' I nodded, slightly dumbfounded. 'How ... brilliant.'

I wasn't entirely sure how I felt about it. I was tantamount to staggered, if you want the truth. Yes, we quite often had boys playing female parts in our school productions – it was a case of needs must in a predominantly male environment – but, as far as I was concerned, Nancy was an icon, and had the show's paramount and most dazzling number – 'As Long As He Needs Me' – so there was a heck of a lot to think about. I mean, which rendition of the song would I do, for example – the Shirley Bassey or the Judy Garland? I'm very fond of both! And what does one do, outfitwise? I would, for instance, favour a plunge neckline, something slightly Nell Gwynn-ish; but could a fifteen-year-old schoolboy credibly pull that look off? I just didn't know. And bosom. What do I do about a bosom?

'Oh! For fuck's sake, sir!'

A voice from the back of the hall: the odious but brutally handsome Jason Lancaster, whose dreadful family have, for as long as I can remember, resided in my street at number eight, a mere seven houses from my own. Jason loathed me, pegging me as the school sissy and therefore fair game, and my stomach lurched at the very sound of his scornful tone.

'Isn't Starr bent enough already?' he called out. 'You don't want to make him any more of a pansy, sir, he'll explode!'

He and his cronies' spiteful laughter clattered around the lower hall, kicking off a domino effect of ruthless mirth. My face flushed and burned suddenly, eyes smarting. And although I grinned valiantly, I felt as though my guts had once again been ripped out. Why me? Why the fuck was it always me they singled out for their infantile malevolence? Was it just because I studied hard and handed my homework in on time, or because I hated football and didn't want to play? Was it because I'd lovingly put together and dutifully handed out the Dog Kennel Road school newspaper every fortnight for a year and a half before the headmaster banned it for being semi-revolutionary? Was it perhaps because I had a vocabulary of more than fourteen words and I preferred Kate Bush to Thin Lizzy? Yes. It was all of those things, and much, much more. I sank low into my chair, making myself as small as I could, and then I caught a glimpse of Frances, her eyes flashing pity at me.

'Just ignore him, David,' she advised sweetly, touching my arm.

As if I could. I knew Frances understood all too well, though.

'They don't bother me,' I lied to her. 'They're a bunch of dense wankers.'

Jason was evidently not going to give up.

'He's already a Nancy, sir!' he bawled across the assembly hall.

More hysteria. Hamish McClarnon slowly stood up, visibly fuming, and I turned around in time to see Jason's mouth shut like a trap: as if he knew, suddenly, that he'd crossed the line. Hamish raised an ominous ringed finger.

'Lancaster, you don't use words like "bent" in front of me, boy, or anywhere, come te that. You know as well as everyone else in this room ma rule on that, son. I'll tell ye, it's more than your life is worth, which, let's face it, isn't all that much te begin with. Now shut ye mouth, or leave. Do ye understand me?'

Jason looked down at his feet with a tight smirk, rain still glistening on his quarter-inch crop.

'Sorry, sir! I didn't mean you, sir,' he mumbled.

'I'll bet!' Hamish said. 'But I don't care who you're talkin' te, I don't want te hear that rubbish in my class-room or anywhere else, is that clear?'

'Sir!'

'Anyway, you'll be on props duty, Lancaster, for this

show, if you're te be involved at all, understood?'

'Yes, sir!'

Hamish McClarnon was, pretty much, my hero. I don't imagine for one moment that he was the first homosexual I'd ever encountered, but he was certainly the most ebullient and self-assured. He'd arrived at the Dog Kennel Road Secondary Modern last January in a flurry of pastel knitwear, and had made his mark with some swiftness. He was one of what us kids might call the 'lefty' brigade of teachers in the school: a small but evolving assemblage of staff who wore jeans and badges with political slogans; and, unlike some of the Christian Conservative contingent, fronted by our very own headmaster, treated us like young adults rather than silly children. In our very first drama lesson with him he had told the assembled class, with a hand's flourish, that he was, in fact, an openly gay man – one of a very small handful within the Inner London Education Authority, apparently – and proud of it. The ensuing sniggers and attempts at jeering were cut mercilessly short by Hamish, who, in no uncertain terms, informed the culprits and their would-be aficionados that there were to be no such anti-gay or homophobic shenanigans anywhere even approaching his earshot, and that the same went for racism. Further to that, were there any breach of this rule, chastisement would be prompt and severe.

The punishments that Hamish had gone on to delineate were wide-ranging and far-reaching. They included regular and protracted silent detentions or being put on report, where teachers sign a form, drearily commenting on your behaviour, at the end of every single lesson; even suspension wasn't out of the question. However, the jewel in Mr McClarnon's castigation crown, as far as I was concerned, was the threat of being banned for the rest of term from taking part in all after-school sports, including football: both practice and matches. This, of course, horrified Jason Lancaster, who naively saw himself as the next fucking Kevin Keegan, and his similarly sporty pals; and they left me alone, on the whole, during Mr McClarnon's classes, despite the unpleasantness of today.

As last term progressed, a small group of us older kids – including Frances and myself – had started to actually socialize with Hamish and some of the other like-minded teachers, including Mr Peacock and Miss Jibbs, outside school. We went on theatre trips to *An Inspector Calls* and *Hello, Dolly*, and to the Rock Against Racism gig at the Alexandra Palace. We even went to the Palmerston pub with them on a few occasions, which is just far enough away from the school not to get caught supping lager shandies by the less enlightened teachers. Then, during the summer holiday just gone, Frances and me were invited to Hamish's flat for supper, with Mr Peacock and his wife, Annie. We had something vegetarian and drank Sainsbury's vin rouge, and then we listened to Marlene Dietrich and smoked a joint – it was very sophisticated to my mind, and Frances and I had been thrilled. The thing, though, that impressed me about Hamish the most was that he didn't seem to give a fuck what people thought about him being 'one of them', as my nan might say – a homosexual. It was someone else's problem as far as he was concerned, and that, to me, was gob-smacking: the idea of admitting thoughts like that even to myself, let alone divulging them to another living soul, made me want to hughie. But Hamish was seemingly fearless.

The school did have another gay member of staff up until a couple of months back, as it happens: a timorous and nervy creature who taught French, and, in his patchwork denim and multicoloured braces, looked like he'd been left behind by a travelling pro-duction of *Godspell*. His name was Mr Majors, and some of the children – well, most of them, actually – called him Farrah Fawcett. In stark contrast to Hamish McClarnon, Farrah held little to no authority over any of his classes, most of whom had decided he was a homo the minute his *'Bonjour, mes enfants'* got under way. He fared, I believe, slightly better with a handful of the younger boys – the first and second years – who hadn't quite worked out the implications of his rather liberal hand gestures and assorted silk necker-chiefs, but once the boys hit about thirteen, any wide-eyed notions of Mr Majors being anything other than a 'raving arse bandit' went straight out of *la fenêtre*.

During almost all our lessons with Farrah, there had been a steady stream of random, smart-alec remarks bandied across the French room by the clever little so-and-sos who knew, with some certainty, that poor, wretched Mr Majors would rather stick his tightly permed head into a textbook, or fuss around with something unimportant in a stationery cupboard, than confront their cruel slurs, and, indeed, his own demon. So Jason Lancaster's cries of 'Where's your girlfriend, sir?' and 'Does she like it up the bum?' went, for the most part, unchecked.

I, of course, felt horribly sorry for Mr Majors at first; but then sometimes – when the name-calling spilled over, consuming me in its putrid wake – I would catch him studying me, as if I might be party to some hitherto unspoken secret method of deflecting the spiteful tongues of fifteen-year-old schoolboys. He never once stood up for me. He never once told Jason and his friends to desist as they pointed and laughed at me each time we read aloud the word *'pensée'*, on the afternoon we learned the French names for popular flowers. It was something of a breather for him, I imagine. Anyway, after finally more or less convincing most of the fourth and fifth years that he was, in point of fact, engaged to be married and therefore not gay, someone spotted Farrah on the night bus with a man in cerise angora – so that was the end of that. Two weeks later he handed in his notice and fled the school, unable to endure the unyielding derision.

At least he had that option. I, of course, don't. I'd thought a lot, recently, about the obvious similarities between Mr Majors and Hamish McClarnon . . . both teachers, both gay . . . and the striking differences. I'd thought about which one of them *I* would rather be . . . which one of them I might well be.

* * *

'What about Bill Sikes, sir?' Frances called out across the hall, heroically navigating attention away from my still fresh mortification. 'Who's playing evil old Bill?'

'Oh! Yes! I nearly forgot,' Hamish whooped, sounding uncannily like Molly Weir from the Flash commercials. 'The part of Bill Sikes will be played by Maxie Boswell.'

Who? Who the fuck was Maxie Boswell? I'd never heard of him. I followed a sea of rotating heads, now all looking in the direction of said Maxie, who was sitting at the back of the hall on his own, and discovered a blond, hazel-eyed creature I don't think I'd ever once spotted at the school, or anywhere else in the locale for that matter. I would have remembered. I indisputably would have remembered him.

'Do you know who he is?' I quizzed Frances.

'I've not ever seen him,' she said, 'but I've heard about him. He started this term – transferred from St Joseph's. And he's put a lot of noses out of joint cos after the football trials the day before yesterday he got made captain. He's a bit tasty, actually.'

I looked around at the boy once more. He was leaning back on his chair and his right hand was between his legs.

'D'you think?' I said. 'I wouldn't know.'

Then the pips went for the next lesson. Frances and I began to gather our bits and pieces together, but Hamish, evidently not quite finished yet, started clapping his hands together and shouting over the resultant din.

34

'Wait a minute! Wait a minute!' he yelled. 'We've got our first read-through *and* sing-through tomorrow afternoon, so can everyone be here prompt after last period, please? Mr Lord will be accompanying us on piano, so start learning these scripts and songs now, ma pets.'

'Mr Lord, the PE teacher?' I squawked at Frances, aghast, as we filed out of the hall. 'Playing the bloody piano?'

'Believe it or not, Bob Lord's a veritable Winifred Atwell on the ivories, as well as being Greater London's forty-eighth strongest man,' Hamish assured us as we passed him.

'And he's a born-again Christian, sir,' Frances reminded us.

'Yes, well, nobody's perfect, dear,' Hamish said, handing us each a script and ushering us through the swing doors and into the corridor. 'Now, quick smart te your next lesson!'

The aforementioned Mr Lord, in fact, taught my next lesson, technical drawing. Technical bloody boring I call it: why on God's green earth I ever let my father talk me into taking the subject is a constant and bewildering mystery to me.

'You've got to have a practical option in amongst all the arty-farty bollocks,' Dad had said. 'Drama, music, French ... fuck that. You need to do something that might be a bit useful in the outside world, son.'

But I loathed it, and was rubbish at anything technical or scientific, or, indeed, mathematical. What I loved was drama, history and music, and, of course,

English language: I didn't even have to try at that, and I'd sat my English O level, and passed, a year early along with another fourth-year boy. In the end, though, it had come down to a toss-up between technical boring and metalwork, but the thought of coming home from school twice a week with iron filings in my freshly Alberto Balsamed hair was too much to bear, so TD – or should I say, TB – it was. Apart from that, Bob Lord also presided over the Physical Education department, PE being the other subject I loathed with all my being, so there was double the reason to hate him. He wasn't that fussed on me either, really, particularly as far as any sports-related classes went. Only last week he'd pulled me aside in the changing room before games, virtually yanking my arm out of its socket.

'You can't wear cut-off denim shorts to play basketball, Starr!' he'd spat.

'My shorts are in the Hotpoint, sir,' I said as astringently as I dared, 'so it's this or my sister's old ballet tutu.'

It was the first TB lesson of the fifth year today, so there were a few fresh faces in our class, odds and sods who had defected from other art-based curricula within the school – pottery mainly, as the headmaster's much-heralded promise of a new kiln had finally fallen flat after almost two years. As I turned around to see exactly who had rocked up for this funfest, I found myself practically nose to nose with the mysterious Maxie Boswell, who was sitting at the desk behind me, smiling and chewing a protractor. I noted his sturdy jaw; his full and crooked mouth; his thick, dirty-blond eyebrows above eyes one might bathe in: nothing to write home about, I said to myself – though I suddenly found myself only semi-detached from a swoon.

'So you're my Nancy,' he said, almost bashfully.

'I guess I am.'

'Well, that's all right then, ain't it,' he said.

And I supposed it was.

When the lesson had finished, he grabbed the back of my blazer as I was headed for the door.

'What you doing lunchtime?' he said. 'We could go through the script together if you like.'

I stopped in my tracks and turned around, intrigued, as the rest of the exiting class shoved past me.

'Well, we 'ave got quite a lot of lines together,' he said. 'And it's still pissing down with rain, so we might just as well find a quiet corner in the library and get a head start on it – what do you think?'

I suddenly had butterflies, and felt slightly clammy. What the hell was happening?

'Well, yes, I suppose that would be really rather sensible,' I said.

Maxie seemed pleased that I'd agreed to his plan.

'Great!' he said. 'What 'ave you got next?'

'Double music,' I said, hauling myself together. 'We're discussing *Evita*, and whether the tight bun might have been a contributing factor in her early death.'

'Oh!' Maxie said, visibly baffled. 'Well, I've got double PE, and the showers weren't working this morning so I might be a bit sweaty come lunchtime.'

'I'll live,' I giggled.

Why did I feel so strange? What was going on with me? Before I knew it, Frances was upon us, waving bits of printed paper in my face.

'Hiya!' she shouted. 'I hope you've not forgotten about helping me with my leafleting this lunchtime, David.'

My heart sank. I had. Maxie stepped forward.

'What are you leafleting about?' he asked Frances.

'Blair Peach,' Frances said proudly. 'Oh! You're Maxie Boswell, aren't you?'

'I am,' Maxie confirmed, 'but who's Blair Peach when he's at home?'

'Well, he's not at home any more,' I muttered. 'He's dead.'

'He was an anti-Nazi protester who was killed by SPG while he was demonstrating against the National Front earlier this year,' Frances elaborated. 'So far the police have fucking got away with it – got away with murder. But there's gonna be a march and a demo in a couple of weeks, with a concert at Brockwell Park, so that's what the leaflets are all about.'

Frances had been a vigorous campaigner for the Anti Nazi League ever since Hamish took us to the Rock Against Racism gig in June. Maxie looked at her, and then back at me.

'Well, that sounds important, doesn't it?' he said. 'Maybe I should help too.'

'Brilliant!' Frances yelped: her favourite word. 'Brilliant!'

Then she grabbed an armful of leaflets from her

shoulder bag, dumping half of them on me and the rest on Maxie.

'Make sure you do the whole school this lunch,' she said.

And she trotted off.

I turned back to Maxie, who was busy studying one of Frances' pamphlets.

'This is awful,' he said, 'really awful.'

I nodded solemnly.

'I'd better get off to my next lesson,' I said.

'Oh yes,' Maxie said. '*Evita!*'

I turned and headed along the whitewashed, bricked corridor towards the music room, and Maxie suddenly shouted after me.

'We can go through our lines tomorrow if you want. Lunchtime. I've got footy after school.'

'All right!'

Well, I practically floated down that long hallway, quite giddy. I didn't know what it was about that boy, but I was strangely and undeniably taken with him: bowled over, if you like; and then I caught myself. What the fuck was I thinking? I mean, what could I possibly do about it anyway? Nothing. Absolutely nothing. Why can't things be different, I thought, why?

'Why?' I said aloud, as I turned the corner.

Jason Lancaster was coming out of the science lab with biro ink all down his white shirt.

'Why what, Starr?' he said noisily. 'Why are you such a fuckin' faggot?'

And then he laughed, a couple of his granite-faced mates joining in.

'I s'pose it's no surprise you're playing Nancy anyway,' he went on, raising his voice even further. 'Seems to me like you were born to play it, you sad fuckin' fairy.'

The peal of spiteful laughter rang through the school corridor, and I slipped into the music room and shut the door. That's why things can't be different.

Three

Love and Lunacy

It was raining for a spell, but it's stopped now, and the air seems cleansed and revived as I promenade along Lordship Lane, swinging my mother's loaf as though it were an Indian club. I've been turning things over in my mind for a while and, I must confess, I'm moderately baffled now. What on earth have I been daydreaming about? I seem to have persuaded myself that this apparition ... this boy ... this ... 'Maxie Boswell' – a nom de plume if ever I heard one – has captured my heart in some way. It has to be said, thoughts of him, and him alone, have been affecting me all day. I'd been, for instance, scandalized to find, during English lit this afternoon, that I'd recklessly felt-tipped his name across the dust cover of my *Cider with Rosie*. Fortunately, it being a wipe-clean frontage, I managed to render this imprudent dedication an unsightly red smudge, but it's not funny. How could I allow myself to even consider the possibility that I could fall in love ... be in love with ... NO! It just isn't possible. I'm fairly certain that even thinking along these lines is akin to embarking on some grisly and ceaseless fairground roller-coaster ride, which would without doubt transport me, ultimately, to the certain annihilation of my very soul. Perhaps I'm being a teeny bit dramatic, but it is no small thing I'm contemplating here; and then, of course, there's the likes of Jason Lancaster and . . .

'OY!'

My sister, Chrissy, is standing by the little grocer's on the other side of the main road, and is hollering at me to come over.

'All right, bruv?' she smiles as I reach her. Then she frees a cigarette from the golden trappings of a Benson & Hedges packet, and places it between her lips, immediately staining its filter bright pink with lipstick.

'OK?' I say brightly. 'What you up to?'

'Just waiting for Abs. She's gone in the Wimpy for a bender and chips,' Chrissy says, flicking her hair out of her eyes. 'You know Squirrel, don't ya?'

And she gestures towards the boy to the left of her.

'All right?' he grins, blowing out smoke.

One might peg them as a fairly odd coupling, Chrissy and her latest boyfriend, Squirrel, as they slouch against the outer wall of the shop, puffing on fags. Chrissy is relatively voluptuous for a fourteen-year-old, and, as we speak, she's teetering on skyscraper heels and is clad in a tight grey pencil skirt and an even tighter mohair sweater. Her bleached-white hair, still damp from the early evening downpour, is fashioned into a rather severe wedge at the back. At the front, it falls forward over her right eye, affording her a quality of significant and, it has to be said, effortless mystique. That is, until she tosses her head, or flicks the hair away from her face, revealing her wide blue eyes and trademark petulant smirk. It is this particular trait that the boys at her school can't seem to get enough of – that, coupled with the fact, of course, that Chrissy has the largest breasts in the fourth year.

In stark contrast, Squirrel, as he is known – principally due to his aptitude for concealing stolen goods about his person, usually without detection – is a somewhat weaselly apparition. Our mother, Kath, has suggested on several occasions that Squirrel – real name unknown – appears more than a little undernourished, and would almost certainly profit from a few hearty lunches. And if you ask me, I don't think Chrissy is entirely sure what she sees in him, but she seems to cherish him nonetheless.

'I just fuckin' love the way he dresses,' she'd told me only this morning over her Ricicles. 'He's dead fuckin' kushdi – don't you reckon, David?'

I guess he is a rather well-turned-out boy at that. This evening, for instance, Squirrel is sporting a tonic-green three-buttoned box jacket; grey Sta-Prest trousers that seem to give up at the ankle; thick white socks and shiny black tasselled loafers. I'm led to believe that he has aligned himself with the most recent of youth cultures, the growing throng of south London mods: teenagers, and older, in fact, who have embraced and revived the clothes and music of the early sixties youth cult of the same name, though I believe a lot of them now call themselves rude boys. They're all obsessed with a band called the Specials, and a new film just out, *Quadrophenia*, which apparently concerns itself with young men without aspiration hurtling around Brighton on scooters, and which looks deadly dull to me. Well, certainly not as good as *Abba: The Movie*, anyway! Regrettably, a few of these mods, and quite a lot of their skinhead counterparts, appear to be leaning towards light Nazism, despite the fact that most of the bands that supposedly inspire them are racially mixed. Squirrel, however, seems to have little time for politics, and just likes the outfits ... and possibly the dance. He eyes me nervously for a moment as Chrissy stubs her cigarette out underfoot; and then he turns to her, earnestly.

'So going back to what we were talking about earlier,' he says.

'Yes,' Chrissy sighs, rolling her eyes to the heavens, and sparking up another B&H almost immediately.

'Well,' he says, 'would you let me finger you or not?'

My mouth drops open and Chrissy draws heavily on her fresh fag. Then she looks evenly at Squirrel, whose eyes are farcically wide.

'Not outside the mini-mart, no,' she says, only marginally irritated.

'No, obviously not outside the mini-mart,' Squirrel laughs, 'but I mean, would you – in theory – let me finger you?'

I turn away, agog. Surely Chrissy has never done

anything like that. Not my little sister. She's not fifteen for two months, for Christ's sake. She can't be more sexually qualified than me – can she?

'Well, what do you wanna do that for?' Chrissy says, slumping further down the wall. 'I'll tell you what you can do, Squirrel, you can buy me a bottle of cider – that's what you can do.'

'It's not the same,' Squirrel sulks. 'We've been going out three months now; you don't let me do nothing.'

I pitch forward.

'Can you not discuss this in front of me, please?' I shriek.

But Chrissy completely ignores me.

'We kiss, don't we?' she says to him, taking another elongated drag on her fag. 'I let you feel me tits, didn't I? Stop fucking moaning, Squirrel, for fuck's sake!'

And with that my sister's best pal, Abigail Henson, arrives on the scene clutching a large bag of overly ketchupped chips; Squirrel, mercifully, falls silent.

'Hi, David,' Abigail breezes, fluttering seriously made-up eyelids when she spots me. 'I thought that was you, what a great surprise. Are you coming out with us tonight, then?'

Abigail is two years older than my sister, and, to my mind, a bad influence. She's still in her school uniform, or at least the remnants thereof. Her white blouse is dragged open across her shoulders to reveal much more of her undergarments than I'd have chosen to see, and her once thigh-covering school skirt has been rolled over so many times at the waist it has become little more than a belt.

'Where are you all off to?' I say.

'We're going up the Crystal Palace Hotel,' Abi says, gesturing with a chip. 'They've got some good bands on – you should come.'

'I'd better not,' I say. 'I've got to go home and think about stuff. I've got a lot to think about tonight.'

Abigail shuffles towards me slightly, and fiddles coyly with the ends of her dark-brown curls.

'Oh, go on, Dave, I've just had a demi-wave specially; besides, thinking is boring,' she says, as if she'd ever tried it. 'Come out and have a laugh with us.'

'Go on,' Chrissy suddenly interjects. 'You know Abs fancies you, David. You might get your leg over.'

Well, I'm mortified.

'I'm sure I never knew any such thing,' I say, my voice leaping up about an octave.

Squirrel is chortling irksomely behind my sister. Abigail at least has the good grace to blush slightly.

'Well, you do now,' Chrissy laughs, 'so why don't you come? All you do is sit in your room and listen to Blondie and bloody Abba, you boring fucker. Come out and 'ave a giggle with us.'

'No. I won't. Not tonight – sorry.'

Abigail looks vaguely crushed; Chrissy just shakes her head while stubbing out her latest cigarette on the pavement.

'All right then, I'll see you back 'ome,' she says. 'Abs, let's go and get changed at mine. I need to put me goin'-out face on.'

And off they go, Squirrel sauntering two paces

behind the giggling, chattering girls, head down. I start back along the high street, somewhat bemused. Abigail Henson? But why me? I'd never given her any reason to . . . so why would she even think that? Me and Abi Henson? Whatever bloody-well next?

I'm distracted, for a moment, by a tempting waft from the Wimpy bar, but I shan't succumb; there are more critical matters afoot. I'm casting thoughts of l'amour aside for the time being and heading for the paper shop, having spotted a fourth-year boy at school with the new *Record Mirror*. Debbie Harry is on the front cover: I simply have to own it. Perhaps I'll read it as soon as I get home, while listening to the twelve-inch version of 'Sunday Girl' – perhaps not – I don't know. I need to do something when I get home to take my mind off all this love and lunacy, that's for sure. What *shall* I do this evening?

I settle on masturbation as I've not really managed to find occasion for it the last three or four nights, what with one thing and another. My dad stashes smutty magazines beneath an empty fishing-tackle box in his wardrobe: well, I say smutty – it's *Penthouse, Men Only*, that type of affair. It's not really my cup of tea, truth be told. I can get the job done with that type of pornography, yes, but I can never quite grasp why men feel the urge to gawp at dim-looking women playing golf or washing up while naked. I mean, waxing the Cortina just doesn't strike me as the type of task one would undertake with one's tits out, to be frank. Some of the sixth-form boys carry much spicier porn: dubious publications featuring men and women

47

– German, I presume, or perhaps Norwegian – performing the most filthy deeds one could ever imagine. It would take me less than a minute to come, armed with this type of literature, despite the off-putting hairstyles so, quite apart from being supreme masturbatory fodder, I consider this type of magazine a real time-saver. And after I've done with that, I think I'll learn, by heart, the words to the entire *Voulez-Vous* album. It's the only Abba LP I don't have down off pat: sociology can go fuck itself, and so can the rest of my ever-accumulating homework. I'm fed up with being goody-bloody-two-shoes. And with that significant decision under my belt, I do a little dance as I pass by the next parade of shops on the main road.

For some reason, I stop outside the French bistro that used to be David Greig's years ago. I close my eyes for a second and squeeze my left hand shut tight, as if I were holding my grandad's hand like I used to, right here on this spot, and I try hard to picture his face. He used to come and collect me from our house, my grandad, each Saturday morning.

'Come on, Melksham,' he'd shout out from the passage. That was his nickname for me, after the town in Yorkshire where he was born. And we'd be off to Lordship Lane with two big shopping bags: one red, one black. Most of the shops in East Dulwich were different in the late sixties. There was no Mace, or Wallis; there wasn't even a Wimpy Bar. We'd always come to David Greig's first – a long shop it was, with fancy glass-covered counters running down both sides. Counters with meats, and huge blocks of cheese, and pies, and pastries – a food hall, I suppose you'd call it. Greig's had all the old Edwardian fittings, and it was emerald and brown shiny-tiled from top to bottom. Grandad would buy best back bacon, and mature Cheddar, and all the men serving us would wear boaters, and aprons around their waists and down to their shoes. Next to that was the green-grocer's; that's still here.

'A nice cauliflower,' Grandad would say, 'and some new potatoes; I don't need runners, I'm growing my own this year.'

Then we'd get kippers from the fishmonger, and at a quarter past five on a Saturday, after *Grandstand*, I'd watch *Doctor Who* while my nan grilled the kippers; Grandad would eat them while he was watching *Dad's Army*. We'd get our eggs from Tucker's the butcher's, which I thought was odd at the time. Every single week, without fail, the nice man in Tucker's with the twinkly eyes would ruffle my hair, which was white-blonde when I was little; and one Saturday he gave me a toy – a bendable PG Tips monkey with a shopping basket and a pink hat. I've still got it some-where. If I was very well behaved while we did the shopping, Grandad would get me a comic from Tom's Newsagent, or a bag of Revels – they were my favourite, apart from the coconut ones. Then he'd hold my hand really tight as we crossed the road, and say, 'Come on, Melksham! Let's get home, or we'll not catch the wrestling.'

Of course, as time went on and I got older, I tended to skip our Saturday-morning shopping more and more in favour of playing out with the other kids, or sitting in my room listening to records – that all seemed far more important. Things change, don't they? But it seems to me that they just get thornier and more convoluted most of the time, when you don't always want them to. You have to start making decisions about things that you'd rather shut away in a Tupperware container in the cupboard. When Grandad died a few years ago it was too late to go back to our Saturday shopping excursions, and sometimes, like now, I really, really want to. My grandad and his kippers, his wrestling, and his Kathy Kirby LPs; those days hadn't been at all thorny or convoluted. It was all unfussy and joyful then – not like now, not like today. Today was a bit like the Big Dipper at Brighton: happy one minute, scared and anxious the next, and all the time feeling like I might be sick. This can't be what love's about, can it?

A big drop of rain smacks me straight in the eye and brings me back to the here and now. I'm immobilized, still, in the French bistro's window. It's closed tonight, but if I lean right against the dark glass I can just about see the emerald and brown shiny tiles – they've kept them. They're still here. I take a step back and I'm frowning at my reflection: I'm not a bad-looking chap, am I? Not unkind on the eye? I've had many a female admirer, after all – just look at Abigail Henson: there's the proof. I mull on this self-appraisal for several minutes, taking in my slim frame, my grey eyes and pronounced lips, my hair: straight on top, then tumbling about my ears in modest curls. No, I'm not bad-looking for fifteen, nearly sixteen, not bad at all.

'What's wrong with me, then?' I say aloud, glancing round to see if anyone's within earshot. 'Why do they all call me bent? Is that what I am if I feel like this? Bent. What the fuck does that even mean?' I wonder, for a moment, why on earth I cheerily accepted a girl's role in the school musical, but that's a mystery as well. It's like I can't stop myself. Like I'm asking for it. And now, on top of it all, this Maxie Boswell character. I shouldn't even be thinking about this. Entertaining thoughts about love! About him.

Once I've got my magazine and a bottle of Cresta I head for home. I can hear 'The Logical Song' by Supertramp blaring out of the Wimpy Bar and I catch myself humming along.

'Won't you please, please tell me what we've learned?
I know it sounds absurd.
Please tell me who I am . . .'

Then I spot Jason Lancaster, alone, puffing on a roll-up outside the working-men's club that I work in part-time, still in his school uniform. He sees me, too, but turns away at speed, unable to look me in the face. And I know very well why.

Four

Tossed

Shutting the front door, and safe in the shelter of number twenty-two Chesterfield Street, I head down the passage to discover mum and my Auntie Val – who lives two doors down with my nan – parked in the lounge with wine and nibbles, screeching the names of old movies at the television.

'*The Bridge on the River Kwai!*' roars Aunt Val. '*A Bridge Too Far! Waterloo Bridge! Waterloo Sunset! Sunset Boulevard!*'

They're watching *Give Us a Clue*, but clearly do not have one to give.

'Where have you been, David?' Mum asks, looking up. 'You've been ages.'

'She asked you to go and buy a loaf, not fucking bake one!' Aunt Val laughs, jumping up to kiss me. 'Hello, darlin'!'

'Sorry, Mum, I got waylaid,' is the best I can come up with, and I hand my mother her ciggies.

'So, did you get a good part in the play then, love?

They'd be bloody barmy not to give you one, with your singing voice,' Aunt Val enthuses.

Mum jumps up abruptly, knocking over her plate of Twiglets.

'Ooh yes, I forgot to ask earlier. How did it go at the casting today?'

Both women are now clutching a hand each, beaming at me eagerly.

'I did get a part,' I smile. 'I did . . . it's a great part . . . I'm gonna to be playing . . .'

A voice booms from the passage, quite unexpectedly.

'Chrissy's got fucking nail varnish on that new kitchen table. Jesus Christ, look at it! I'll bloody kill her!'

Dad strides into the room and inadvertently crushes a batch of Mum's fugitive Twiglets into the gold and green shagpile beneath his boots.

'Oh bollocks! Who left them there?'

'Shut up, Eddie!' Aunt Val dismisses him. 'David's telling us about his school play.'

Val, I suspect, is the only living person not afraid of my father. She'd had Eddie's card marked ever since she and my mother first clapped eyes on him running the waltzers on Peckham Rye funfair in the sixties.

'Never mind the school play,' Dad hollers. 'That nail varnish has dried now – I'll never get it off. She's left all 'er fuckin' make-up all over the kitchen – she's got no respect for anythin', Kath.'

Mum puts her hand on Dad's arm and gives him a gentle – or perhaps nervous – smile.

'Eddie, she's a teenage girl, that's all,' she says.

'It don't matter how old she is,' Eddie barks, pulling away from her. 'I don't want fuckin' nail varnish on me new kitchen table.'

'Well, Eddie,' Aunt Val chimes in, bravely stepping into the breach, 'I doubt if Kath wants pigeon shit all over her clean sheets while they're drying, but that's what she's got for the last fifteen years, isn't it?'

Dad grits his teeth and looks somewhat mental.

'Mind your own business, Valerie, please,' he says, with a slightly more hushed, but equally menacing tenor. 'Shouldn't you be at home, anyway – makin' up spells or summink?'

'Well,' Val huffs. 'All this furore over a dab of Hot Pink on a bit of shitty old smoked glass. Get some Pledge on it, why don't ya?'

I make an attempt to back out of the lounge, still carrying a now rather sad-looking Vitbe loaf.

'I'll fill you in about the school play later,' I say softly, and to no one in particular – they're not listening anyway.

'It's no wonder you're not fucking married, Val,' Eddie scoffs as I duck out of the door surreptitiously. 'Who'd put up with that fucking gob?'

I head up the stairs towards the relative sanity of my bedroom, leaving the three of them to fight it out, with Una Stubbs and co. still gesticulating madly on the television behind them.

On the landing I hear more rowdy voices: Chrissy and Abigail are in Chrissy's bedroom trying on clobber with The Boomtown Rats' 'She's So Modern' full pelt on the stereo.

'I'd say it was more of a porridge colour, that jacket,' Abi is remarking to my sister, who is admiring herself from all angles in the mirror on the wardrobe door. 'Have you got any oatmeal-coloured shoes?'

'Who the fuck has oatmeal-coloured shoes, Abigail?' my sister snaps in semi-despair.

Then she spots me at the top of the stairs, and breaks into a smile.

'What do you think, Davey? What should I wear? This one or the . . .'

'I think you should wear your black and white dog-tooth skirt, the black polo neck – or perhaps the halter top if you're feeling in the mood to show your cleavage off tonight – and the black suede winkle-pickers,' I suggest, entering her unbearably messy bedroom. 'That's what I'd . . . I mean that's what I reckon. Where's Squirrel?'

Abigail, who is slumped on Chrissy's unmade bed, licking her middle finger and flicking through last week's *Jackie* magazine, rolls her eyes.

'Gone to meet some of his wanky friends,' she says. 'You know a lot about women's fashion, don't you, David? I've noticed that before.'

'He's got a very good eye for a frock-and-shoe combo,' my sister agrees. 'He always knows. I reckon you'll be a fashion designer one day, Davey.'

'Perhaps.'

Then Chrissy strides over to the bed, dragging her

friend up by the elbow, and marshalling her towards the door.

'Now, can you take Abs up to your room and play some records or something for twenty minutes please, David. I've got to get under the shower and run a flannel over me baps before I go out. I've had netball today and I'm a bit tacky.'

Abigail's all smiles.

'I'd love to see your room, David,' she gushes. 'All your bits and pieces.'

Chrissy stifles a snigger, and winks at me. There goes my early-evening wank.

'I hope you're not too embarrassed about what Chrissy said earlier,' Abi says, plopping herself down on my bed. 'Do you mind if I do me nails?'

I shake my head as Abigail unleashes a revolting shade of coral-pink polish from her bag and proceeds to daintily varnish her long manicured fingernails.

'You are a nice-looking chap, David,' she goes on as I head for my record collection. 'A lot of the girls think so, even girls my age in the sixth form, but I've never seen you with a girlfriend. Have you had one? Don't you want one, David? You never seem to be that fussed, really – unless Frances Bassey is your girlfriend, and I've never seen you two kissing or even holding hands, but you're always together and so . . . as I say . . . Christ, you've got a lot of Abba posters.'

'Yes, I suppose I have,' I say, looking around at my scrupulously considered wall design.

'And Debbie Harry,' Abi says. 'Do you like blondes?'

For some strange reason I have a transitory vision of Billy Blue Cannon from *The High Chaparral* – we'd watch that on a weeknight when my grandad babysat, and I was allowed to stay up past nine.

'Yes, I suppose I do,' I agree again.

And then I study her for a moment. She's a very pretty girl, is Abigail – even now, sitting under my favourite poster of Kate Bush, Abigail is tremendously pretty. She drops the nail varnish back into her bag and gives me a wink.

'Why don't you put a record on and get on the bed with me?' she suddenly suggests.

Well, I'm knocked for six by her brazenness. What on earth does she think is going to occur?

'I'm just looking for something,' I all but stutter.

'Come on,' she says. 'Chrissy'll be an age yet.'

I flick through my singles until I come to S for 'Summer' and then pop on a twelve-inch while Abigail flaps her hands around violently in an attempt to dry her freshly decorated nails at speed. Out of the blue, something takes hold of me and I move, albeit timidly, towards the bed. Hmm ... I'll show them who's bloody well bent.

'You know what, Abi?' I say, sitting down beside her. 'If you cut your hair a little shorter, and messed it up a bit, and bleached it white, you'd look a bit like Debbie Harry ... sort of.'

'Really?' Abigail squeals jubilantly. 'Well, perhaps I should do it, then.'

And with that she swoops forward and secures me in what I take to be a French kiss. Interesting. I close my eyes tight as Donna Summer's honeyed tones drift languorously out of the one functioning stereo speaker and across the bedroom: 'Down Deep Inside', a song in which Donna seductively implies that there might be a place deep inside me that I'm longing to explore – only I'm not entirely sure there is. I'm really not. As it turns out, this record is fairly lengthy – a good six minutes – and I've started to wish I'd put on something a little shorter: Blondie's 'Hanging on the Telephone', for instance, which comes in at a bijou two minutes twenty-three. Then at least I could have jumped up and changed the record for a bit of respite – my lips are red raw already. Eventually, though, Abigail comes up for air, and I find myself panting slightly. She clearly takes this as a sign of arousal on my part and goes for gold.

'Shall I toss you off?' she suggests, and she gets up and turns the key in the lock on my bedroom door.

When she sits back down again I chew over the proposition at hand for a moment, and I decide, possibly recklessly, that having Abigail take a crack at pleasuring me in the comfort of my own bedroom mightn't be such a shoddy notion. I mean, if I can handle that, then perhaps the recent trepidation I've had surrounding my sexuality might be unfounded after all. Perhaps I could like Abigail in the same way I like Maxie. Why not?

'Oh, go on then,' I say before I know it. 'You'd best

be nippy though, Chrissy'll be out of the shower in a minute.'

So away she goes. There's a certain amount of fumbling at the outset, as the button on my Lois jeans can be a bit pernickety, but once Abigail negotiates that, things get going at a reasonably fair old pace. I'm pleased to report that my penis is quite credibly stiff – though I am intermittently glancing down at Abi's discarded *Jackie* magazine, which, conveniently, has fallen open at a poster page featuring a shirtless Paul Michael Glaser. Just to be on the safe side.

'You're quite good at that, Abi,' I say cheerily, sensing that there might be a result in a minute or two.

'Shhh!' she snaps. 'I'm concentrating.'

So I sit back, watching her salmony pink-painted fingers move up and down my cock – it's fascinating, to be honest, and, as I say, she's quite adept: not too hard, not too soft.

'Have you done this before?' I grunt.

'Not really,' she says, 'but I secretly spied on someone doing it to my younger brother this summer when we went to our chalet in Leysdown, so I think I know what I'm doing.'

'Oh!' I say, intrigued, as she picks up speed. 'Your younger brother's in my year – who was wanking him off, then?'

'My older brother,' she says. And that's what takes me over the falls.

When Abigail and Chrissy eventually head off to locate Squirrel, I potter downstairs for a spot of post-coital veal and ham pie and some pop, and I'm not entirely sure how pleased with myself I'm supposed to be. I mean, on the one hand – if you'll pardon the idiom – I had managed to bring about an agreeable finish to the proceedings upstairs with Abigail, but to be honest, I'm not altogether sure if my heart was really in it, let alone my undivided attention. I don't think it answered any of my questions at all, if you want the truth. Bollocks! As I walk past the door of the lounge towards the kitchen, Aunt Val grabs me by the sleeve of my T-shirt.

'Hey, you!' she says. 'You've still not told your mum and me about the play. You know I'm dying to hear all about it.'

She was, as well. Mum's younger sister has always pegged me as her golden-haired boy, and I in turn adore her. Along with my mother, my nan and my Aunt Val have been pretty much everything to me ever since I was little – especially after lung cancer had viciously snatched my grandad from us all. Mum relies on Aunt Val too – more, I think, than she knows – chiefly as an ally against my father, who is prone to griping and light bullying at the very best of times, and has a furious temper at the worst. Having her sister in such close proximity has always been, I feel, a safety net for my mum – for all of us, really – and my nan's house a close-at-hand haven of calm and good cooking.

Mum, it seems, is also on tenterhooks re my starring role in the school production, but Dad's just lying on the settee with his shirt off, leafing through the

Exchange & Mart, when I come into the lounge. At least they've all stopped bloody shouting at one another!

'So,' Mum says, smiling, 'who are you playin' then, love – Bill Sikes? Mr Bumble? I expect you're too skinny for Mr Bumble, aren't you? Ooh! The Artful Dodger!'

Everyone is waiting. Even Eddie has glanced up from his paper now. I take a deep breath.

'Nancy!' I announce haughtily, and almost certainly ill-advisedly. 'I'm playing Nancy.'

Silence. Nobody speaks for what seems like a decade, and then Dad says, 'Oh Jesus fucking H. Christ!'

'Nancy?' Mum repeats quietly, as if making completely certain she's heard correctly.

'Yeah.'

More silence.

'Well, I think you'll be fuckin' fabulous, darlin',' Aunt Val says finally.

Then Mum breaks, and gives me a little smile.

'Me too!'

'Thanks!' I say, quietly relieved. 'You'll have to make the costume, Mum. D'you mind?'

'Course I'll make it,' she says. 'I always do, don't I? Just let me know the colour scheme. I've got some peacock taffeta left over from the frock I made your nan when she won the ladies' darts trophy the year before last, will that be any good?'

'I'm not sure Nancy would have worn taffeta, Mum,' I laugh. 'Mind you, she was a nineteenth-century singing whore, so I suppose anything's possible.'

I turn to look at Eddie, who, it has to be said, doesn't appear best thrilled. Within seconds he's off the sofa again and bellowing as per.

'You shouldn't fucking encourage him, you two,' he screams at Mum and Val. 'You'll turn him into a right little poof! He'll be a laughing stock. Nancy! Fucking Nancy! Why couldn't he be bloody Fagin or the other little cunt with the top hat? I blame you, Kath. You took him to see too many fuckin' Julie Andrews films when he was a kid – that's his trouble.'

It was always the same with Eddie. Whatever Chrissy and me did wrong, it was always Mum's fault in the end.

'Oh, cobblers, Eddie!' Aunt Val snaps. 'There's no girls at his school – someone's got to play the part, and he's got the best voice. Take no notice, David.'

But Eddie is on a roll, and they're off again.

'Why don't you mind your own fuckin' business for once in your life, Val. Is that too much to ask, eh? Is it?'

And it's time for me to slip quietly away once more.

Up in my pop-star-wallpapered attic bedroom, I turn Debbie up so loud on my headphones I can scarcely hear myself think, let alone my dad's incensed ranting.

Debbie is singing a song about a man who is evidently sinking, hopelessly, in a sea of love, and I guess I can identify with that. I wilt on to my bed and pick at the woodchip paper that I've recently painted turquoise, and gaze up at a photograph of Agnetha and Anni-Frid from Abba that I've Blu-Tacked to the ceiling. Suddenly I am standing there in front of them, a warm but forceful wind almost knocking me over. There they are – right there – wearing white jumpsuits and clogs and standing beside a helicopter, as one might were one as famous and as rich as they purportedly are. I look down, and discover that I too am wearing a white jumpsuit, and matching white clogs, and I am now walking towards Agnetha and Anni-Frid who stand, glorious, beneath the rotating blades of the chopper, blonde and auburn hair fluttering in the slipstream. When I reach them they smile at me, but say nothing.

'It's all your fault,' I tell them. 'I should never have listened to you.'

The girls stand either side of me and take one of my arms apiece, tenderly; and as the din of the helicopter engine subsides, they are humming softly – the first few bars of 'Chiquitita' – and I close my eyes. When I open them, I can hear the bongs from *News at Ten* coming from the lounge downstairs, but no more yelling, thank God; and then, suddenly, I can smell semen. Oh, Christ-on-a-bike: Abigail Henson! What was I fucking thinking?

I finally get undressed and put on my pyjamas, climbing into bed early; I'm dog-tired. Well, it's been a jam-packed day, what with one thing and another. I mean, I might well have fallen in love with one person, I had a very unexpected sexual skirmish with another, *and* I got the leading-lady role in the school musical, and just look where that got me! I consider, for a moment, what my grandad might have made of all this, and then my thoughts switch to Dad. I wonder whether his words will forever make me feel this bloody awful, and whether the taunts of Jason Lancaster will always follow me, stinging me – just like they always have.

Five

Rough Boys: a Naked History

It's always been the same for me, as far as Jason Lancaster and his clique were concerned. It had certainly been no picnic a few years earlier: particularly if in 1975 you were an eleven-year-old boy living in south-east London with a heavy fringe and a picture of Abba glued to your satchel. No, sir! There was a warped hierarchy in play even then, a junior pecking order in which, I confidently pressumed, I languished fairly far down. At the very top of this pre-pubescent social pile were the boys who rode skateboards in the Co-op car park, the boys who kicked footballs against the garages in the flats: the ones who swore, and smoked Rothmans at the bus stop. These were the boys who packed a punch – then and now, the same ones who name-called us across the street as we walked home from school. The rough boys, we called them; and they were all-powerful.

Me and Frances Bassey were fairly frequently the unfortunates who were singled out for sundry abuse by the rougher boys around and about East Dulwich and, in particular, the street I lived on, Chesterfield Street. I was generally 'bender' or 'poofter' as far as they were concerned – I could never quite grasp why – whereas Frances, more often than not, was nig-nog. Not especially inventive, I grant you, but these invectives, though deficient in originality, got the point across. Frances, my dearest friend and closest ally even then, was always far sharper than me. Once, during half-term, Gary Hoskin dared to shout 'golliwog' after her as she sauntered up the road with a Jubbly. Frances turned on her heel and without missing a beat warned Gary that her uncle was Idi Amin, President of Uganda, and that if he cussed her once more Idi would be around to fuck him up. I recall thinking at the time that this was a fairly savvy retort for a twelve-year-old, and I wished that I'd had the wherewithal to be even half as canny as Frances was; but I, typically, at the first sign of altercation, put my head down and ploughed on to the sanctuary of number twenty-two, mortified and completely unable to fathom why, of all people, these repugnant boys had singled me out as a queer.

I suppose it has to be said, though, looking back, that I was never likely to garner a huge amount of street cred, what with my mum coming out at six thirty every weeknight into the tree-lined road where we all played, shrieking, 'David, *Crossroads* is starting!', particularly since none of the other kids my age, boys or girls, seemed to recognize the intrinsic wonder of soap operas in the way that I did. I followed, for instance, *The Archers* with my nan every single lunchtime in the school holidays, and adored the magnificent Elsie Tanner in *Coronation Street*. Most of all, though, I was absolutely and completely fanatical about the five-nights-a-week, continuing story of a family-run motel in the Midlands that was ... *Crossroads*.

'Let's play at *Crossroads*!' I would oft demand of Chrissy during the summer holidays, insisting that she play the part of Meg Richardson, the show's formidable middle-aged matriarch and motel owner; while I would, more often than not, take the part of the alluring and, to my mind, glamorous waitress, Diane Parker – who was blonde and had astonishingly shiny hair. Our version of *Crossroads* was actually set in our father's pigeon loft, and some of the episodes I concocted and directed there were, I felt, even more thrilling and nail-biting than the real thing. These included storylines involving multiple-car motorway pile-ups, stillborn children, and once – in a genius cross-procreation with my other favourite television show – Daleks invading the motel and exterminating all the guests in the dining room who had failed to use their silverware in the proper sequence. Chrissy and I dearly loved our own private Crossroads motel with its wooden hatches and its cooing, seed-pecking patrons, but it was a game I could never share with the other children on Chesterfield Street – and especially not with the rough boys. They surely wouldn't have understood, and I'd have been cut down yet again.

* * *

I seemed to fare little better on the social scale in the cut-throat environment we light-heartedly called primary school. Boys like me, who fled from a football and winced at war games, dared not hobnob with the girls (much as I was drawn to them, in terms of the playground at least). This would merely antagonize and incite the more boorish soccer captains and would-be Lotharios amongst the boys, exposing their ineptitude and inability to relate in any way to the opposite sex outside of a hand up the skirt. Therefore, boys who fraternized with girls were themselves considered girls and would, at some juncture, get a decent kicking for it. My own wretched downfall in the classroom had come swiftly, and without warning, one rainy afternoon shortly before my eleventh birthday. Mrs O'Beng had set our class an essay, mapping out what career paths we thought we might like to follow when we eventually left school. She had then chosen a selection of the completed essays to read aloud to the class, including, rather unnecessarily, I felt, my submission, in which I'd expressed my fervent ambition to become Doctor Who's assistant. There was no coming back from that, really. That's where the downturn started, and the rise of the rough boys became evident. Even the happy-go-lucky Frances copped it more often than she'd have liked, despite her sustained and evident pluck. On more than one occasion at playtime, or as we'd wander along Lordship Lane with our swimming stuff, she'd sob silently, as one of those wretched boys would shout at us. Something along the lines of 'Look at the gay Starr and his darkie girlfriend,' it would be, or, if they couldn't be bothered to cobble together an entire coherent insult, 'Wog' would ultimately suffice.

'It's just words, Frances,' I would say in an attempt to console her. 'They're just fucking kids. It doesn't actually mean anything.'

'You don't understand, David,' she told me once. 'It's not just me. I hear people say those things to my mum and dad, too. Not children: grown-ups, saying those things to other grown-ups. It doesn't get any better when you get older. You just wouldn't understand.'

And then she'd always turn around and stick two fingers up at whichever little tosspot had been hurling the abuse.

'You've got big mouths and small dicks,' she'd shout.

And I don't think I did really understand. Not then.

On one sticky Saturday three years ago, when the men of Chesterfield Street had stripped to the waist to wash their Ford Capris, my nan and my Auntie Val had been off to the shops for a quarter of boiled bacon and some pearl barley, so I'd trotted along. As we passed number eight, there was Jason Lancaster, swinging on the gate of his untidy front garden. Jason had cultivated a deep loathing of me ever since I'd dressed his flock-haired, eagle-eyed Action Man up as Laura Ingalls from *Little House on the Prairie* when we were nine, so I tended to give him a fairly wide berth whenever possible. I remember I'd nestled myself snugly in between my nan and my Aunt Val as we walked past, secure in the knowledge that Jason would never dare commence his customary public haranguing of me while I was flanked by two redoubtable ladies such as these. No way! On this occasion, however, I was horribly mistaken.

'Oh! Hello, ducky,' he shouted in a macabre pantomime-dame tone as he spotted me. 'You look very gay today.'

I stopped in my tracks, the ugliness of what had happened swallowing me fast. I'd been used to this kind of remark, yes, but this was surely the first time that anyone in my family had witnessed it. What could they possibly think Jason Lancaster had meant by that remark? Were they appalled by some unspeakable realization about me? I suddenly felt as if the safe arms of my home life – a world in which I had always felt cosseted and loved – had been sullied in the most terrible and irreversible way: my grandmother and my mother's sister had been exposed to all my hitherto private uncertainties and terrors in one split second. I have never forgotten the cringing and knotting of that defining moment: desperate to be noble and clever and composed, in truth I was just an unshielded little boy. I felt naked.

Aunt Val, of course, had snapped back at Jason as quick as you like.

'Get out of it, you snotty little fucker!' she barked.

'And tell your mother she needs to wash them nets out, dirty bastard,' Nan added matter-of-factly as

Jason scuttled away. It was some paltry retribution, I suppose, but the damage had been well and truly done.

That night when I got home I told Mum I didn't want to watch *Crossroads* any more.

The weird thing was, I didn't even particularly understand what a poof was, or what a queer did to incite such disdain. If television was anything to go by, a lot of them seemed to host game shows, or were featured in situation comedies in fashionable clothes, and those ones seemed enormously popular as far as I could make out, so quite why being queer was considered so bloody god-awful I couldn't fathom. On a chilly evening just before Christmas in 1975, though, things became a little less cloudy when I sat down with my mother and my Auntie Val to watch a new TV drama called *The Naked Civil Servant*. The turbulent life story of Quentin Crisp had been somewhat of a revelation to me, to say the least. Quite apart from the fact that this outrageous, fearless and, in my opinion, rather fantastic creature had been parading around London fifty years ago, wearing mascara, nail varnish, lipstick and attire that wouldn't have looked out of place on the King's Road in the present day, another significant part of the equation had also been filled in for me. Queers had sex with other men.

'He was a very brave man,' my Aunt Val had remarked as we all sat glued to this enthralling tale. 'In those days, being a homosexual was illegal – you could get put in prison.'

'Really?' I'd said, sipping my R. Whites cream soda, not quite believing her. 'Just for wearing a bit of make-up?'

'Not so much that,' Mum said, appearing a little uncomfortable. 'But for doing it with another man; you could have certainly been banged up for that.'

'Doing what, exactly?' I asked her.

'Sex!' Aunt Val said loudly. 'It was against the law for two men to have sex up until a few years ago, you know.'

'Oh!' I said. 'How strange. And do they do the same as what men and women do when they have sex?'

'Sort of . . .' Mum said.

'But they do it up the back passage,' Aunt Val clarified, 'which, I should imagine, is quite bloody painful.'

Mum nodded.

'It is,' she said, under her breath.

I remember, quite clearly, being intrigued and appalled all at once as I mulled over this fresh information during the adverts. So that's what all the fuss was about, I said to myself as I watched Rodney Bewes extolling the virtues of Bird's Eye Cod in Parsley Sauce to busy housewives countrywide. That's why the rough boys considered being queer so ghoulishly abhorrent: they must have known about this all along – so why didn't I? And come to think of it, how did any of this apply to me anyway? I didn't have sex with men. I hadn't had sex with anyone, or even considered it. It wasn't something that I felt was high on my list of priorities, to be frank – not like getting my *Look-in* comic every week, or saving up for a Three Degrees LP. And as for make-up, well, I didn't wear that either – so that was that theory out of the window. In fact, apart from trotting round my nan's front garden in a pair of my Aunt Val's lilac suede ankle-strapped platforms a couple of times the previous summer, I really couldn't think of anything that would induce those terrible boys to tar me with any sort of 'homo'-related brush. I was sure of one thing, though, as I watched the end credits of *The Naked Civil Servant* roll, the very next day at school, some smart arse would undoubtedly – in front of an entire class, or playground full of people – call me 'Quentin'!

And sure enough . . .

Six

A Golden Boy

'What are you doing, wankin' off them light ale bottles or stacking them on the shelf?'

I look up, somewhat appalled, at Marty Duncombe: droll bar steward extraordinaire, and my boss at the Lordship Lane Working Men's Club.

'I'm wiping them off, they're dusty,' I offer. 'Folk don't appreciate grimy beer bottles, Marty.'

'Well, get a trot on, love,' he says. 'It's twenty past seven and I want that bar open in ten: we've got a dance on tonight – it's not like a normal night, y'know.'

'Oh, shut up, Marty, you fucking idiot,' comes the clarion call that is the voice of Marty's wife, Denise. 'Leave the boy alone.'

Denise saunters over to the front bar and hauls up the shutters, puffing on a Rothman as she goes.

'Take no notice of 'im, darlin'. He couldn't get it up this mornin' and he's 'ad the 'ump ever since – miserable bastard! You all right, sweetie? You're looking a bit peaky.'

74

'Yeah, I'm fine, thank you, Denise,' I smile, getting up. 'Did Mum tell you, I got a part in the school musical, *Oliver!*? I'm playing Nancy.'

'Haaaaa ha!' Denise screeches, with a good inch of ash dangling hazardously from her cigarette end over the vodka and orange she is preparing for herself. 'I bet that pleased yer father no end.'

'He wasn't too impressed, I don't think.'

'No, I shouldn't imagine 'e was,' she laughs, swabbing out an ashtray with a bar towel. 'Well, fuck 'im – that's what I say.'

Denise downs the majority of her drink in two gulps, and then throws me a slightly befuddled stare.

''Ere, Dave, don't they 'ave any birds at your school? How come you're playin' a tart's part anyway?'

'We only have girls in the sixth form at our school, and none of them can sing, apart from Barbara Saville, and she looks like something out of *Star Trek*,' I explain.

'Well, fuck me!' Denise says absent-mindedly as she replaces the bottle on the Malibu optic.

I get back to the bottling up and then Marty swishes past me, shouting once more and slapping my arse hard as he goes.

'Come on, Mary-Anne,' he says, putting the drip trays in place. 'Look sharp! I want you workin' in the dance hall tonight with the wife.'

And then he turns to Denise.

'Couldn't get it up, my bloody eye!' he says. 'What bloke could with the look on your mooey half the fucking time?'

Marty and Denise Duncombe are a reasonably attractive, if slightly rough, couple in their late twenties, and they're from somewhere horrendous, originally – I think it's Dagenham. Denise regularly sports an unfeasibly staunch perm, and seems to possess a bewildering array of low-cut satin tops, while Marty, still fancying himself a bit of a lad, harbours a teenage twinkle in his eye that he regularly trots out for the benefit of some of the younger ladies propping up his bar – when he's out of the wary eye-line of his wife, that is. All in all, they've been pretty decent to me – I'm actually, legally, not supposed to serve behind the bar, as I'm not even sixteen for another month, so I'm officially just the pot-washer. Everybody knows me here, though, and Marty has told me that if anyone should question me, I'm to say that I'm just the pot man, and that a working-men's club has different rules. It is slightly different to a pub, as one has to be a member and pay a yearly sub-scription, and everyone knows the ins and outs of absolutely everybody else's business.

The Lordship Lane Working Men's Club (the working men can even bring their working wives, if they've a mind to) is quite cosy, in a red Dralon sort of a way: smoky, and just the wrong side of tatty. But there's undeniable snug banality in seeing the same faces sup the same tipples every weekend, while the same dreary three-piece band of geriatrics hammer out tunes that should have been lain to rest fairly brusquely after the Battle of the Somme. I mean, really: does anyone in 1979 know what a kitbag even looked like, and whose troubles could possibly fit inside one these days anyway? Does anyone know, or indeed care, who the fuck Dolly Gray was to say goodbye to? I don't think so. I try to sneak the French version of 'Sunday Girl' on the jukebox whenever I go out to collect some glasses and the band are on a break, just to annoy everyone. Still, I love working here as it makes me feel rather grown up; and as my dad's on the committee, he and Mum are here most nights, so they don't mind either. At least I can keep an eye on him, Mum had oft remarked to Denise.

I can't quite seem to focus on getting a good head on a pint of mild tonight, though. My mind is on other issues. Try as I might – and God, I've tried over the last few days – I can't stop thinking about him. Maxie. Maxie the divine, Maxie the brave, Maxie the beautiful ... I am far beyond being in love: I'm contiguous to obsessed. In fact, it's getting to the stage where I'm past caring about the convolutions of my burgeoning sexual proclivities. Maybe I am gay. To be brutally frank, if Abigail Henson jerking me off has made anything clear, it's these two imperative facts: a firmer, more masculine hand would doubtless have made the experience considerably more pleasurable; and, secondly, getting dried coral-pink nail varnish off one's cock is no mean feat.

'A pint of Kronenberg!' Dad shouts across the bar.

'And I'll have a pony!' my nan adds, appearing from behind him.

She's wearing an astrakhan coat she's had since the

fifties, and her unyielding lilac hair has been set in an 'Italian boy' as usual – almost certainly by my Aunt Val in Nan's scullery.

'What's the matter with you?' Nan says to me. 'Looks like you lost two bob and found a shilling.'

'Nothing, I . . .'

'Can you bring me drink over, love? I'm sitting in the blue room with your mum and Auntie Val. Your father'll pay.'

Nan throws Dad a sardonic smirk; she doesn't much care for him either, and makes little secret of it. Dad slams the money down on the bar, not even looking at me – evidently he's not forgiven me for my impending foray into public transvestism, but I'm far too engrossed in my quixotic musings to concern myself with his shitty mood.

'Are you going to the dinner and dance?' I ask him brightly.

He slurps on his lager but still doesn't look up.

'I expect so,' he mutters.

I endeavour to fill the silence as he seems to have no intention of moving away from the bar.

'I do like a good dinner and dance,' I say. 'Everybody having a bit of a knees-up, all kitted out in his or her finery. The ladies always look so nice in their long frocks . . .'

Oops. Finally Dad looks up at me, but it is with such disdain that I feel I might melt like the Wicked Witch of the West at the tail end of *The Wizard of Oz*, when Judy Garland chucks a bucket of water over her.

'You'll be in a long pink frock behind the bar yourself next,' he says blankly.

Pointing out at this juncture that I'd be far more
suited to something in midi-length cobalt, I feel, is
unwise, so I just smile and say, 'Nuts?'

Mercifully, within seconds, Marty is back –
salvation! Suddenly Eddie is smiling again.

'All right, Mart?' he almost bellows. 'Come and 'ave
a pint wiv me.'

Marty swaggers over like Edward G. Robinson in
track pants and puts his arm around Dad's shoulder,
planting an overzealous kiss on his cheek, in what I
presume is jest. Though Marty is a few years younger
than Dad, the pair of them are as thick as thieves –
literally, as it turns out – and have been ever since Marty
took over as bar steward two years previously.
Marty had evidently discovered that some of the committee members, including Eddie, had been fiddling the
fruit machines of a Sunday morning when it was their
job to empty them, pocketing sizeable cloth bags of fifty-
pence pieces for themselves. Marty, instead of berating
Eddie, or, indeed, dobbing him and the other pilfering
committee members in to the club chairman, had
insisted that Dad cut him in on the deal, so to speak, and
that had apparently been the beginning of a beautiful if
somewhat illicit friendship. What neither of them knew,
however, was that I, on discovering this sumptuous
titbit of information, chiefly through loitering outside
the appropriate doors and keeping my shell-likes open,
would in turn help myself to some of this perfidiously
acquired bullion – the odd tenner out of the bar till,

perhaps, or a fistful of fifty-pence pieces from Eddie's ill-concealed cloth bag (it was right next to the porn in the wardrobe, for Christ's sake) – and I'd use the cash to bolster my already enormous record collection. Eddie would be livid if he ever found out the number of Boney M singles he'd unknowingly stumped up for from Follett's record shop on Lordship Lane.

'Another pint of lager, David,' Dad demands.

'And get a move on, lady – I want you in the dance-hall bar with Denise in five minutes,' Marty adds, guffawing.

Dad joins in the hilarity. Cheers, Marty. That's all I'm fucking short of.

I bumble about behind the bar during the dance, not able to concentrate in the slightest. Denise does most of the serving.

'You're neither use nor ornament tonight,' she says. 'Like a spare prick at a wedding.'

At about half past nine, Nan, Mum and Aunt Val all rock up to the bar together in their evening frocks, breathless – exhausted, apparently, after a spirited turn around the floor to 'Cracklin' Rosie'.

'Two medium white wines, a barley wine and a couple of bags of dry roasted,' Aunt Val pants, leaning across the bar in cinnamon crêpe. 'I'm still fucking hungry; that dinner wouldn't have kept a sparrow alive. David! David, are you listening?'

'He's in another world,' Denise says, reaching for a bottle of Black Tower, ''as been all night. I reckon 'e's in love, aren't you, Dave?'

'Yes . . . NO!'

And they all shriek with laughter. It's like some sort of chiffon-swathed coven.

'His 'ead's full of lines,' Mum says. 'He's been rehearsing for the play all week and he can't think about anything else.'

You're almost right, Mother, but not quite. I can think about one other thing, and that's Maxie. He's the reason I can't flaming concentrate tonight.

It's been a week and a half since the commencement of *Oliver!* rehearsals, and I think they've been the happiest days of my life, with the possible exception, perhaps, of the day Frances and I met all four of Abba outside the Thames Television studios last February after standing in the freezing rain for two and a half hours – but in the happiness stakes, this last week has unquestionably been up there. From the very first day of rehearsal I just knew there was a spark between Maxie and me – I just knew it. When Mr McClarnon and the dramatis personae all piled into the hall after lessons had finished, the day after the cast had been announced, Maxie sat down on the stage right next to me before even Frances (who'd now been cast as chorus/flower-seller/sundry black-toothed whore) could get there. She wasn't pleased, and gave Maxie an untrusting sideways glance, her pretty eyes almost flashing fury for a split second, and parked herself the other side of him. Then, as the read-through of the script got under way, I could feel Maxie's shoulder rubbing against mine, and my mouth got dry.

'I can't wait till it gets to our scene, can you?' he

turned and said to me after a few minutes, and I nodded and gulped, trying not to make full eye contact with Frances, who was peering at me curiously over Maxie's shoulder. But as it went, we didn't get that far along into the play on the first evening's rehearsal and I'd been disappointed. On the second evening Hamish was otherwise engaged, so Bob Lord presided and we just hammered through a bunch of the songs. Even then, though, Maxie pulled his chair right up next to mine around the piano and shared my song sheet, our hands actually touching three times: twice during 'Food Glorious Food' and then again – this time with the lingering implication of intent – during the opening few bars of 'Who Will Buy This Wonderful Morning?' It wasn't until the third rehearsal on Monday just gone that Maxie and me actually got to walk through our first scene together, and then he really knocked me for six.

'I want te move on te the scene wi' Nancy and Bill at the Three Cripples Inn,' Hamish had announced, after a cheerless eternity watching our chosen – and to my mind woefully miscast – Oliver struggle through the first few bars of 'Where Is Love?' with a defiant lisp. 'Let's give it a go, shall we?'

Maxie and me wandered over to the chalk mark on the hall floor that was designated the imaginary doorway we were to appear through. Quite unexpectedly he took my hand and I virtually leaped out of my skin, but he just turned to me and grinned like some handsome fool.

'Come on then, Nance,' he said, and I heard a few sniggers from the ensemble.

Maxie's hand felt hot. Mr Lord, who'd been sitting behind the piano with his nose in the *Daily Mail* until this point, suddenly jumped up: he looked a bit flushed.

'Err . . . I don't think Bill Sikes would have been the holding-hands type, Boswell, thank you. What do you think, Mr McClarnon?'

Hamish looked over at me, standing there with a cocky, beaming Maxie clutching my sweaty hand.

'Perhaps you're right, Bob,' Hamish said softly. 'It's not *Mr and Mrs*, boys – drop the hand-holding.'

Maxie's grin got even wider, so I pulled my hand away sharpish, and I clocked Hamish smirking.

'Let's get on now, kiddies,' he trilled, clearly trying not to laugh.

'Don't we need Bet somewhere along the line?' I said, scanning the room for Sonia Barker. 'It'll be "Oom Pah Pah" before you know it.'

She was in the corner sucking an Ice Pole.

'And Sonia Barker, too!' Hamish shouted. 'Quick smart!'

The run of the scene went moderately well, despite the off-putting vision of Sonia's purple tongue every two minutes, as did the whole rehearsal, and afterwards Maxie and me stayed behind to go over lines for the next day. The hall had emptied, and the smell of new-term floor varnish caught my nose as Maxie sat opposite me in the middle of the vast room, our knees touching like bookends with no books in between.

'How come you're doing this musical as well as playing in the football team?' I asked after we'd run a couple of pages. 'You mustn't ever go home.'

'It is quite a lot to take on,' Maxie said, 'but I promised Mr Lord faithfully that I'd keep up with the footy if I did the play – he made me promise.'

'He doesn't like me, Mr Lord,' I said. 'He never has, ever since I suggested that découpage might be more use to me in later life than technical drawing. He thinks I'm a sissy.'

Maxie laughed out loud.

'Well, I'm his golden boy,' he said. 'He certainly likes me. He made me football captain after one match when I first joined the school, and I made the running team when there were definitely a couple of kids who were much faster than me at the time trials. Every time he claps eyes on me mum and dad, he tells 'em how fucking wonderful I am. I think I must be like the son he never had.'

Then Maxie glanced over his shoulder and around the room, as if to make quite certain no one else could hear him.

'More often than not,' he said, hunching forward conspiratorially, 'Mr Lord will find some excuse to make me stay later than the other kids after games: discuss match strategies, pick the team for the next game – you name it . . .'

Maxie was close to me, and the tang of varnish was replaced by his own scent.

'Really?' I gulped.

'Yeah, I reckon he's lonely, poor bastard.'

'But he's married!'

'I know,' Maxie said, 'but he just seems to like having me around. Not in a creepy way. I mean, he don't stare at me in the showers or nuffin' like that. Not like some blokes I've caught lookin' at me . . . as if they . . . you know . . . like me.'

I bit my bottom lip, hard.

'Looking at you? What, in the showers?'

Maxie nodded.

'Don't you ever get that? Other geezers looking at you like that?'

I shook my head.

'I try to avoid the showers if I can, to be honest,' I said.

Maxie stared into my face and nodded his head again, slowly, as if he understood.

'I know I'm good-looking,' he went on. 'I know why they look.'

'You do have very nice eyes,' I said earnestly. 'That's probably why they look.'

Maxie leaned back, balancing on the two back legs of his blue plastic chair.

'Possibly,' he said. 'But I reckon I've got a fairly big knob for my age. I think it's more likely that they're looking at that.'

And he chuckled quietly.

'Long as they don't touch me, they can look all they like.'

'Quite,' I said nervously.

Then I felt myself blush, and harden slightly, so I adjusted my script accordingly.

'Why did you do that earlier, the holding-hands thing?' I asked. 'Don't you know what it's like for me at this school?'

Maxie looked slightly embarrassed.

'It's only actin',' he said, and he winked at me. 'Why d'you give a shit what those other kids think, anyway, David? They're fuckin' wankers.'

'You don't have to put up with it day after day,' I said.

'I s'pose,' he said.

Then he screwed up his face for a moment and said, 'Shall we walk 'ome together? Frances said you live on Chesterfield Street; I can get a bus from there.'

'All right,' I said, 'but . . . kids might see us.'

He laughed.

'There you go again, so fuckin' what? You're a weird one, you are, David. I do like you, though. You make me laugh.'

'I aim to please,' I smiled, getting up and hoping against hope that the semi-protuberance in my pants might subside sometime soon.

And off we went.

What I really couldn't fathom was, why me? Why would someone of his social standing within the school want to chum up with someone with my reputation – the class clown, the class fairy, the boy who only hung around with girls from the sixth form and his own sister? Maxie didn't seem bothered about any of this – he was entirely unfazed, and I think *that* is why I felt myself fall for him. There, I said it. I fell for him. I'd fucking fallen for him and I didn't care. If that made me a one hundred per cent, fully fledged homo-sexual then I actually didn't care.

During the rest of the week I could see that even Frances was coming round to Maxie's evident charms, and the three of us would wander the ten-minute route down the hill from school towards Lordship Lane each afternoon after rehearsals, gossiping and laughing about Sonia Barker's atrocious acting, or little Oliver's un-fortunate speech impediment. On Wednesday evening, which was particularly clement, we bought a bag of chips between us from Elvis' fish bar, and then we walked down Chesterfield Street and perched on the swirly black iron railings outside my nan's house.

'I live right there,' I'd said, brazenly putting one hand on Maxie's shoulder, and pointing at number twenty-two with the other. 'That's my sister Chrissy in the white trilby and the boob tube, having a ruck with her boyfriend outside, in the front garden.'

Frances laughed.

'As per!' she said.

'It's nice, your gaff,' Maxie said. 'We live in a little house, modern. Me dad's always fuckin' moving with work, so we never stay anywhere for more than about two years. It gets on my wick. I'd love to live in a big old house like yours, though.'

'Really?' I said. I could scarcely take my eyes off him when he was talking, to be honest. It was like I was hypnotized or something.

'I live in the flats,' Frances interjected urgently, almost shouting. 'Don't I, David.'

But I didn't answer her; instead I said to Maxie, 'You'll have to come for your tea one night, maybe this week.'

And I heard Frances huff and kiss her teeth. Whether she realized how I felt about Maxie, I wasn't sure, but I did catch her looking at me in a bizarre, unearthly way as we waved him on to the 185 bus at the bottom of my road that night, just as it was getting dark.

'Has he ever mentioned a girlfriend to you or any-thing?' I said to Frances as we ambled towards her flats afterwards.

'No, why?' she said. 'Do you fancy your chances?'

Then she caterwauled a raucous laugh and shoved me playfully into the doorway of the dry-cleaners. Maybe she does realize, I thought.

Then yesterday – Friday – Frances went to the dentist at two thirty with suspected junior-onset gingivitis, so she didn't walk home with us. Maxie had slung his school blazer over his shoulder and was kicking an empty Fresca can down Lordship Lane as we reached the bottom of Chesterfield Street, and he looked slightly gloomy.

'I've missed quite a lot of footy practice this week,' he said as we reached the bus stop, and he booted the now semi-crushed can clean across the main road. 'Mr Lord isn't happy.'

'I know what you mean, Maxie,' I agreed. 'I've not done any homework or any sort of revision since I met . . . since the play started, I mean, and I've really, really let my "two new words a day" rule slide as well.'

Maxie looked mystified, and he leaned against the bus stop.

'What the fuck is the "two new words a day" rule?'

I felt myself redden.

'Well . . . I like to find and learn the meanings of two new words a day,' I muttered, 'and then use them in sentences on the following day. I've done it since I was twelve.'

Maxie still looked confused.

'I don't do it at the weekends, you know, only in the week,' I said, as if that might sound slightly less mental. 'Like, up until a month ago I didn't even know what libidinous meant, or prurient.'

'Really? And what do they mean?' Maxie asked.

'Well, they're both something to do with the expression of sexual desire,' I said, rather too persuasively.

And I suddenly hoped that an approaching Ford Granada might mount the pavement and knock me down stone dead. Maxie stared at me for a moment, then he smiled and put his hand on my arm.

'You're a fuckin' geek, David,' he said. 'But a very funny geek. Sweet.'

Sweet? What did he mean, sweet? Suddenly I spotted a 185 bus coming, which Maxie was bound to jump on if I didn't do something about it fast. I took the bull by the proverbial horns.

'Why don't you come for tea at mine now,' I spouted. 'My mum won't mind and we can listen to Blondie.'

'Oh!'
'Well, you don't have to, I . . .'
'OK! I'll just have to ring my mum.'
'OK!'
'Right!'

He was lying face down across the beanbag in my bedroom when I came upstairs with two cups of Mellow Birds and a packet of Rich Tea. I felt my heart somersault in my chest.

'Do you fancy her?' Maxie looked up and asked, as he pawed through my albums. 'Debbie Harry?'

I told him I wasn't sure, and then I went over to my music centre and put on a cassette of something I'd recorded off the radio the day before: it was the brand-new Police song, 'Message in a Bottle'.

'Do you think Sting is good-looking, then?' he asked.

'I guess,' I said. 'I think you look a bit like Sting, apart from the hazel eyes – have people told you that?'

'No,' Maxie said. 'But I like it that you did. Is Frances your bird?'

Jesus, he's inquisitive.

'Oh God, no. She's nobody's bird. She's just my best friend. I haven't got a bird. Well, Abigail Henson wanked me off in here the other day, but I don't particularly want to go out with her.'

Maxie's face was a comic portrait: mouth open, eyes bulging.

'She wanked you off?' he gasped, and he sat bolt upright.

'Yes.'

'Fuck! Did you like it?'

'Not especially.'

'Oh. Why?'

'I don't know,' I said. 'Perhaps I would have if it had been somebody else.'

His eyes narrowed.

'Who?'

I didn't dare tell, so I said, 'Debbie Harry, perhaps.'

We both laughed raucously, rocking back and forth on the cream and brown carpet-tiled floor of my bedroom.

'Or Sting,' Maxie suddenly suggested.

And we both stopped laughing; staring at one another for a moment, silently – just as the record started to fade and disc jockey Dave Lee Travis began yabbering over the end of the song. Then the tape cut off and I said, 'Tea will be ready in a flash. We're having Findus Crispy Pancakes.'

I remember I'd sounded a bit like the Queen Mother when I said that, aside from the fact that she would almost certainly not have been having Findus Crispy Pancakes for her tea. Maxie nodded.

'That sounds very good,' he said.

When the bottle smashes on the floor of the bar I almost have a coronary. I've been so lost in my fucking daydream, I don't know where I am for a moment.

'Oh, for Christ's sake,' Denise snaps, and I realize suddenly that it's me who's dropped the bottle – Guinness all over the place.

'Dolly Daydream you are tonight, Dave,' she laughs.

91

'Well, you can bloody well tidy that up yourself, and do the glasses. I'm going home to watch *Police 5*. I do love me Shaw Taylor.'

Denise gathers up her Rothmans and the long black cardigan she wears over absolutely everything, and heads for the bar hatch.

'Keep 'em peeled!' she says, waving her fingers.

And when I look back, I realize that the dance hall has virtually emptied without me even noticing. I didn't even see my mum and Aunt Val leave.

As I pop the final load into the glass-washer, Marty comes up from the cellar and reminds me that the prawn cocktail crisps are dwindling and to get another box down.

Heading to the storeroom, I can hear Marty and my dad chatting at the now deserted bar.

'Do you fancy some afters, Eddie?' Marty says. 'Scotch?'

'Nah, I've got an early airport run tomorrow,' says Eddie. 'But are we going sea fishing next weekend or what, Mart? You can bring your little lad if you like; David won't wanna go.'

No. You're perfectly correct there, Father dear, I reflect as I unlock the large storeroom cupboard. The last time I went sea fishing with you was at Littlehampton when I was eleven. I got a clump around the head, I recall, for aiding the liberation of a large floundering cod back into the sea, and then I knelt on the worms and got another clump – plus I ruined my best Wranglers.

'Yeah, that'll be good, Eddie!' I hear Marty say. 'I'll look forward to that. See yous later.'

I stretch up to the top of the cupboard to reach the box of prawn crisps. I have a theory that prawn cocktail crisps are tremendously common, and I have to say, that theory is often borne out by a few of the people I witness purchasing them at the Lordship Lane Working Men's Club. To my mind, ready salted or cheese and onion are far more acceptable as a fried-potato seasoning, but that's just me. I stand on tiptoe to reach the box, and I'm suddenly aware of a presence behind me; and then there's a hand on my stomach, below my exposed navel, fingertips brushing my pubic hair. It's gone as quick as it landed there.

'Look at you, you dirty little sod, showing all your belly off!'

I whirl around, dropping the crisp box, to face a grinning Marty.

'Fuck off, Marty!'

I half laugh in shock, pulling my face away from his, sharply.

'Don't worry, darlin',' he smirks. 'I'm not gonna kiss ya. I'd fuck you, if I didn't 'ave to look at you, but I wouldn't kiss ya!'

Marty evidently finds himself hysterical and roars with laughter at his own disgusting wisecrack.

'You stupid bastard, I nearly had a heart attack,' I say, yanking my shirt back down. 'You can sort the fucking crisps out yourself now.'

I push past him angrily, and head for the coat rack. Marty looks slightly remorseful.

'Sorry if I made you jump, mate,' he says as I collect my bomber. 'Your wages are on the desk.'

At home, and tucked up in bed, I have Debbie on the headphones.

'Darlin', darlin', darlin' . . . I can't wait to see you,
Your picture ain't enough,
I can't wait to touch you . . . in the flesh!'

I reflect on Marty and his crude remarks, and for a moment I'm horribly aroused; so I turn my thoughts to Maxie, and swiftly he washes through me like morphine. Maxie! You're the one I can't wait to see. Ten minutes later, though, as I tug at my cock, I'm nowhere near a climax, so my mind drifts back to Marty. I don't want it to, but it just does. I think about him touching me in the stockroom . . . in the showers, maybe . . . oh fuck . . . it's then that I come.

Seven

Top Hat and Tales

Mum and Aunt Val have cut out the pattern for my First Act Nancy frock, and it's spread out all over the lounge floor.

'If your father sees me doing this, I'll be mincemeat,' Mum says, hacking her way through a carpet of emerald cheesecloth with her best pinking shears. 'I do hope he doesn't decide to come back from fishing earlier than he said.'

'Oh, let 'im shove it up his arse; he'll 'ave to get over it sooner or later,' Aunt Val interjects helpfully. 'Now, David, do you want a nice nipped-in waist? I would if I were you, and not too flared, skirt-wise, else you'll end up looking hippy. Your mother's bought a dirndl pattern, but to be honest, I'd 'ave said that was more your Lady von Trapp than Nancy, meself.'

'Just shut up and let me get on, Val,' Mum snaps, crawling around the floor with a tape measure and a mouthful of pins. 'I'll be 'ere all night otherwise.'

Aunt Val looks at me and rolls her eyes.

'She's like a mad thing once she's got them scissors in 'er hand,' she says.

Mum and Val's banter was the stuff of legends as far as I was concerned. They often bickered, yes, but there was love behind every slur, and woe betide anybody else that joined in on either side: they'd more often than not end up doing battle with the pair of them. Different, they were indeed: Mum was a true English rose, an almost ridiculously beautiful woman with a gentle soul, who was kind, pliant and, sometimes, just a little bit nervy – though this was probably due to being on the receiving end of Eddie's yelling for the last fifteen or so years, poor cow. She did on occasion, however, demonstrate a ferocious stubborn streak, and if she was of that mind, even Eddie couldn't win a battle, let alone us kids. Valerie, on the flip side, was very unlikely to hide her light under a bushel in any given situation. Like my nan, she spoke as she found, and I had seen grown men reduced to near whimpering wrecks after receiving only a small slice of the rough end of her tongue. Aunt Val was my fashion icon. I'd almost wet myself with glee pawing through snaps of her taken during the sixties, in which she'd be wearing white leather miniskirts and Chelsea boots, or skin-tight embroidered lemon organza with matching satin-covered slingbacks. She'd be sitting, invariably, on the bonnet of an Austin Healey with some handsome boy, or posing outside the GPO Tower where she'd worked. It all looked so much more glamorous back then; perhaps it was the black and white. Val's dark features and beehive hairdo would always put me in mind of Sophia Loren or Gina Lollobrigida, while Mum was more of a Jean Simmons or Liz Taylor type. And I loved nothing more than sitting with them on Saturday nights, listening to tales of when they'd go dancing in the hall above the Co-op down Rye Lane, before me and Chrissy were born.

'They were a couple of bastards,' Nan would chip in while sipping her barley wine. 'Specially your mother. All the lads were after her, and she wasn't as fussy as she might 'ave been.'

'I'd have to fight all the bloody horny Teddy boys off while she just stood there lookin' pretty,' Aunt Val told me one night. 'She was a bloody nightmare, your mum.'

'It's not my fault I was stunningly beautiful,' Mum retorted. 'They all wanted my virginity, that was the thing, David.'

'Well, little did they know that ship had long since sailed,' Aunt Val said. 'It was halfway to China by then.'

And we'd all howled with laughter.

'Right!' Mum says triumphantly and finally, holding the freshly cut-out dress shape up against me. 'That's gonna be fantastic. You'll be the greatest Nancy ever in this, David.'

Who could doubt it?

'And with that nice-looking chap playing opposite you, I think you're gonna knock 'em dead,' Aunt Val adds. 'What's his name again?'

'Maxie,' I say dreamily.

'Very good-looking boy,' Aunt Val says. 'I see him sittin' outside with you the other night, David; 'e'll break a few hearts, won't he, Kath?'

'He certainly will,' Mum agrees. 'He was over here a few times this week, wasn't he, Dave?'

'Mmm.'

I'm giving nothing away.

'In fact, I think it was three nights on the trot he had his tea with us this week, wasn't it, Dave?'

'Mmm.'

It's true – Maxie and I have been even more indivisible this last week. In fact, every time I turn around, there he is, beaming sunshine at me and dragging me off to rehearse our lines alone: it's been virtual rapture, to my mind. He'd even, yet again, daringly ducked out of after-school football practice so he could come over to my house and run lines. That had not gone down especially well with Mr Lord, who finally put his hoof down and gave Maxie an ultimatum.

'One more missed practice, Maxie, and you'll have to choose between the play and the team,' he'd warned in a sing-song tone, as Maxie and I turned up ten minutes late for technical boring on Wednesday. 'We don't want that, now, do we?'

And then he'd scowled at me as I sat down, with a glare that quite plainly said: I know you're to blame for this, Starr. I didn't give a shit, though. Maxie had confided in me that if push actually had come to shove, he'd have chosen the play over a stupid football team any day; but just to keep Bob Lord sweet, he'd agreed to turn up for all scheduled footy practice in the future. Frances – who's supposed to be my friend – said she too is getting pretty sick of seeing Maxie and me huddled together in corners, hashing out our banter, but, as I pointed out to the daft mare, Maxie and I have a lot of scenes together and I feel very strongly that I need to submerge myself utterly into the role bestowed upon me.

'I've got an idea of what you'd like to submerge yourself in!' Frances had taunted on Friday afternoon during my wig-fitting, and we'd both cackled like fish-wives. Surely she must know, I thought; must have realized by now. But then I thought: realized what, exactly? There was nothing to know yet . . . was there?

'Oh my gosh, Starr! Ye canna wear that bloody wig!' Hamish said, bustling into the costume room with his arms full of orphans' breeches, pointing at the sleek, blonde-bobbed hair I was fussing with. 'You're a Georgian whore, not one of Charlie's Angels. I'm certain we can find a more suitable hairpiece for you than that.'

'Yes, sir!' I said, feeling thwarted.

Hamish threw the trousers into a pile and said, 'I'd actually like a word, David, if you don't mind . . . in private, please!'

His face was solemn, and I became slightly alarmed, turning to Frances in a hushed panic, but she was no use.

'I'll meet you by the football pitch after last bell,' she whispered.

And then she disappeared, leaving me perched anxiously on a hamper in the cramped costume room – formerly the art cupboard – with Mr McClarnon.

He looked on edge, and he was wearing a singularly unconvincing grin and fidgeting with a mob cap. What the hell was all this about? I felt myself flush slightly, and the longer he said nothing, the worse it got. Was there something amiss with my portrayal of Nancy? Maybe he'd decided that having a boy play her wasn't such a good idea after all. I finally decided to pre-empt any possible denigration of my artistry and speak up.

'Is it my performance in the tavern, sir?' I said assertively. 'Is that what you want to talk to me about? Only, if it is, I have to say in my defence that I'm entirely hampered by an extremely shoddy Bet. Sonia Barker is wholly inept, and not nearly good enough to play her, particularly with those cuts all up and down her arm; and unless we write it into the script that Bet has consumption or some other life-threatening, lung-related ailment, I think we should try to get her to stop coughing every five minutes and wiping her nose on her leg-o-mutton sleeve: she's second-row chorus at best, sir!'

Hamish laughed, thawing instantly and pulling a packet of cigarettes out of his tan jumbo corduroys.

'Do ye mind?'

I shook my head and he lit up.

'You want one?'

I shook my head again, and he sat down next to me on an upturned dustbin.

'No, it's nothing to do with your performance, David. I'm very happy wi' that,' he said softly. 'The thing is, though, I've observed your behaviour around young Maxie Boswell and I wanted te talk te ye about it.'

I was shaken, and felt like I might vomit into the Artful Dodger's top hat, which was sitting beside me on the hamper. Hamish put his hand on my shoulder, evidently sensing my agitation.

'Now, don't go fretting. You've done nothing wrong in my eyes, son, but I notice how animated you become when the lad's about, and I detect a certain . . . what can I say . . . chemistry, almost . . . perhaps even . . . flirting, on your part. Would you agree with that, or am I talkin' outa my behind?'

I could feel the corner of my eye twitching, and I got the distinct feeling that Mr McClarnon was now wishing he'd never started the conversation at all. But I was intrigued and somewhat delighted, to be honest, not to mention flattered, that someone had noticed the apparent bond between Maxie and me. Hamish ploughed on, clearly selecting his words with some prudence.

'I'm just worried, David. I know what some of the other kids call ye sometimes, and I see how ye get when you're around him . . . and . . . well, ye might not be doing yourself any favours running around like Marianne Dashwood, if ye know what I mean. *Do* you know what I mean, David?'

There was a snow globe on the shelf opposite me. It had a fairy in it. I looked into it, unable to speak,

unable to answer Mr McClarnon. But I had to answer
him. I had a choice to make, and I had to make it then
and there – for myself if for no one else.

'Do ye . . . like him?' Hamish almost whispered.

'Yeah.'

'Are ye attracted to him? You're very tactile with
him, I notice. I think other people might – Bob Lord
said something to me just yesterday about how he
thinks you're distracting the boy from his sports. And
besides that, I'm not sure if Maxie would . . . I'm
uncertain that he's . . . David, do ye think you might be
gay? There, I've said it!'

Hamish took a huge drag on his Marlboro.

'It's no bad thing if y'are – and if you're not, I'm
dead sorry for bringing it up; but you see, being gay
myself, and having been a gay kid myself, I sorta
notice this kind of thing, d'ye ken?'

'Yes!'

'Yes what?'

I gathered every bit of courage within myself, as if I
were about to leap off a high ledge into a swollen river.
I stared directly at the fairy trapped in the glass bubble
of the snow globe, and I said, 'Yes. I think I might be
gay. I think I'm gay. I like boys. I fancy boys. I fancy . . .
I'm in love with Maxie Boswell.'

And right then and there, I was sick in the Artful
Dodger's top hat.

Frances was loitering by the goalposts, chomping her
way through a bag of Frazzles, when I arrived at
the pitch to meet her twenty minutes later. An

uninterested goalie was kicking up bits of turf beside her, and there were jackets and sports bags strewn all around the vicinity.

'What was that all about?' she muttered, not taking her eyes off the ongoing Friday-night footy training.

'Nothing.'

'Well, it must have been something,' she bristled. 'He wasn't coming on to you, was he?'

'Don't be soft,' I said.

And I leaned on the goalpost she was resting against, so we were shoulder to shoulder. The goalkeeper, who was now having a crack at spitting, ignored us.

'Mr McClarnon wanted to know if I was gay, that's all,' I said casually, and reasonably quietly.

'Oh! And what did you tell him?'

'I told him I was. Can I have a Frazzle?'

Frances offered me the packet, glaring at me attentively.

'Oh!' she said again, clearly desperate to sound matter-of-fact-ish about the whole affair. 'And what did he say to that?'

'He said that I could go and talk to him at any time, and about anything, even things about sex, and that I was to go careful around Maxie Boswell and try not to flutter my eyelashes at him.'

'Yes, I've noticed you do that,' Frances affirmed. 'And?'

'And that there is nothing wrong with me, and that I should be proud of who I am.'

'And who are you?' Frances laughed. 'Martina Navratilova?'

That started me off laughing too, but then Frances went all serious.

'Are you, then?' she said. 'Proud?'

She stepped in front of me, and glared at me with a sudden gravity in her eyes that jarred me.

'Are you?'

'More terrified than proud,' I said. 'I've never said it out loud to another living person, to be honest, and I'm not quite sure why I'm saying it now.'

I looked towards the sky.

'Perhaps love has made me brave,' I said.

Frances rolled her eyes.

'Oh, Jesus!' she snorted.

At that moment the ball rolled towards us and stopped only yards from our feet. Hollering and whistling from the pitch ensued, and one of the players came racing up to us. It was Maxie.

'Hey, you two!' he said.

He was bathed in evening summer light and looked quite beautiful. Suddenly I knew I'd done the right thing.

'I didn't know you were practising tonight,' I said breezily, struggling not to admire the thick shape detectable under his snug shorts.

'Afraid so,' Maxie laughed. 'Mr Lord's roped me in on the fucking swimming team as well, now.'

'Really?' I semi-lunged forward, surprising even myself.

'Oh, for fuck's sake!' Frances interjected. 'Hadn't you better get back to the game, Maxie? You'll be in the shit if you hang around over here.'

'It's half-time,' Maxie said. 'Anyway, I wanted to ask you two what you were doing next weekend? My mum and dad are going to Southend, so I thought you could both come over to my place. We could get a Chinese, and maybe do some line-learning after.'

Frances kissed her teeth.

'I hain't got n' damn lines,' she laughed, exaggerating her West Indian twang, which she knew I loved. 'And you two fuckers should know all yours backwards by now, the amount of time you've spent cosying up together learning them.'

I felt myself redden, and Maxie giggled.

'Anyway, we're going to the Rock Against Racism gig in Brockwell Park next Sunday, aren't we, David?' Frances went on.

'Well, it's not definite, is it?' I said. I'm a fickle spirit, to be honest.

'Really?' Maxie looked excited. 'Ah! I'd bloody love to go to that with you guys. That'd be fantastic! Do you mind?'

Frances seemed pleased.

'The more the merrier, crushing the rise of the Nazi scum, as far as I'm concerned,' she said. 'Mr McClarnon is going with us, and Mr and Mrs Peacock. It'll be a right laugh! There'll be wicked bands playing, too!'

'Yeah!' I said. 'It'll be amazing!'

I was suddenly coming round to the idea, for some reason.

'Cool! It's a date!' Maxie declared.

Date! He actually said, a date! I thought for a moment I might faint.

'Brilliant!' Frances concluded. 'Bring some cider.'

The three of us chattered on, propped against the goalposts, scheduling our upcoming excursion as a burst of deep September sun fell across the green of the school football pitch. Presently Mr Lord headed towards us with a few of the team – including Jason Lancaster, who was rummaging around inside his shorts as per. I had a feeling there might be a bit of bother, so I stood up straight.

'Are you coming back to us again, Boswell?' Mr Lord enquired superciliously. 'Or are you stopping here with these girls?'

Bob Lord was a short man with a shiny face and head to match. He was from Wigan, or somewhere equally grim, but affected an inexcusable Cockney accent: nobody knew why. He was also a so-called born-again Christian, and as far as I could fathom, his particular rebirth into the faith must have entailed an acquisition of sneering sarcasm and mean-spirited malevolence.

'What is your story, Starr?' Mr Lord said, turning to me, his voice measured and contemptuous. 'Why are you here? You don't like football. Seems like every time I turn around you're hanging round this lad.'

He nodded towards Maxie, beads of sweat on his nose.

'Do you fancy him or something? Have you got a bit of a thing for him?'

Mr Lord laughed and gave me a little shoulder

punch. Before I could answer, Jason Lancaster piped up for the benefit of the other boys.

'Of course he fancies him, sir! He's a bloody queer!'

He laughed uproariously.

'You can see him in the showers looking at our willies!'

The boys all whooped.

'He'd have to have a bionic eye to spot your dick, Lancaster,' Frances gallantly yelled over the laughter.

I began to unravel inside. Not now, please. Not in front of him. Oh God, no!

Then Maxie strode forward, teeth gritted, fists clenched.

'Shut your mouth, Lancaster, or I'll knock you out.'

'You see, sir?'

Jason Lancaster was almost frothing at the mouth now, and he lurched towards Maxie, meeting him face-on.

'Protecting his little lover boy, it's obvious. Dirty queers!'

The team all whooped again, whistling and slapping Jason's back. Bob Lord loved this. This was just what he'd hoped for. He harboured a deep loathing for me, and any other boy who didn't relish the thought of running around a footy pitch or hanging upside down off a rope in the gym. Quite suddenly, though, a calm washed over me, and I collected myself, stepping forth in the brouhaha, and facing Jason down.

'I don't think you really mean that, Jason, do you?' I said evenly. 'I mean, *really* mean it.'

Jason glared at me, and the boys fell silent, evidently wondering why their pal hadn't laid me out flat. There was turmoil in Jason's expression, though, and he took a step back.

'Think very carefully before you answer,' I continued.

He attempted a look of menace, but I valiantly stared him down.

'Let's get back to the game, boys,' he spat, turning away. 'It fucking stinks around here. You coming, Boswell?'

Maxie, too, looked confused for a moment, but then gave Frances and me a defeated smile and sauntered back towards the centre of the field. Bob Lord leaned in, jamming his face up close to mine.

'Look at the trouble you're causing that boy,' he hissed. 'Is that what you want?'

Out of the corner of my eye I saw Frances shake her head and look down, and I shrugged my shoulders.

'Why don't you just leave him alone and stick with the girls, eh?' Mr Lord suggested. 'I'm watchin' you, Starr; just you remember that, lad.'

'I don't really care what you are, David,' Frances said, taking my hand as we walked along Chesterfield Street later that afternoon. 'But you wanna be careful of people like Mr Lord and Jason: blokes like that always come out on top.'

I stopped and faced Frances.

'Do they?'

'Yes, they do. And the way you goaded Jason back

there, you're lucky he didn't smack you one – in fact, I'm not at all sure why he didn't.'

I took in Frances' luminous beauty. She was stunning, almost perfect, with elegantly defined cheekbones, soft lips and fiery eyes: so why didn't I want to kiss her like I did Maxie?

'Jason's terrified of my dad, that's why,' I reassured her. 'Always has been. Don't worry, I can handle him.'

And we walked on.

'So do you think Maxie is gay as well, then?' Frances puzzled as we reached number twenty-two.

'I don't know. Do you?'

'I don't know either,' she said. 'But he certainly fills out those bloody football shorts, doesn't he?'

Frances sniggered lasciviously.

'I don't know,' I coyly replied. 'I can't say as I've noticed.'

We both laughed loud and long. We laughed until we cried, dropping our satchels and falling against the front-garden wall outside my house. We laughed and laughed, until a Vauxhall full of rough boys sped past, and a twisted face hung out of its window and shouted, 'NATIONAL FRONT! BRITAIN FOR THE WHITES!'

We stopped laughing, and I looked at Frances: ruined and sad in a split second. It made me fucking furious.

'They're wankers,' I said, and she nodded glumly. 'And that's exactly what next week's rally is all about, love, getting rid of 'em.'

'I know,' she said.

And as we waved one another goodbye, and I headed up our front path, it suddenly dawned on me: I'd recognized one of those scowling faces in that car. I definitely had.

By the time Eddie gets back from his Sunday fishing trip, Mum has hidden all the dressmaking paraphernalia and has managed to cobble together a late tea. Aunt Val's made herself scarce, so I decide to take my milk and a liver-sausage sarnie up to my room and listen to a bit of X-Ray Spex – I'm in that sort of mood. I do hate Sunday evenings, and the looming prospect of the school gates. Well, I usually did. At least, I suppose, now I have Maxie to keep me going. Or do I? I mean, how does he feel about me? I've said it out loud now – actually said it out loud to another human being – two, in fact. But Maxie, well, he probably just thinks of me as any other ordinary chum: blissfully ignorant, is Maxie. He doesn't know – couldn't know – that I love him. And what the fuck would he do if he did know?

Eight

Doomed?

That night I dream I'm feeding the ducks in Dulwich Park with Debbie Harry. She's wearing the yellow dress and the same hairstyle that she wore on *Top of the Pops* when she performed 'Picture This', and she's tossing stale Hovis into the mouth of a gluttonous mallard on the bank. I do hope it is a dream, because I appear to be dressed in a calf-length, burnt-orange dress with a plunge neckline trimmed with white lace, and leg-of-mutton sleeves – something Nancy might wear, I suppose. Peeking down, I discover my footwear to be heavily scuffed, button-up Victorian ladies' boots that come up to meet the bottom of my rather tatty frock, and I suspect that my hair is piled high on my head with unruly wisps falling about my forehead, but I've no mirror to corroborate this supposition so I try, in vain, to find my reflection in the water. The weather in this dream is especially stunning, and, as I watch the ducks and swans glide on the still glass of the pond, it is entirely tranquil.

'So you think you love this boy?' Debbie Harry asks, eventually turning to me.

I nod.

'Well, honey, it's not gonna be easy. You know what people are gonna say.'

I glance around me at the other folk in the park: the children in breeches and buckled shoes; the women sporting bonnets and twirling parasols – it's like a painting by Seurat.

'You know what people will say, David,' Debbie says again.

I nod again (can I not speak? It's Debbie Harry, for Christ's sake).

'Do you think you're tough enough for this?' Debbie asks. 'Do you think this boy feels the same about you?'

'I don't know.'

'Well, you'd better find out fast,' Debbie smiles, dispensing the last of her crusts, 'cos I'll tell you one true thing . . . there's nothing more painful than unrequited love, baby. It's always doomed.'

Unrequited. Doomed. Alarm clock.

Chrissy and I are wolfing down the last of our breakfast while our cleaner, Moira, stands at the sink, rinsing the remnants of last night's supper off the plates before she stacks them in the dishwasher – an appliance we all imagined would end the relentless barneys about whose turn it was to wash up; now we just squabble about who'll load the fucking thing. Chrissy, in preparation for a normal Monday at school, has decided to cake her face in overpriced American cosmetics she'd seen advertised by Lynda Carter, I believe, on television the other week. Now, when I say overpriced, what I mean is that they might have been overpriced had Squirrel not pinched them for her from the Co-op chemist at the weekend, along with a huge stash of sanitary wear, which my sister refuses point-blank to be seen purchasing because she has to request something for a medium to heavy flow. Chrissy is also – and this is at the breakfast table, mind – sporting a pork-pie hat, and more gold belchers than one could shake a stick at.

'I'm a rude girl now,' she'd announced to us during *Sapphire and Steel* a couple of weeks back, wearing bright-pink lips and a low-cut T-shirt.

Mum had just tutted and gone back to her *Family Circle*, but Nan, who had popped in for a visit, said to her, 'You ought to be wearing something a little less revealing, young lady. It's not that long since they blew up Lord Mountbatten, you know.'

Chrissy didn't give much of a fig what anyone thought, anyway. As far as she was concerned, she and Squirrel were something approaching the Bonnie and Clyde of East Dulwich: untamed free spirits who could do pretty much as they pleased, as long as our dad didn't find out.

'Your hair looks ever so nice today, Moira!' Chrissy shouts over, with a mouthful of Special K.

Moira spins around at the sink.

'Do you like it?' she beams, fingering the blue-black curls about her shoulders. 'I got it from a Paki shop in Penge!'

Chrissy and I both gasp in horror at the same time.

'We don't say Paki, Moira,' I scold, and I point at the Anti Nazi League badge on my blazer lapel. Chrissy is shaking her head.

'It's Pakistani!' she says. 'Not Paki.'

'It's Pakistani if the person in question comes from Pakistan, Chrissy,' I correct. 'They might come from India or Mauritius, or Bradford.'

Moira laughs nervously, her eyes blazing.

'Oh! I don't mean nothin' by it,' she says. 'I'm not a racialist, I can promise you that – I used to go out with one meself.'

'One what?' Chrissy asks.

'An Indian fella! I dated him for quite some months, as it goes, till all the drug-taking fucked it up.'

We're intrigued.

'Drugs?' I say.

'He was taking drugs?' Chrissy gasps.

Moira looks misty-eyed.

'No, I was,' she says. 'Oh, he was gorgeous, though – beautiful wavy 'air and green eyes – and an absolute gent the whole time we were together. Took me places I never thought I'd go: Hampton Court Palace, Garfunkel's ... it was tough, though, kids, it really was.'

'What was?' I say. 'What was tough?'

'The pressure of stepping out with an overseas-type gentleman,' says Moira, sticking out a large bosom. 'People are unkind; they don't want to understand anyfin' different. I'd 'ave women lookin' daggers at me in Victor Value – oh yes, cutting remarks on the bus

114

from all and sundry, people expecting me to like hot food. No, kids, other people's prejudices tore me and my Sajan apart, I can tell you that. We were fuckin' doomed from the start.'

There's that word again. Doomed.

Moira looks wistfully, and somewhat over-dramatically, out of the kitchen window for a moment, while fiddling with a Brillo.

'I wonder whatever 'appened to him,' she muses.

'Well, I think you should have bloody well stayed together,' I say, banging my spoon down rather too vehemently on the glass table. 'It's nobody else's business who one chooses to love, is it? You should have stuck it out. Fuck what anyone else thinks – that's what I say.'

'S'pose you're right,' Moira says, now bleaching down the draining board. 'But if it wasn't meant to be, darlin', it wasn't meant to be. I guess it just wasn't in the stars for little ol' me to spend my life with an Indian man. Which is probably for the best if you think about it. I mean, they're very studious and clever an' all that, but they don't really 'ave the big willies like the blacks, do they?'

And with that she starts singing along with Sad Cafe's 'Everyday Hurts' on the transistor – gathering up our breakfast bowls as she goes.

There's a thump on the front door and before I know it, Squirrel has locked Chrissy in an earthy clinch in the passage. When they're done, he bowls into the kitchen, whistling, and wearing ankle-swinger school trousers that have been crudely taken in at the leg to

115

make them into drainpipes, with a skinny chequered tie over a white shirt with rolled-up sleeves. He looks ever more gaunt, and decidedly shifty this morning. When Chrissy goes upstairs to get her schoolbag, he sidles over to Moira, who's still singing at the sink, and motions to her with his eyes when he thinks I'm not looking. Strange. Moira looks back at him and shakes her head, eyes bulging, teeth gritted: I can see them in the mirror on the wall opposite – what on earth are they up to? I didn't even know Squirrel knew Moira that well. I decide to pop out to the utility room, and I pretend to rifle through the laundry basket for something. Then, when they think I'm out of sight, I peek back into the kitchen through the crack in the door. Moira is bending down and she takes something out of her tote bag – it looks like a little package – and she hands it to Squirrel, who bungs it into his pocket as quick as you like. Then she shoves him away, like she doesn't want him near her, gritting her teeth again and shooing him off. This is all very odd, I feel – should I mention it to Chrissy? Perhaps not. At least not until I know more.

'Let's go!' Chrissy shouts from the passage, and I reappear from the utility room, smiling knowingly at Moira as I pass her. She doesn't twig.

'Don't be late, I promised your mother,' she says.

It's a greyish morning and I think it might be spitting, so I pull up the hood on my duffle. Chrissy lights up the minute the front door's shut behind her, and she links arms with Squirrel, dragging the heels of her slingbacks along the pavement as she goes. The three of us plod towards our respective schools, and when we get to the end of Chesterfield Street, Abigail, who becomes animated to the point of virtual apoplexy when she spots me, tags along with us. Shit!

'Hiya, Dave,' she gushes as we head along Lordship Lane.

'Hi, Abigail,' I mutter back.

To be honest, I'm mortified at the very sight of her after what had occurred between us a couple of weeks back – particularly since I'd finally admitted to myself that coral nail varnish on my private parts was, perhaps, not something I'd be altogether thrilled about from hereon in.

'I'm glad I've bumped into you,' she goes on. 'Do you know what I was thinking?'

Surprise me.

'I was thinking we could go out together, Sat'day – you know, just us. Me an' you. What d'you think?'

'Why?' I say.

'Well,' she says, 'I thought after what happened the other week – you know . . .'

And she leers at me as if she might eat me. I'm affronted, and I stare blankly at her as we walk, almost crashing into a lamp post outside the off-licence.

'What do you mean – after what happened the other week?' I enquire foolhardily.

Chrissy and Squirrel start laughing, and I turn to them open-mouthed.

'What?'

'It's all right, Davey boy,' Squirrel chuckles. 'We all

know Abi gave you one off the wrist up in your bedroom the other week. She told us straight after.'

I stop dead in my tracks. She fucking told them.

'You fucking told them?'

Abigail looks down at the pavement and fiddles with one of her bunches.

'I had to,' she says. 'I 'ad spunk on me pleated mini, and your sister noticed. Anyway, we tell each other everything, me and Chrissy – don't we, Chris?'

She's brazen.

'Yeah!' Chrissy laughs. 'And some things I'd rather not know, thanks very much: like me brother being jerked off to a Donna Summer record by me best mate being one of 'em.'

They all find this highly amusing, and Squirrel is almost frenzied with laughter at this juncture. I feel slightly queasy and I lean against the window of the dry-cleaners.

'For fuck's sake, Abigail.'

'I'm sorry, David,' she says.

And I can see that she is, so I decide to let her down gently.

'The thing is, Abigail,' I say cautiously, 'I've actually met somebody else . . . met somebody . . . you know . . . that I like in that way, and I . . . er . . . well, I can't really go out with anyone at the moment, because I like this person, you see.'

'Oh!'

Abigail sucks in her cheeks and looks down at her moccasins.

'I thought you said I looked like Debbie Harry,' she says quietly.

'Oh, you do!' I say, gripping her by the shoulders. 'You really do. It's just that . . . well, I'm not sure that I'm looking for someone that looks like Debbie Harry, much as I enjoy her music. Do you understand?'

'No, I don't,' she snaps, and she pulls away from me.

Chrissy and Squirrel suddenly stop giggling and pay full attention. Abi goes on.

'All I know is that you took my virginity, and now you don't want to go out with me. Typical boy. You think I'm a slag, don't ya?'

'I don't think you're a slag,' I say, agog. 'And what do you mean, I took your virginity? We didn't even . . .'

'My hand virginity,' Abigail clarifies. 'You took my hand virginity. I'd never touched anyone like that before, down there before.'

I think she might cry.

'Oh, Jesus!' I say. 'Don't be so ridiculous, Abi. Look, I can't go out with you, and that's that – I'm really sorry.'

Squirrel elbows me, hard, in the ribs.

'Ooh! Right little minge-teaser, you are, Davey,' he squawks. 'Didn't think you 'ad it in ya, mate.'

This exhausts me, and I turn my back on the lot of them.

'Whatever,' I say. 'I'm going to school.'

And I start to head along Lordship Lane again, alone. Suddenly, Chrissy shouts after me.

'Who is she, then? This girl!'

But I don't turn back.

'He's making it up,' I hear Abigail say. 'He hasn't got no one.'

You're probably right, Abigail, I decide. You're probably absolutely bloody right!

I'm pondering my Debbie dream when I finally wander into school, and I've just stopped to consider Moira's insight into the numerous pitfalls of star-crossed love outside the science block, when a voice calls me from across the playground.

'What are you doing out here, David? It's twenty past nine, son, you're late.'

Luckily it's Mr Peacock in a pea-green cagoule carrying a clipboard.

'Nothing, sir! I didn't realize what the time was, sir, sorry!'

He strides over towards me, eyes squinting against the spitting rain, which is dripping off his loosely permed fringe.

'Haven't you got technical drawing first lesson?' he says. 'Mr Lord won't be best thrilled if you're late, will he?'

I shake my head.

'I don't think I'm in Mr Lord's good books anyway, sir,' I smile.

'Oh, and why's that?' he says, and then he holds up his hand.

'Actually, David, you don't need to answer that.'

And he chuckles.

'Are you looking forward to the rally and the concert on Sunday?' he asks me, then. 'Annie and I are, very much – I think it's going to be a really good turnout.'

I nod enthusiastically.

'I really am, sir, so is Frances. And Maxie Boswell is coming along, too, did you know?'

'I somehow thought he might be,' Mr Peacock smiles, and I look up at him, slightly puzzled by the remark.

'Well, you just go easy, David, eh?' he says softly.

I nod again, but I'm not sure quite what he means; then he looks down at his clipboard.

'I won't put you in the late book today, David,' he says.

'Thanks, sir!'

I turn and head, then, towards the main building. I'm thinking about Moira and her kind, gentle, Indian man and their ill-fated romance; and I wonder, just as I reach the dreaded technical boring room and a red-faced Mr Lord, whether all misunderstood love – and indeed, my love – might well be doomed.

Nine

A Moment of Unity

The day of the Rock Against Racism rally and concert is upon us and all I can say is Wow! Brockwell Park is awash with punks, Rastas, hippies, students and all sorts of homosexuals, male and female, under a seemingly endless canvas of azure sky. Everywhere you look, large-breasted, dungaree-clad women and their offspring are skipping about plaid blankets that all seem to be covered in nut roasts, discarded sandals and Sainsbury's red wine in ribbed plastic bottles, the smell of ganja pricking the air. The sound system is now so implausibly loud that the dub and reggae coming through its speakers just sound like a low buzzing thump echoing around the park, but nobody seems to mind at all; everyone just keeps on dancing.

This is my second Rock Against Racism gig – we'd been to one with some of the 'lefty brigade' teachers at the Alexandra Palace earlier in the year and Frances and me had adored it. There, we hadn't felt different:

wonky or out of place. We felt like we were part of something that made up something that counted for something, and we vowed to go to every subsequent RAR event that we could. Frances has now got quite into the whole Anti Nazi League scene and has learned practically everything there is to know about it. She'd explained to me, for instance, that the Rock Against Racism movement had originally been launched after Eric Clapton, who I felt had never made a decent pop single, had stopped one of his concerts to make a speech in support of the intolerant and bigoted diatribes of Enoch Powell. She also knew all about 'the battle of Lewisham' in 1977, which, people say, brought about the formation of the Anti Nazi League.

'Ever since then we've had the NF on the run,' she'd say with pride, 'and we're getting stronger all the time.'

She was a right little militant. Of course, Margaret Thatcher being elected Prime Minister earlier in the year wasn't ever going to be a help to any kind of left-wing group, particularly as the news and media slant seems to have taken a very sharp – and in my opinion, unpleasant – turn to the right these days. Still, though, Frances can oft be discovered outside Chelsea Girl in Peckham of a Saturday, doling out paraphernalia, and shouting up for her cause. And for that – and for the astute and compassionate eyes through which she views the world – I admire Frances utterly.

I suppose I'm seeing the universe in a whole new light as well, as it happens. I'm actually fast growing used to the fact that I am what all the other kids always said I was: homo, queer, bent, shirt-lifter and all the other choice and exquisite pet names I'd collected over the years. The difference is that now it is *my* declaration and no one else's. Not Mr Lord's, not my dad's and not Jason Lancaster's. I am the one affirming who and what I am. I have taken back the power. I am something approaching Wonder Woman and I'm rather enjoying it. Not that I've been able to caterwaul about my sexuality from the proverbial rooftops or, indeed, make public my feelings for Maxie. But just to have finally said the words 'I'm gay' to myself without actually combusting, or melting, or turning bright pink, is extraordinarily empowering. Having Hamish McClarnon and my best friend, Frances, tell me 'it's OK' is like breathing a new and exhilarating oxygen. And as the days go by, and the fruit of this fresh revelation ripens, my vim and vigour are shooting up like wild corn, along with a new sanguinity.

Maxie and me have settled on the grass towards the back of the park where the crowd is a little thinner. We've decided to catch the first band while Frances goes on the hunt for a food stall, and Maxie is actually lying here in his crisp white shirt with his head virtually in my lap, chewing a long stalk of grass. It's *très* Evelyn Waugh, I decide, but he doesn't appear to be in the least self-conscious about it. I'm resisting the urge to run my fingers through his hair when he suddenly bobs up.

'Hey! There's Frances!' he shouts, pointing through

the throng at an approaching juvenile covered in badges.

'Oh yes!' I concur. 'And she doesn't seem to have my fucking hot dog. The greedy cow has probably scoffed it herself!'

'She's been ages,' Maxie says, gazing across the bustling park. 'Do you think she's met a lesbian or something? There seem to be an awful lot of 'em here.'

'I should think she's probably met several lesbians,' I suggest. 'But I'm pretty certain that when push comes to shove, our Frances has a preference for the penis.'

'What, like you?' Maxie laughs, lying back down and looking up at me with saucer eyes, and I feel myself crimson: what does he think he knows? I've not actually told him anything!

When Frances eventually reaches us, hopping over a dwarf punk couple, I can tell that all is not as it might be.

'There's been trouble. There's been a lot of fucking trouble outside the park gates,' she says.

She's quite breathless, and her Bob Marley T-shirt is soaked through. Maxie and I sit up straight.

'Really?'

'Nazis. The National Front, shouting, throwing bottles at the people coming in, doing Heil Hitler. I got hit in the face with a Kia-Ora carton,' Frances says, looking like she'd just run with the stampeding bulls in Pamplona. Her hands are positively trembling.

'Well, it could have been worse, lovey, couldn't it?' I say, quickly pulling myself up from the ground and giving her hand a little comfort squeeze. 'A carton's not as bad as a bottle, is it?'

Frances, however, begins to cry.

'It was filled with piss,' she whimpers, 'and somebody shouted nigger at me. I just went to that hot-dog man by the gates, because the sausages looked better than the ones from the man by the portable toilets. And then, on the way back – I was soaking wet – one of the skinhead girls grabbed my arm through the fence – she really pinched me. She called me a black bitch.'

And she sobs some more. I am unreservedly horrified.

'Fucking cunts!' Maxie shouts, jumping up. 'Are they still there? I'm gonna go out there if they are! I'm gonna fucking go out there.'

He turns to make a dash for the gates, but I grab his arm.

'Oy, simmer down, Batman, for fuck's sake!' I say urgently. 'Let's calm down a bit . . . what happened next, Fran?'

'The pigs waded in and the NF have been moved on – those that weren't carted off in a meat wagon. The thing is, though, half the people that were arrested were our lot – the anti-Nazi brigade. The police don't seem to care that it's our festival and that those fuckers have come to spoil it.'

I put my arm around my friend's shoulder, and pull her close to me.

'It was horrible, really horrible, and you'll *never* guess who I bloody well saw,' she goes on, her distress now morphing into something approaching fury. 'Right in the thick of it: swastika on his jean jacket, Nazi salute – the lot!'

'Who?'

'Jason pigging Lancaster!' Frances announces, with the emphasis on the 'pigging'. 'Right at the front of the mob, *and* with another goon from our year: Bernard . . . I can't remember his surname . . . the one that had a wank during the RE exam last term. There was a few of them from our school I recognized, as it goes.'

Now I'm furious too, and Maxie and I stare at one another in disbelief.

'The bastards!' I spit. 'We should tell Mr McClarnon when he gets here – tell the whole school, in fact, they'd be expelled.'

'What's the fucking point?' Maxie says, getting between us and putting one arm around me and the other around Frances. 'Jason will only lie his way out of it and say he was just here for the gig or something – people like him always get away with it. I think we just need to try to forget it now and enjoy the day, eh? Don't let 'em fuck it up for us? What do you think, Frances?'

Frances sticks her bottom lip out and flutters her dazzling eyes at Maxie.

'Do I smell of piss though, Maxie?' she says pathetically.

'Yes, Frances,' Maxie says, smiling. 'You actually do.'

As a big auburn ball of late summer sun sinks over Brixton, and the park revellers get progressively and

127

jubilantly more stoned and pissed, my sister Chrissy and a fiercely sunburned Abigail join us with a practically full bottle of Cinzano Bianco.

'You said you'd be by the fuckin' stage,' Chrissy snaps at us, Abigail nodding furiously behind her.

'Sorry, sis,' I say. 'I didn't know you were definitely coming, and it's too crowded up there. Where's Squirrel?'

'I've no idea where that prat is,' Chrissy says, 'and I don't fucking care to be honest. He's always disappearing lately.'

She holds up a large checked laundry bag.

' 'Ere, look what I nicked out of Nan's ottoman,' she says.

When we all sit back down again, it's on one of my nan's old eiderdowns, and we decide to smoke the weed that Frances had pilfered from her older brother that morning. After a couple of puffs I can't seem to stop myself giggling.

'Your face is ever so red, Abi,' I splutter. 'Do you not think you should cover up a trifle?'

Abigail, who is in an aubergine tank top and cut-off denim hot pants with scarcely any of the original trouser-leg left to speak of, looks at me with only thinly veiled abhorrence.

'It's called being sun-kissed, David,' she barks. 'We don't all want to be sheet-white like you, do we?'

'I'd say it was more of a slap than a kiss,' I laugh, and Maxie starts to giggle too.

'Shut up! It's from sunbathing, if you must know,' Abigail says. 'I've been sunbathing.'

Chrissy shrieks.

'Where, on the fuckin' sun itself? You look like a tomato with teeth, Abi!'

And with that we descend into merciless hysteria. Poor Abigail. Frances is practically slapping her thigh with delight.

'Oh, Lard! Dat is too damn funny,' she screams, and we roar even louder.

At least she's laughing again. Abigail, however, is incensed.

'I slavered meself in Hawaiian Tropic – Number Five,' she continues to protest, 'but I'm very susceptible to the elements. Mum says I've got thin skin; you shouldn't laugh.'

Nothing can stop us now, though, and as the strains of 'Take Me I'm Yours' by Squeeze float across the park, I have tears running down my face and an aching side. Brilliant!

Eventually we're all flat on the ground, pretty much done in, and I tip my head back and soak myself in the pulsating music, enjoying the feel of Maxie's head on my chest as he lollops from side to side, slowly. I virtually leap out of my own hide when a familiar voice says, 'Are ye gonna give me a toke on that joint, or what?'

It's Mr McClarnon, looming over us with an open, half-drunk bottle of Sainsbury's red.

Maxie sits up sharpish, clearly aghast at the fact that we've all been caught red-handed smoking an illicit substance by a member of staff, but Frances and I just giggle as Chrissy, also open-mouthed, hands Hamish the joint, and he inhales, long and deep. For most of the day thus far, Hamish has been hands on at the 'Schools Against Racism' information stand on the far side of the park, but he's evidently ready to relax and enjoy the concert now, and he joins us all on the ground in his green cap-sleeved T-shirt, covered in badges. My eye is drawn to the pink one with the black arrow: it reads 'Gays against Nazis', and it makes me smile.

'Well!' Hamish says after I've introduced him to Chrissy and the now lobster-coloured Abigail. 'This is a nice surprise indeed. It's food for the soul te see you kids getting involved with this sort of thing.'

He takes another huge pull on the joint, and as he coughs and puffs out the smoke, says, 'It's important!'

He stares at me for what seems like a very long time, and then I follow his eyes down to Maxie, who is clearly stoned and has gone back to using me as a pillow. Hamish nods slowly.

'It's nice te see you two boys here together too,' he says softly, and I'm almost certain I detect him chase away a tear before taking an enormous quaff from his wine bottle.

'I'm proud of you, David,' Hamish says. 'Right proud! I know you've had a difficult time this week.'

And Maxie looks up at me, puzzled.

Hamish wasn't bloody kidding about me having a difficult week; I'd have said monumental was nearer the mark. It had all kicked off on Wednesday afternoon, when Jason Lancaster and his friends had ribbed me horribly as I rehearsed the number 'I'd Do Anything' with the repulsive little first-year who was playing Oliver.

'Do I have to hold the little brat's hand?' I'd complained to Hamish. 'He's no Mark Lester, you know, and I don't think I've once seen him without his finger jammed up his nose. That coupled with the fact that Sonia Barker can't pronounce her Rs, so it's bloody "catch a kangawoo" every time she sings it, and this number's turning into an absolute fiasco!'

'Of course ye have te hold his hand,' Hamish had instructed, just at the inopportune moment when Jason was shifting the long and weighty workhouse table across the hall with a couple of his mates.

'Go on, Starr, you know you want to,' Jason had bellowed at me the minute Hamish had disappeared off to the loo. 'Stick his willy in ya mouth while you're at it!'

Charming!

Then, on Thursday lunchtime, there had been what I'd call a major incident – well, two, actually. Maxie and me were sitting in the costume room off the lower assembly hall, sipping Tab in amongst the half-finished papier-mâché scenery, when Maxie said to me, 'Do you reckon people think we're bum chums?'

'What?'

'You know,' he said. 'Some of the other kids. Do you think that's what they're thinking? Half the footy team

131

hardly speak to me since the other night at the field when I squared up to Jason.'

I stared into his face, blinking.

'They don't call you names, though, do they?'

Maxie shook his head, and then he got up and started pacing around the tiny room.

'Not like they do you. But I reckon they all think it just the bloody same.'

I fiddled with the buttons on Mr Bumble's frock coat, which was hanging on a clothes rack next to me.

'And does that bother you?' I enquired cautiously.

I felt horribly anxious. Had Maxie, at last, cottoned on to my feelings? Was he about to run a fucking mile? If the penny had dropped then there wasn't much I could do about it, but if it hadn't, I would have to discourage him from any further suspicions of it. I couldn't chance losing Maxie, not now.

'Well, it's not true, is it?' he finally said, crushing his drink can. 'I've never even fuckin' kissed a boy, have you? Have you kissed a boy, David?'

I shook my head slowly.

'Mind you,' he went on. 'I do think there is something a bit . . . weird with us, though, don't you?'

My heart almost flew out of my mouth.

'Is there?'

Maxie sat down again, and then leaned right back on his chair – he was always doing that. He closed his eyes tight for a moment, as if in deep thought.

'Well, I've not known you for that long, have I?' he said, 'and we're already so . . .'

'What?' I said.

Then he got up again, but this time he walked straight towards me, his brow in a deep furrow. He put his warm palms on either side of my face, and for a second or so I thought I might be sick again. Then, just like it was nothing, he planted a light – almost silly – kiss on my mouth and laughed.

'There you go,' he said. 'Now I *have* kissed a boy. Don't make me queer though, does it?'

'Doesn't it?' I said, but the words barely left my mouth, and I felt myself crumple slightly, sliding down in the chair.

I lifted my hand and touched my bottom lip softly with my index finger to check that it was still there, because I wasn't sure it actually was, and all the while Maxie was saying something to me – well, I thought he must have been because his mouth was moving. I couldn't hear what he was saying, though; I couldn't hear him at all. All I could hear, loud in my head – filling the room, in fact, as far as I was concerned – was The Crystals singing 'Then He Kissed Me'.

Then the pips went for the end of lunch, and I heard Maxie say, 'What have you got next?'

And I said, 'I don't know . . . Sociology, I think . . . and I've not done my essay or . . .'

'Well, I'll catch you after school,' he said.

And he was gone.

When I followed Maxie out into the hall I felt flushed, and ever so slightly feverish. I didn't feel as though my legs were functioning all that well, but Maxie was striding ahead swinging his Arsenal sports bag as if nothing had happened. Unfortunately for me, Bob Lord had been hovering over by the piano, and when he clocked me following Maxie out of the costume room he got this look on his face that, I must say, unnerved me somewhat. It wasn't one of the routine looks he trotted out whenever he saw me approaching: menacing, disdainful, irritated; it was more a look of concern – fear, almost. I thought he might burst into tears. I couldn't work it out, but he didn't say anything, just looked. Things became crystal clear later, however, when Mr Lord arrived at the tail end of my English lit class, last period, and requested the pleasure of my company in his office.

'Off you go,' Miss Jibbs, my English tutor, said. 'We're just about done here any road, Bob.'

I felt as though she was sending me into the arena with a particularly unpleasant lion, but I didn't have much choice but to go, did I? So I packed up my books and toddled along after him.

'You're a bright lad, aren't you, David?' was his opening gambit as I wriggled uneasily in the tatty calico armchair in his broom cupboard of an office.

'I suppose,' I said.

'Oh, there's no suppose about it, son,' he said with a slightly ominous edge. 'One of only two students to take his English O level at the end of the fourth year, and passing with an A; editor of the school newspaper two years running; top of your class in almost all of your humanities subjects, and a lexis that most of the staff here would envy.'

I'd looked up the word 'lexis' only last month, so I knew what it meant.

'Some folk might just call that having a smart mouth,' I laughed, attempting to lighten the mood.

'They might indeed,' he semi-sneered.

Then he went quiet and sank back in his swivel. I looked around the room, perhaps for an escape route – I'm not entirely sure. The place was crammed with sports equipment: a locker with a broken door almost bursting with rugby balls and tatty-handled hockey sticks; a net on a hook on the back of the door full of cricket balls; and a Tesco bag spilling over with unclaimed articles of football kit. I decided to rupture what seemed an inordinately protracted silence.

'Anyway,' I said, 'it's not all good news, aptitude-wise, with me. I mean, hand me a Bunsen burner or ask me about algebraic variables and I'm at complete sixes and sevens, and don't even get me started on homeomorphism.'

Mr Lord grunted a laugh to himself.

'My point exactly,' he muttered. 'An answer for everything.'

Another long silence. Then he said, 'I've been chatting to some of the other staff, David, and they seem to think you're letting things slide a bit so far this term: assignments not handed in; lateness a routine occurrence; not paying attention. I mean, you're in a world of your own most of the time in my classes, son, I can see that for myself. Do you think the school musical might be diverting your focus from your studies, given your evidently faultless previous diligence, I mean? Or do you think, perhaps, it might be something or someone else cocking it all up? Eh, son?'

Mr Lord's demeanour was now vaguely menacing, so any thoughts I had of a swaggering retort were dwindling by the second.

'I'm sure I don't know to what you're referring, sir,' was the best I could do.

Mr Lord smiled at me with all the sincerity of Uriah Heep, and then he said, 'We're on the second floor here, aren't we, David. Overlooking the car park?'

Oh shit, he's not going to throw me out of the fucking window, is he?

'And what,' he went on, 'do you think I'd see if I looked out of this window right now, David?'

'I'm not sure, sir,' I said. 'Probably not Niagara Falls. Why?'

'I think I'd see young Maxie Boswell out there right now,' he said, 'and do you know why?'

'I don't.'

By now, any bluster I'd had was completely gone and I could feel the sweat building under my collar. Whatever this was, I thought, it wasn't good.

'I think I'd see Maxie Boswell outside because the pips went two minutes ago, and because he'll be waiting for you to come out of your English lit class, which is just below this window. That's what I think.'

I wriggled a bit more.

'And?' I said.

'And that's what I've seen every night for the past two or three weeks, Starr. Him hanging around waiting for you, or you skulking about the football pitch when there's a practice on, waiting for him.'

'I don't skulk, sir,' I almost whispered. 'I just go and meet him, and we walk home together – well, for part of the way, anyway. I'm sure lots of other kids do the same. What's the problem?'

Bob Lord slithered around the table and sat on the edge of his desk facing me. He almost looked compassionate.

'Well, my problem is, David, that you're a lot more sure of yourself, and what you're about, than Boswell is, and I think he might be a little bowled over by you. I think he might think some things are OK, or acceptable, when they really aren't. Do you get me?'

'No.'

'Well, what I see is the two of you behaving in a way that might be construed as . . . odd for a couple of lads of your age – not, dare I say it, Christian. And I think that you, as the older of the two boys, need to address this and put a stop to it before it goes too far up the wrong path.'

I resisted the urge to raise an eyebrow.

'Maxie is three weeks younger than me, sir. We're both sixteen in the next few weeks.'

'Yes, in years and months you might be the same age,' Mr Lord said, rather creepily putting his hand on my shoulder. 'But, as I've said, you are much more sure of yourself than Boswell, and I guess you have already made choices about who and what you are. I think he's a lad, however, that could be swayed into doing something that he might not naturally do otherwise.'

'Like macramé, sir?' I said.

'I think you know what I'm getting at, David,' he said, his voice remaining spookily measured and serene. 'I've seen the two of you together, and I think you do know what I mean.'

I said nothing.

'Do you?'

I looked down at my shoes, as if I should be ashamed. I don't know why, it just seemed the right thing to do. When I lifted my head again, Mr Lord was smiling and nodding.

'Can I go now, sir?' I said.

'Go on then.'

As I reached the door, though – eyes fixed on the net bag full of cricket balls – Mr Lord surprised me with a little gasp and said, 'Oh! We didn't check, did we, Starr?'

I turned to see him beckoning me over, and I crossed the room as he yanked up the venetians. Then he chuckled as we both looked out of the window at Maxie, two floors below, leaning against the lamp post in the car park outside what had been my English class.

'Well, well, well,' said Bob Lord.

And so, yes, it had been a bloody difficult week, to say the least. But I'm certainly not going to let that spoil today: today in the park, in the sun, with my friends, and with Maxie.

* * *

Hamish is now lying face down with his eyes shut. In fact we are all now pretty much just grinning patches of jelly on the cool grass of Brockwell Park, so it's a fairly rude awakening when Maxie leaps to his feet and screams at the top of his voice, 'Yeah! I fucking love this song: it's The Specials! Get up, get up! I have to dance!'

Somehow everyone manages to haul him or herself upright, and suddenly we're all moving to the now clearly audible and perfectly superb music. We're a bit shaky at first, it has to be said, but once we get into our stride we all dance like we're possessed and we throw our hands into the sky, singing:

'Why must you record my phone calls? Are you planning a bootleg LP?'

Around the park, everyone is dancing: the white boys and the black girls, the queers and the mums, the punks and the rude boys, the dykes and the Rastas. This is a moment of complete unity – this is what we came here for. My sister Chrissy grabs my hand and we are dancing together, whooping and laughing.

'Said you've been threatened by gangsters; now it's you that's threatening me.'

Chrissy spins round and then grabs Abigail around the waist, while Maxie takes my hand, swinging my arm back and forth with his. I close my eyes for just a second to savour the moment, and when I open them, Maxie gives me a wink. I am very happy. We are all roaring with laughter as we watch Frances and Mr McClarnon dancing the moonstomp together, and then hearing our teacher shout out, *'Don't call me scarface!'* at the appropriate moment just about finishes us off. As the song ends we collapse like cards back down on to the grass.

'Perfect!' shouts Hamish McClarnon. 'Absolutely fucking perfect!'

I couldn't have agreed more.

Ten

The Balcony Scene

It's a good six hours since we left the park by the time Maxie and me get to Moira's flats, and as we step out of the sour-smelling lift and head along the covered walkway, Maxie says, 'Are you sure she won't mind?'

I'm not really sure at all, but I ring the bell anyway. No answer. I ring again, a longer blast this time, and now I can see through the ribbed glass someone shuffling along the passage. When Moira opens her front door, it's only by about two inches and she warily peeks out as best she can on to the balcony. A brass chain across the door prevents it from opening any further.

'I've told ya, I've got nothin' till tomorrow,' she says curtly.

I turn to Maxie; he looks as puzzled as I am.

'It's me, Moira,' I whisper. 'David! I've got my friend Maxie with me.'

'Oh! Come in, boys, come in!' she says with some

surprise, and she undoes the chain and swings open the door to her council maisonette.

'What the hell are you doing out this late, David? It's half past one in the morning.'

Maxie and I bundle into the hall and Moira pokes her head out of the door, scrutinizing the balcony in both directions – for what, I've no idea.

'I told me mum I was staying at Frances' house, Moira,' I say as she darts back in and puts the catch on. 'You won't grass me up, will you?'

'Don't be daft,' she snorts, herding us along the passage and into a lounge chock-full of decorative no-no's. 'As if I would! Where have you been till this time, anyway?'

'We've been to the Rock Against Racism gig,' Maxie breezes proudly.

Moira stands back with her short arms folded and takes in Maxie, giving him the full up-and-down inspection.

''Ave you now?' she laughs. 'And who the fuck are you when you're at 'ome, anyway?'

'This is Maxie, Moira. I told you about him last week, remember?'

Moira sparks up a Superking and plonks herself down on the peach World of Leather recliner she's always rattling on about.

'I must 'ave had me head in the oven,' she smiles, and then she notices: I knew she would, you can't bloody miss it.

'What's with the fucking black eye?' she says.

Maxie puts his hand up to his face and rolls his eyes.

'We 'ad a bit of trouble at a party,' he mutters. 'It's all right, though, it's not that bad – no real damage done.'

'Speak for yourself,' I say. 'My beige soul sandals are ruined.'

Moira's looking confused.

'I thought you said you were at a concert,' she says, 'not a flamin' party; and even so, it's a Sunday night – where 'ave you been till this time?'

'Just walking,' I shrug. 'Walking. We lost track of time and then Maxie realized that he didn't have his Chubb key. His dad puts the mortise on at half past ten.'

'They've been in Southend so they probably think I'm staying at my sister's,' Maxie says. 'I often do on a Sunday.'

Moira eyes us askance, flicking her ash into a depleted fruit bowl on the nest of wicker tables beside her.

'So what 'appened at this do, then?' she asks. 'How did Joe Frazier 'ere land up with a fuckin' shiner?'

Maxie and I park ourselves on the couch beside Moira's chair, and I relieve her of her cigarette, taking an elongated drag. I don't always smoke but this has been quite a day, what with one thing and another.

'Well, after we left the RAR gig about eight thirty-ish,' I say, 'we all get invited to this random party by Chrissy's mate Abigail. It's some bloke she knows on the Aylesbury estate who works in John Colliers on a Saturday and sometimes DJs at the CPH.'

'The what?' Moira says, pushing back on her recliner and letting the footstool shoot out.

'Crystal Palace Hotel,' Maxie clarifies.

'Oh!' she says. 'That's the pub where your sister and all the mods go, isn't it?'

'Yes,' I say. 'Anyway—'

Moira interrupts again.

'And it's bloody rough, that Aylesbury estate,' she says. 'You kids shouldn't be knocking around there at night.'

'Well, we know that now,' I laugh. 'Anyway ... so ... we all get on the bus from Brixton and head over there, and at first it was a really cool house party. Me and Maxie went, plus Chrissy, Abi, Frances and even our drama teacher, Mr McClarnon, went for a bit – mind you, he was so pissed by that point I don't think he knew where he was. Anyway, we were the youngest bunch there. A lot of 'em were eighteen, nineteen, but they were really cool with us because they knew Chrissy and Abi from the pub. And we were dancing ... the music was boss, wasn't it, Maxie? They played loads of ska and new wave, and we all ended up dancing out on the balcony with the sound system blaring out across the estate ...'

It was true, at least half the party had trundled out into the night air to dance with the moon above them.

'I reckon this balcony's gonna come away from the bleedin' wall in a minute,' Frances warned us as the music thumped out through the doors and windows of the flat, which was positively quaking.

Whoever was playing the music though, as far as I was concerned, had unimpeachable taste, and when I heard my absolute favourite new record – one I'd only just taped off the radio the previous morning and already knew by heart – I was off and running with the rest of them: jumping up and down on the tenth floor of a council estate on the Walworth Road under the stars on a Sunday night – who'd have fucking believed it?

'I bought my baby a red radio.
He played it all day a-go-go a-go-go.
He liked to dance to it down in the streets.
He said he loved me but he loved the beat.'

Even some of the neighbours didn't seem to be too fussed about the noise. Some young punky types from the floor below had heard the music and popped up to investigate, and then a lady in a black bra and her teenage daughter came out of the flat two doors down, grabbed a tin of Heineken from a passing Rasta and joined in – grooving with the multitude.

'It was about then that the ructions started,' I say to Moira, who by now looks nigh-on fascinated and has lit up another super-sized ciggie.

'Go on,' she says.

'Well, me, Maxie and Frances were all standing by the stairwell sharing a smoke I'd bummed off Chrissy, and suddenly out of the lift pour about ten or twelve boys who we'd have rather not bumped into, if you know what I mean.'

'Who were they?' Moira says.

'The little NF contingent,' I say grimly.

'Led by a kid from our school,' Maxie interjects.

'Jason Lancaster, his name is,' I continue. 'A right nasty little bleeder; hates me with a passion. Anyway, him and his fucking brownshirts – as I call them – come along the balcony where we all are and start mouthing off. Some of them infiltrate the party but a couple of them start throwing beer over two black kids that are stood outside, thinking it's hilarious. Then another boy has a go at Frances; starts pulling her hair and shoving her about. So Maxie bowls over to this kid and yanks him away by the arm, tells him to get his dirty fucking hands off Frances—'

'Hence the black eye,' Maxie smiles bravely.

'Hence the black eye,' I repeat. 'Well then, all bastard hell breaks loose. Some of the party kids get wind and come over to sort Jason and his mates out and suddenly it's bedlam. Huge fucking bundle.'

'Ooh my gawd!' Moira says, clutching her throat. 'No one was 'urt, was they? There weren't no stabbin's or nuffin'?'

'No, the police were called,' I say, 'and apart from Maxie's shiner, none of us lot were really hurt; but Abigail said that one of the NF boys had tried to finger her while she was passing a bowl of Monster Munch through the serving hatch in the kitchen.'

'Shockin',' Moira says.

'I know,' I say, and I take another long drag on her fag and flick the ash in the fruit bowl. 'The worst part of it was poor Chrissy.'

Moira's eyes bulge.

'Why? What the fuck 'appened to your Chrissy?'

'Well, nothing happened to her,' I tell Moira. 'She'd been in the kitchen with Abi and she came out to see what the noise was. Course, who was she faced with when she comes out of the front door?'

'Who?'

'Squirrel! Her boyfriend!'

'And?'

'And,' I say, 'he was one of them. He was the one shoving Frances and pulling her hair. Squirrel was the one that gave Maxie the black eye.'

Moira stares down at her ski sweater, somewhat guiltily, I feel, and picks at some loose wool. Is she about to come clean, I wonder, about her and Squirrel's little secret – whatever it may be? Should I inform her that I'd witnessed her passing him an unidentified package in our kitchen the previous Monday, in a manner one might only describe as surreptitious? I decide against confrontation, principally as I'm angling for her to let Maxie and me spend the night, and I don't want to piss her off.

'I knew he was a bad lad, that Squirrel,' Moira eventually says softly, but that's all she does say.

'Chrissy was devastated,' I tell her. 'She knew Squirrel was into the mod scene, but not hanging around with the NF kids – she never knew that. She was livid. Anyway, in amongst all the fighting and the loud music, suddenly I heard sirens, and then the police pour into the flats and come dashin' up the stairs, don't they? Mr McClarnon managed to shepherd all of our little mob along the balcony and into the lift, and we legged it out of there, thank God. Some mad fucking party, though, eh?'

'Fuck a duck,' Moira says breathlessly.

'Two ducks,' I say. 'Anyway, that was about

ten-ish, and since then we've just been . . . just . . .'

'Wandering around East Dulwich,' Maxie says.

'Yeah. Just wandering,' I say. 'And now we've got nowhere to stay.'

I stare wretchedly at Moira, who just looks back at me, stony-faced, and sucks hard on the remainder of her fag.

We hadn't exactly been wandering around East Dulwich for the whole time. Maxie and I had first ushered a more than slightly shaken Frances safely back to the flats where she lives. I felt horrible about what had happened at the party, especially with Squirrel, but I must say, Frances was putting on a valiant front when she kissed us both at her door, waving her finger at us like a mother hen, and advising us to get along home. After that, we left Chrissy and Abigail drinking cider out of plastic bottles outside the dry-cleaners at around ten thirty. Then, deciding that the night was still young – probably foolishly – Maxie and me had set up camp in the Wimpy Bar until it closed and then we'd just walked and talked, though I've little to no idea where or what about. I was practically a giddy 1950s schoolgirl by then, if you want the truth – one of the four Marys from *Bunty*, perhaps – and why not? I'd had one of the most thrilling, if at some points a little scary, days of my life and now I had Maxie Boswell all to myself, to boot.

'I can't go home now, me dad'll 'ave locked the door,' Maxie said. 'I stay at my sister's nine times out of ten on a Sunday, so he'll think I'm over there. I could stay at yours though, couldn't I?'

I think I was a little bit sick in my mouth, and then I shouted, 'NO! . . . I mean . . . my old dears think I'm at Frances'. I was supposed to be staying there tonight, wasn't I?'

'Well, why didn't you then?' Maxie said as we stopped outside the brightly lit window of Marriot's toyshop.

I thought for a moment. Yes, that was a good question, as it goes. Why hadn't I stayed at Frances'? I turned to Maxie, who was staring in the window, utterly transfixed by an almost life-size model of the much-heralded and purportedly terrifying creature from the new movie *Alien*. It was perched in what looked like a giant Noddy car next to a superstar Barbie fashion face, which I felt slightly detracted from any real terror it might otherwise have instilled.

'I suppose . . .' I mutter. 'I suppose . . . I didn't stay at Frances' place because . . .'

Maxie turned around and I felt nervy all of a sudden, but I soldiered on regardless.

'Because . . . I didn't want today to end.'

He leaned against the toyshop window, and then he looked at me and laughed, and I thought: what's funny? But then he said, 'Well, it doesn't 'ave to, does it? Isn't there somewhere else we can go?'

It was then that I thought of Moira's. She's always up late. She watches telly till all hours now, since my dad got her that knocked-off video recorder.

'I know somewhere,' I said.

'Well, let's go,' Maxie smiled.

Of course, I don't tell Moira all that. Just that it's much too late for us to go banging on either of our own front doors now, so here we are.

'All right,' she says dubiously. 'You can stay 'ere tonight but you're up for school in the morning, seven o'clock, so you've got time to pop 'ome and get your school stuff. You'll 'ave to 'ave my bed cos me spare room's got all me wigs in it. I'll sleep on the recliner – I don't really mind, I've still got three episodes of *Quincy* to get through. And I'm gonna get you a bag of frozen runners to put on that eye, Maxie, cos it'll come up nasty in the mornin' if you don't – do you 'ear me?'

Maxie and me are both smiling and nodding; what an adventure we've had. Moira drags herself out of her chair and heads towards the kitchenette.

'Do you want a tin of lager to take up, lads?' she calls out, swinging open the fridge door.

'Go on then,' I say. 'Just the one.'

By the time Maxie finally comes into the cerise-painted bedroom from the loo, I've got a partially bald avocado candlewick bedspread hauled up to my neck in an attempt to conceal my lean arms and puny chest – not having ever seriously considered the possibility that we might, in fact, be sleeping in a double bed together. It suddenly dawns on me, though, that I might look vaguely like a jumpy Victorian virgin on her wedding night, so I bravely let the cover fall, exposing my torso.

'I think I'm a bit tipsy,' Maxie says, swaying slightly in the doorway. 'Are you?'

'No,' I say. 'I'm not.'

And I take a huge gulp from the can of Carling Black Label that's sitting on the ugly Formica bedside drawers next to me. Maxie undresses with the lamp on, and he is not in the least bashful, throwing his shirt and jeans off and shoving his hands into his pants to adjust himself before hopping into the bed beside me. Oh, God. Maxie *is in* the bed beside me. I'm picking at the woodchip paper on the wall next to me, and fretfully chewing on my lip as he snuggles down. Oh, Christ on a bike!

'You're shivering. Should I pop that fan heater on?' he says.

'I'm all right, as it goes,' I assure him, and then he leans across me and switches off a small pottery lamp that hasn't got a proper shade but is draped with a half-finished Holly Hobby cross-stitch picture.

Then it's dark. 'As black as yer hat', my grandad would have said. And for a while I don't have even the wherewithal to move, and I can't hear or see a bloody thing. Then I hear him breathing: it's a fast, shallow semi-pant and my own respiratory rhythms seem to be in sync with his. I realize, quite suddenly, that I am actually aching for Maxie to touch me – even accidentally – but still I dare not move in case he thinks I'm some kind of voracious teenage molester; so I am lying rigid and damp with sweat. Inert. Confounded. Hard.

*   *   *

After jerking awake several times, and desperate not to fall into a deep sleep and miss any of this implausibly perfect night with my boy right here beside me, I turn on to my side and he is facing me: yes, facing me – we are now only inches apart. Near enough, in fact, to feel breath. I'm longing to make a seductive and sexy move, but I have absolutely no idea how to achieve this in my present predicament, or any other predicament, come to that, and I'm not entirely sure what sexy and seductive actually is, anyway, so I think – what would Debbie Harry do? Oh, it would be so much easier for her, all this. She'd be so much wiser and womanlier; plus she has much longer and blonder hair and I would assume that could only be a bonus, to be honest.

Quite suddenly there's movement: definite, tangible movement. Am I deranged with fatigue or did Maxie just shunt closer to me? Then, closer again . . . then . . . oh, God! There is no kiss. A kiss was anticipated, expected almost, but there is none. He's tugging gently at my hand – guides it downward and on to his . . . oh good grief . . . that's ridiculous on a boy his age, surely! That's just silly! No kiss still. Well, I suppose that's not what a teenage football captain wants, is it? He doesn't want romance and kissing; he wants someone to play with his dick. Isn't that what I want? Isn't that what I was hoping for too? And anyway, let's face it: beggars can't be choosers, can they? This is actually happening. It *is* actually . . . Oh! I'm not very good at this. It's tricky . . . difficult doing it to someone else; it's a whole new manoeuvre. You have to get your arm in a whole new position and . . . it's stressful. Maxie's breathing is quickening now and . . . his arms are around me . . . he's moving over me, I can feel his thighs around mine and . . . he's making a noise like he's . . . Ah! And there's the kiss!

When Debbie Harry smashes the tennis ball at me hard, it comes with heaps of top spin.

'So now what?' she shouts across the grass court.

'Well,' I grunt, whacking it back with the sun fierce in my eyes, 'at least I know he's into me now, right?'

'Well, yeah,' Debbie laughs, hitting an offensive lob that I am forced to chase down. 'You could look at it like that, but now you gotta keep it going and that's the hard part. What happens tomorrow? That's where the real work starts, baby.'

To be honest, at this point – match point – my peroxide idol's platitudes about love and gay romance are wearing a little thin, and the fact that she's playing tennis so very adroitly in high-heeled shoes is just adding to my exasperation. Besides that, it is scorching hot and I am dry and flagging in this vast and unoccupied stadium. I manage, despite all this, to wallop the ball high, just by the skin of my teeth.

'Don't worry about me,' I yell across the grass court persuasively. 'I know what I'm doing, even in a tennis skirt.'

Why is it that I am always dressed in women's clothes in my dreams? Anyway, Debbie heads for the high-flying ball and comes back with a slam that thwacks the ball down just my side of the net as I dash forward – racket outstretched – too late!

'Fuck it!'

My knees hit the grass in a burning skid, just as the ball comes down for a second time.

'You have to expect the unexpected,' Debbie Harry says, walking towards the net. 'Robinson's Barley Water?'

Eleven

A Beige Hatter

October 1979

To look at us you'd think we were love's young dream, Maxie and me, since that night in Moira's bedroom just over a week ago. Well, perhaps not exactly that, but as good as, at a pinch. For instance, at rehearsals for the now rapidly approaching school production, there had been an effusive quantity of enduring stares across the dolly cart, and a fair few premeditated and what I took to be lascivious hand-brushings between us when we thought we could get away with it. Almost every time, in fact, that we even passed one another at close proximity or rehearsed a scene together, there had crackled a discernible current that I'd sense from my head to my toes. And what's more, the grand illicitness of the whole thing made it all the more exhilarating to me, and, it appeared, to Maxie. As the days went on, and even under the watchful, dogmatic eyes of Bob Lord and the discriminatory gaze of Jason Lancaster, Maxie would find a way to pat

me audaciously between the thighs or press himself
suggestively against me in the costume cupboard, his
face slicked with the filthiest of grins. It was all very
Benny Hill but I loved it . . . and I loved him. To be
honest, the only entity that was absent from this otherwise marvellous panorama was actual sex! Yes, Maxie
certainly appeared to be looking through the eyes of
love at me, it was true. Yes, he'd walked me home
every evening last week after school, carrying my
bulky sociology textbooks as if he were Jim-Bob
Walton and I was Ike and Corabeth's adopted
daughter Aimee, but that's where it ended. Flirtation,
it seemed, was fine, but Maxie hadn't once come up to
my bedroom to listen to Blondie records since that
night at Moira's, and it was starting to get to me.

'Well, you hain't hardly sixteen yet,' Frances Bassey
had ruthlessly reminded me over a Bender Brunch at
the Wimpy Bar on Thursday. 'Perhaps the two a you
shouldn't be damn well havin' sex yet, bwoy! It's
nasty!'

And she shrieked into her lime milkshake, while I
glared at her with pursed lips.

'No, seriously,' she said once she'd stopped
giggling. 'You've had more time to think about all this.
I mean you were building up to it, weren't you?
Perhaps, to Maxie, it came as a bit of a shock. Perhaps
he isn't ready for the whole full-on gay thing – d'you
know what I mean?'

I nodded earnestly as Frances sipped her drink,
thrilled that she seemed at last to be viewing my
dilemma with at least some semblance of seriousness.

'Besides,' she continued, breaking into a snigger again. 'Havin' you do all ya bizness all over d' poor bwoy is enough to send anyone ronnin'.'

And she laughed so hard that she spat fluorescent green liquid all over the table – very much like Linda Blair in *The Exorcist*. Only black.

The horrendous truth of it is, though, that Frances was probably right, damn her! Although Maxie did seem, on the exterior, to be fine and dandy, who knew what sort of ghastly inner tumult he might be harbouring? Granted, he had certainly seemed at peace with himself on the Monday morning after our blissful dalliance at Moira's place. He'd even enthused about the sheer brilliance of the whole previous day, as had I – though we didn't mention, and have not since, the actual dirty deed. But then I suppose it's a big step, isn't it? Going from captain of the school football team to full-out bender in one fell swoop, and after my own experiences of coping with the many and varying complexities of burgeoning fairydom, how could I expect him to be embracing the concept with open arms after only a few days? It was *très difficile*, and there was no getting away from it. Still, Maxie didn't seem to be on the verge of any sort of imminent nervous collapse, and for that I was profoundly grateful. I just wanted to get him alone again, wanted to feel him against me again, and I desperately wanted him to want that too. So, although jamming himself up against me by the costume rack when nobody else was around is all very nice, it isn't enough! It just isn't enough!

* * *

Still, there is more than a faint flicker of hope that things might change: in fact, on this very afternoon. Especially after last night, when Maxie turned up, most unexpectedly, at the Lordship Lane Working Men's Club during my bar shift.

'Maxie! What are you doing here?' I beamed, rather ludicrously.

I was virtually swinging on a crescent moon with elation.

'Just thought I'd pay you a visit,' Maxie said. 'Me mum and dad are parked in front of the telly watching *Tales of the Unexpected* and I can't stick that, so I thought I'd come and see you.'

He was in a black Harrington jacket, with a blue plaid button-down shirt and dark jeans; his blond hair fell sexily over his forehead. He looked adorable.

'Well, that's great,' I gushed, loading some dirty pint pots into the glass-washer. 'Really great! I'm hoping we won't be too busy tonight, so I might have a bit of time to chat.'

No sooner, though, had I uttered those words than an uncouth but all too familiar voice bellowed from the stockroom behind me.

'Oy! Gertrude! Pull your fuckin' finger out; I can see the customers waitin' from 'ere!'

Maxie looked confused.

'It's my boss, Marty,' I explained, rolling my eyes to the heavens.

Maxie continued to look bewildered.

'Why did he call you Gertrude?' he said.

158

'Because he's a cunt,' I smiled, just as Marty marched out into the bar in a West Ham top with a cigarette dangling from between his teeth. 'I'd better go see to these customers.'

I pottered along the bar to serve Mackeson Maude, so called because the only words she ever uttered to anyone were, 'I'll have a Mackeson.' She'd only very recently been allowed back into the club on a trial period, as she'd pissed herself in the snug on Maundy Thursday, and Marty had had to sloosh the place round with Dettol before the cribbage match could start.

'I'll have a Mackeson,' she said, which, as you might imagine, didn't surprise me: I had one ready open for her with a half-pint glass to go with it.

By the time I got back to Maxie, Marty was chatting to him across the bar and my heart sank. What the hell would Marty say about me? He was always taking the piss about something or other.

'Just been chewin' the fat with your little pal, flyboy,' Marty said to me, nodding towards Maxie, who looked very slightly afraid.

'Oh yeah?' I said uneasily.

'Yeah!' Marty said. 'He's a good-lookin' lad, ain't he? I bet he bags most of the snatch when yous two go out on the pull, eh?'

Then he roared with laughter and pinched my arse as he headed back to the office.

'What's he been going on about?' I whispered, handing Maxie a free Pepsi once Marty was well out of the way.

'Nothing much,' Maxie said. 'He told me to watch myself in case you tried to get into my pants.'

And he laughed.

'Bit late for that, ain't it?' he said.

And there it was: concrete acknowledgement from Maxie that something corporeal had happened between us. Joy!

'I was thinking about coming round tomorrow, to your place, after school,' Maxie went on as I buzzed around trying to look busy. 'What do you reckon?'

More joy! Did he actually mean that he was going to cross the threshold of my bedroom? Be alone with me for the first time since Moira's?

'Well, yeah, that would be OK, I guess,' I said, trying not to sound overly hysterical. 'I'm sure me mum would do us a bit of tea; she's been asking why you haven't been around for the last week or so.'

Maxie looked down at the floor, but said nothing.

'In fact,' I went on, 'haven't we got study period all tomorrow afternoon, cos Miss Jibbs is off with her nerves? We could go to mine at lunchtime if you like; there'll be no one in.'

'Oh!' Maxie blushed. 'Nobody in at all?'

I panicked, and had to think fast.

'Yeah, I mean . . . what I mean is, we can play music as loud as we want, or watch a video even – we've got a video, you know – and my dad's got an illegal copy of *The Amityville Horror*, or, if not . . . *The Muppet Movie*.'

Maxie smiled and nodded.

'That sounds good. I like the Muppets.'

'Great! So do I!'

He gulped down the rest of his Pepsi, leaving a nice frothy line around his lips. Panic over. I was happy.

'You fuckin' fancy him,' Marty laughed as he and Denise helped me tidy round the bar at the end of the night.

Denise had just dragged herself down from upstairs to close the bar – she was in her apricot housecoat and fluffy mule-slippers, and had topped the ensemble off with three or four unstrategically placed hair curlers. She rolled her eyes at me as if to say 'he's off again'.

'What?' I said. 'What you going on about now, Marty?'

'That boy that was in 'ere earlier: your mate,' Marty smirked. 'I saw the way you was looking at him. You were all girlie – you got a little crush on him, ain't ya?'

Marty threw a sopping bar towel at me and it hit me full in the face, causing me to flinch and fall backwards against the till, which, consequently, rang up two pounds forty. I almost laughed, and was about to summon up a suitably spiteful retort when Denise jumped in, doing the job very succinctly for me herself.

'Oh, why don't you shut your stupid fuckin' gob, Marty Duncombe,' she spat. 'You don't 'alf talk some shit, you truly do!'

But then something happened; something un-expected, unprecedented, in fact. I turned around to face the pair of them, straight-backed, and I said,

'Maybe I do fancy him. Maybe he fancies me. So what?'

Marty and Denise just stood there, her with a G & T at her lips, and him with a full drip tray.

'Really?' Denise said. 'Well, there's a turn-up.'

She had a gulp of her gin, and I looked over at Marty who was just glaring at me with a ridiculous half-grin, scratching his stomach.

'Well, if you fancy 'im, you fancy 'im,' Denise said breezily, wiping down the bar. 'We've 'ad other queer friends, 'aven't we, Marty? It's no skin off of my arse, darlin', what you like and what you don't. Good for you for shoutin' up for yourself.'

Marty nodded slowly.

'I knew you was a brown hatter,' he said softly. 'Or maybe it's only a beige one at your age – but I bloody knew it.'

'Marty!' Denise snapped. 'Your fuckin' mouth's disgustin'.'

But I just shrugged my shoulders.

'He might be bisexual, anyway,' Denise said, stepping forward and pushing past her old man. 'Are you bi, Dave, is that what you are?'

'I'm not so sure,' I said, fiddling with a tea cloth. 'I do like Lindsay Wagner. I . . . I'm not sure . . .'

All of a sudden it had dawned on me what a truly dire and frightful mistake I might have just made, telling Marty – my dad's best friend – that I might well be a raving poof. I stared fixedly at the beer pump that read 'Courage Best' but all my courage had evaporated rapidly; my previously proud shoulders had sunk, and I must have looked anxious or upset suddenly, because Denise rushed over and flung her arms around me.

'Don't worry, darlin', it's all right!' she said squeakily.

'You won't say anything to Eddie, will you?' I urged. 'Either of you? I'm not sure he's ready.'

Marty laughed loudly.

'Fucking right I won't say anything to Eddie! Not if I value me own life: your old man won't thank anyone for that piece of news.'

'We won't say a word,' Denise promised, still hugging me tight. 'Not a word. Now you get off home, lovey, go on.'

Then she sighed lengthily and looked me straight in the face, her doe-brown eyes misting over slightly.

'I suppose at least you won't be getting any of the little slags round 'ere up the duff, will ya, darlin'?' she said.

Twelve

Whoops!

I'm almost beside myself with elation about Maxie's impending visit this afternoon. I mean, could this be it? Are we going to proclaim and cement our love finally and for all perpetuity? Are we going to at long last unleash our pent-up ardour and have fervent and unbridled sexual relations on my *Bionic Woman* duvet cover?

'Perhaps you're just going to watch *The Muppet Movie*,' Frances suggests mordantly as we bundle out of the art room – she can exhibit a nasty streak, that girl, when she's a mind to.

'We'll see,' I say, winking at her.

It's a crisp day, and for the first time I notice the leaves on the playground trees turning – I hate it when summer ends.

'It's too cold to sit out here,' I grumble at Frances as she drags me towards the currently uninhabited football field. 'And I'm really fucking tired! Dad and Mum were at it till all hours last night – arguing, that is – and I've barely slept.'

Frances seems indifferent to any grievance I might have, and marches on.

'I don't know what's so important that it couldn't keep till tomorrow, anyway,' I say. 'I've got tons to do before this afternoon. Me Auntie Val's made me a lemon meringue pie for when Maxie comes over, and I've got to get that from me nan's, and then put the Scotch eggs that Mum's made into the oven for fifteen minutes, and then run around me bedroom with a tin of Mr Sheen. I'll never get it all done by half past one when he comes.'

Frances huffs.

'You've got an hour and a bit yet, Juliet,' she says. 'Anyway this *is* important.'

And she parks herself down by the goalposts and fishes a bag of pickled-onion-flavour Ringos out of her satchel.

'Do you want one?' she says, proffering the packet.

'No, I don't,' I laugh, 'thank you very much. I want to come over all minty-fresh when I swoop in for my and Maxie's first proper kiss. I don't want to respire all over him with breath you could strip a lavatory door with, do I?'

'Suit yourself,' says Frances.

Then she goes quiet . . . for ages.

'Well?' I snap at her eventually, 'are you going to tell me what this is all about, or not?'

I can't be doing with this today. Not today. Frances puts her Ringos down on the grass in front of her.

'When I was a little girl . . .' she says.

'Oh, fuckin' 'ell!'

165

'When I was a little girl, I had a friend . . .'

'Well, that's more than you'll have in five minutes' time if you don't get on with it,' I guffaw.

'His name was Toby, and he lived along the street from us,' she says. 'His mum used to chat to mine over the gate – you know how mums do when they're on their way to or from shopping, and my mum liked her: said she was the only white lady that gave her the time of day down our street – well, it was very ruched curtain round where we lived, wasn't it? Anyway, sometimes Toby used to climb over the wall of our front garden when our mums were talking and chase me round and round Dad's Johnson's Blue geranium – I suppose we were about four or five then . . .'

I must say I'm unmoved thus far, but Frances carries on despite my marked lack of interest.

'He went to the same nursery as me – this Toby – and every day as we walked through the door he'd hold my hand as we went in, because on the first day I'd cried and cried and my mother could barely get me through the bloody door, but Toby said he'd look after me, and he did. He looked after me every day. When it was milk time, he didn't just fetch his own milk, he'd fetch mine as well, and he'd say, "I got you two straws, Frances," because he knew I liked two straws instead of one.'

I'm about to say something sarky and vile, but I suddenly notice that Frances looks unbelievably sad, so I keep shtum.

'I remember when we were about seven or eight, Toby turned up on our doorstep on Christmas morning on his new Chopper, and he handed me a screwed-up paper Christmas hat with something stuffed inside it. It was a little silver ring with a purple stone – out of a cracker, I expect. He said, "Frances, we're engaged now, and I've got to come in and ask your dad for your arm in marriage . . ."'

'Your arm?' I say, and we both giggle, but then I spot tears. They don't fall, they just sit there in her eyes.

'He was such a smart little boy,' Frances says. 'Always had the tidiest haircut, and nattiest clothes. His family moved out of our street to Camberwell a bit after that, and we moved to the flats, but I always remembered him even though I never saw him again . . . until the other week.'

'Really? Where did you see him?' I ask.

'At a party,' she says in a near-whisper. 'I just turned round and there he was . . . pulling my hair, and punching me in the back . . . calling me a black bastard.'

'Oh no, Fran.'

Frances is nodding, and the tears come down. I put my hand over hers.

'But that was Squirrel that did that,' I say. 'Chrissy's boyfriend, Squirrel.'

Frances nods, and looks up at me.

'I've heard you talk about your sister's boyfriend Squirrel,' she says, 'but I'd never met him, had I? I didn't know Squirrel was Toby. And I never fucking imagined that lovely little boy could ever say those wicked things to me.'

I feel just bloody awful, and I wrench an angry

fistful of grass out of the ground by the roots. I knew it had been Squirrel I'd seen that day in the car full of NF boys outside my house, but I just didn't want to believe that it had been him shouting evil out of its window.

'Why didn't you tell me this before?' I say gently as Frances rests her head on my shoulder.

'I wasn't sure,' she says. 'I really wasn't bloody sure. It was dark out on that balcony at the party, and there were so many people. And don't forget, I haven't seen him for eight or nine years. I thought it was him, but I couldn't be certain then.'

'And you are now?'

Frances nods with absolute resolve, and then she wipes the tears away with the back of her hand.

'Oh, yes,' she says, 'cos I saw him again today – sitting in a Ford Escort minivan outside the school.'

'What, our school?' I semi-shriek.

'Yes,' Frances whispers, leaning forward and swiftly becoming tremendously conspiratorial. 'Outside my sixth-form block – parked there for ages. And do you know who he was with? Do you know who was in the driver's seat?'

It suddenly dawns on me who I know that drives a Ford Escort minivan.

'I think I might,' I say.

'Yes. That bird that does your mum's cleaning,' Frances says.

'Moira,' I say. 'I knew there was something going on with them, but what? What would she want with him?'

168

'I dunno,' Frances says. 'But I was sure it was him then. I was positive it was little Toby, and do you know what the worst part is, David? The worst part is that I feel like he's taken a little bit of my childhood – a lovely, cosy, special bit of my childhood . . . and shat all over it.'

And then she goes quiet for a while, and I don't know what to say. God, I've been so wrapped up in my own romantic drama since the night of that party that I haven't even noticed what my very best friend has been going through. What a prick!

'Look, why don't I tell Maxie that we'll have to hang out at my house together another time? Then me and you can go over to your place and ask your little sister if she'll let us comb her hair out into an Afro and dress her up as Diana Ross again.'

Frances laughs.

'Are you nuts, bwoy? This could be the start of ya big love affair.'

Then she plants a great big teary, pickled-onion-flavoured kiss on my cheek.

'I'll be all right, really,' she says. 'I just wanted you to know about Toby so you can tell your Chrissy, and find out why the fuck your mum's cleaner is knocking around with a little Nazi.'

We pull ourselves up from the grass, which is damper than I thought it was when I sat down, and start back towards the main road.

'Will you be OK?' I ask her.

'I'll be fine,' she smiles. 'Just don't forget to ring me up later and tell me all the gory details about your date!'

'It's not a date,' I laugh, and we head for home.

When we get to the corner of Chesterfield Street we part ways, as Frances decides she can't go another five minutes without a bag of chips from Elvis'.

'Don't get pregnant!' she screams up the road after me.

Maxie is outside my house on his racing bike when I get there, still in his uniform.

'You're early,' I shout on approach. 'I've not hoovered.'

Maxie laughs.

'You don't have to hoover for me, just make me a cup of tea and a sarnie – I'm bloody starving.'

And we head up the front path.

'Mum's done Scotch eggs,' I say, opening the heavy green front door. 'I've got to warm them through, but I'm sure I can manage a cup of Rosie Lee if Chrissy hasn't guzzled all the milk.'

Maxie follows me into the house and leans his bike up against the passage wall. He has a ridiculously toothy smile plastered across his face.

'What are you grinning at?' I enquire, making quite sure Maxie's handlebars haven't marked the Anaglypta.

'Nothing,' he says. 'I just like Scotch eggs. Mum says they're ever so common, but I like 'em. She was open-ing a tin of salmon for her snooty sewing-circle friends when I left – I can't bloody stand that stuff.'

'Tinned salmon,' I laugh. 'She obviously knows how to push the boat out, your mother.'

Then there's a minute or two's awkward silence as we go into the kitchen and I switch on the oven and put the kettle on the gas ring. Maxie sits down at the kitchen table and starts idly leafing through a copy of *The Racing Pigeon* as I turn on the transistor for the tail end of *Newsbeat*.

'What time are your mum and dad getting in . . . and Chrissy?' Maxie finally asks as I hover over the sink with a baking tray of Scotch eggs.

'About half five with Mum, usually,' I say. 'I'm not sure about Chrissy, but I've got an idea my dad might go straight round to the club from work: him and Mum had yet another barney last night. Why do you ask?'

'Oh, no reason, I just wondered,' he says, and I note that he's slightly jittery.

'To be honest,' I go on, 'they've been at one another's throats almost every night lately. It gets on my wick.'

'What do they row about?' Maxie asks.

'Oh, you know,' I say distantly.

'I don't,' he says. 'My mum and dad never row, and if they do they've never done it in front of me and my sister.'

'You're lucky,' I say. 'Mine barely stop.'

Last Wednesday's row, I think it was, had been a real doozy. Eddie had come stomping in at around six and with a face like thunder had skulked straight into the living room, where ten or so minutes later Mum had presented him with a roast chicken dinner – which was a bit of a turn-up for the books midweek, but there it was.

'I don't fancy that, Kath,' I'd heard Eddie snort from the lounge. 'We don't usually have chicken of a Wednesday.'

He was clearly in a foul mood, but not in the mood for fowl.

'Well, we've got it tonight,' Mum said, rather too defiantly for my liking.

She'd got in an hour and a half early and decided to throw prudence to the wind, menu-wise, it seemed; but any sort of culinary spontaneity was, without exception, lost on Eddie, in fact it positively enraged him. Mum well knew this, but had regrettably stumbled on an open bottle of Black Tower when she'd opened the fridge and had, perhaps, let herself get carried away a little. Then, before one knew it, Wednesday's time-honoured shepherd's pie or – at a push – sausage-and-mash option were out of the window, and in went an oven-ready pre-stuffed bird from the Co-op. I'm not sure she'd even defrosted it properly.

'And what's with this fucking gravy?' Dad had gone on, and I crept up the passage to the door of the lounge to see what was what. Eddie was lying flat out on the couch with his boots off, facing the telly, Mum standing over him practically brandishing the plate of food like it was an offensive weapon.

'What's the fucking matter with it?' she said, and I noticed her sway almost a full circle.

'It's thick,' Eddie said. 'You know I only like a couple of Oxo in a bit of hot water; I don't like thick gravy.'

He was seething by this point.

'Well, you do 'ave a choice, dear,' Mum said in a dangerously sardonic tone.

I put my hand over my mouth – she wasn't normally this plucky.

'And what's that?' Eddie snapped.

'Well, you can either eat it or fucking wear it,' Mum said flatly.

And with that it was merry hell. I turned and headed back down the hall just as the plate smashed against the coffee table and Dad shouted, 'You're fuckin' pissed again, ain't ya? Who the fuck do you think you're talking to?'

When he shot out of the room, he had a couple of peas stuck to the side of his face and thick gravy on his shirt collar. He shoved past me like I wasn't even there, and I dashed back up to the lounge, where Mum was sprawled on the carpet. There was food all over the shop, and Mum appeared somewhat disorientated.

'He didn't hit you, did he?' I said, striding over and hauling her upright – she, too, was festooned with mixed veg.

'It was more of a shove,' Mum smiled, and then we heard the front door bang shut.

'He'll be pissed himself when he comes back,' I warned Mum as we sat down on the couch. 'And we'll be up all night with him screaming his head off in a repeat performance of the night before my English O level.'

'You're probably right, David,' Mum had said, brushing a kernel of sweetcorn off her bosom.

And I was.

* * *

'Actually,' Maxie says, snapping me back to here and now, 'I really wanna talk to you about something, so maybe we should have our Scotch eggs later – do you mind?'

He is even more jittery now.

'I thought you were starving,' I say.

'This is more important,' he says gravely. 'Can we go up to your room?'

It's evidently a day for folk feeling the need to inundate me with imperative topics: first Frances' revelation about Squirrel and now this – whatever *this* is.

'OK then.'

Maxie looks nigh-on angelic sitting on my bed beneath my poster of a pouting Kate Bush, his hands tidily in his lap and his head down. I wonder what the matter is with him all of a sudden – he was quite perky when he arrived and now he's gone all sombre and quiet.

'What's up?' I say, popping a bit of Elvis Costello, loud, on the stereo to lighten the mood.

'Come and sit over here,' he says. 'I don't want to have to shout.'

I stroll over and sit next to him on the bed, my heart beating about three times its normal speed, and Maxie says, 'I was wondering what you thought . . . about what happened.'

Does he mean what I think he means?

'What happened?' I say.

174

'Yeah,' he says. 'At Moira's last week. You've not mentioned it.'

'*You've* not mentioned it either,' I say, scandalized.

'You've not,' he insists. 'I didn't know what to say, did I?'

'And I should have?' I laugh. 'It's not something I do every day, ye know. I thought you might be embarrassed, so I kept it buttoned.'

Maxie smiles.

'Well, you've been all lovey-dovey with me ever since – don't think I've not twigged that, David Starr.'

I'm mortified.

'I have bastard well not been all lovey-dovey with you, I just—'

But he stops me in my tracks.

'Do you wanna have another crack?' he says. 'Do it again?'

'Do what again?'

'The fucking Highland fling,' he laughs. 'What do you think?'

Then he puts his hand between my thighs, just as Elvis Costello's 'Pump It Up' is dwindling to nothing.

'I want to know if I liked it as much as I think I did,' Maxie says. 'Have you thought about it much?'

I can tell now he's quite aroused.

'Some,' I whisper.

'When you're havin' a wank?'

Oh, I say!

'Maybe.'

'I have,' he says. 'I've tried not to, but then when I'm kind of halfway through, my mind just goes there even

175

though I try not to let it. I think about you touching me ... like you did ... and I think about what else we could ...'

Maxie starts to undo my belt, and when it's loose I slowly stand up and brazenly let my trousers fall. He follows suit, unbuckling his belt and stepping right out of his trousers.

'Where?' he says. 'On the bed?'

'No, on the beanbag,' I say, shuffling over towards it with my trousers around my knees and guiding him along with me.

Maxie falls back on to the oversized flowery cushion, and I kick off my school trousers and move towards him. I can see him hard through his white underpants, his shirt open, stomach exposed, and his face white with nerves.

'Are you scared?' I say, and he nods.

'Me too.'

Then I move a step nearer, and I lower myself to kneel ... to lean over him ... to ...

WHAT THE FUCK WAS THAT?

'DAVID!'

Eddie's voice booms from the landing. Not from the passage downstairs, no. Not even from the first landing, but from the landing outside his bedroom, which is only five short stairs away from my room. Oh my fucking God! How?

We scramble up, horror-struck, Maxie and me, tearing our discarded trousers from the floor and clumsily hauling them over our feet and up to our knees.

'Yes, Dad, I'm coming down now,' I yell frenziedly.

Maybe he won't come in – trousers up – maybe he'll just head downstairs and wait for me – one button – maybe he won't get up here in time – another damn button. Jesus Christ! I hear his feet, fast on the stairs: one, two, three, four ... and then the door swings open. Eddie just stands there. Doesn't say a word. Not a dicky bird. My entire body, meanwhile, is frozen, as if it were the last moments of Pompeii and I had been engulfed by the lava of Vesuvius while buttoning my flies. My belt is hanging, gracelessly, out of its loops and is dragging on the floor; and I glance up at Maxie, who is in even worse disarray than me, his shirt tucked comically into his Y-fronts, his zipper gaping open. I'm fucking dead, aren't I? But no: Eddie leaves the room and shuts the door quietly behind him.

Oh my God. Oh ... my ... God. Maxie is staring at me, open-mouthed.

'What shall I do?' he whispers, utter panic in his eyes.

'Just go,' I say firmly. 'Just get your bike and go.'

By the time I step into the kitchen, I've managed to splash on some semblance of a smile. Eddie is sitting at the glass table staring into an empty coffee mug, and I head to the sink for a glass of water.

'Marty rang for you this morning, Dad,' I say with as much brazen abandon as I can muster. 'He didn't say what he wanted, but I told him that I thought you'd probably be going to the club tonight as it was committee night. It is Monday, committee night, isn't it? I know it was on a Tuesday for a while, but you changed it, didn't you, because of the ladies' darts matches being on a Tuesday?'

Eddie says nothing, so I chance a peek in his direction. As I do, he lifts his head gradually – almost in slow motion – until his eyes lock murderously with mine. I swallow hard, and Eddie says, 'Don't you ever let me catch you doing that again.'

And then he walks out.

Thirteen

A Meringue in the Offing

Today is my birthday. Sixteen. Mum, Nan and Aunt Val have decided that a 'nice family dinner' is in order to celebrate the fact, though I'm not altogether sure to which nice family they might be referring: surely not ours at the present time?

'Who do you want to invite? You can invite anyone you like,' Mum had said last week, a few days after the appalling debacle with Maxie in my bedroom. I'd thought about it for a moment.

'I'd like to invite Judith Chalmers, and Anni-Frid from Abba,' I said, 'and that's about the sum of it.'

Aunt Val had whacked me playfully about the ear with a tea towel, and then she chased me into Nan's scullery, giggling and flicking me with it as she went. Nan was loitering purposefully around her gas cooker with a variety of pans and cooking apparatus. She was trying out a recipe for jugged lamb that she'd seen on a rerun of *The Galloping Gourmet* – with a queen of puddings to follow – so me and Mum had been summoned in for the result.

'Be serious,' Aunt Val said, leaning against the sink. 'It'll be nice getting the whole family together for your sixteenth, won't it, Kath?'

Mum nodded eagerly, but all I could think about was my dad, who apart from one miserable and brief conversation, had barely spoken a word to me during the entire week. I didn't imagine for one solitary moment that he would be in the slightest bit interested in celebrating my birthday, or anything else, come to that.

'Come and sit at the table, and we'll write down a party plan: guest list, grub, et cetera,' Mum enthused, waving a rather down-at-heel Basildon Bond notepad. 'It doesn't have to be a sit-down; I could do a running buffet if you like, Dave.'

I never understood what that was, anyway – a running buffet – I mean, where exactly was it running, and from what?

We pulled up chairs around Nan's 1940s kitchen table, which was by the big window that looked out on to the Whisky Mac rosebush Grandad had planted a year or so before he died. Mum whipped out a black felt-tip.

'Come and sit with us, Mum, and we'll decide on who's doing what food,' she yelled, but Nan's mind was seemingly elsewhere, and she appeared to be quite eerily spellbound by one simmering pot in particular.

'I won't, lovey,' she replied from the scullery. 'Shout up from where you are. I've just got me veg on the go, and it's very easy to take your eye off the ball with a French bean, I find.'

'All right then!' Mum said. 'Guest list first. Who's coming?'

'Well, there's all of us,' Aunt Val said, counting people out on her burgundy-painted fingers. 'Chrissy and her bloke . . .'

'He's not fucking coming,' I snapped. 'No way. It's my birthday dinner, and he's not coming.'

Mum and Val stared at me blankly.

'Why the hell not?' Mum said, somewhat stunned.

'Well, Chrissy's broken up with him for a start,' I said, 'and besides—'

'They're back together as far as I know, David,' Nan interrupted from the stove. 'Well, they were yesterday teatime if all the face-sucking in my lean-to was anything to go by.'

She had to be kidding, surely. Back together with Squirrel after what he'd done?

'Who else do you want to come, Dave?' Mum said. 'Frances? Your mate Maxie?'

I mulled it over in my head for a second. There was no way Frances was going to set foot anywhere near Squirrel, or Toby as we now knew him, and the chances of Maxie appearing at my house after what had happened a few days earlier were pretty slim, to say the least – in fact, I'd barely seen him the last few days outside lessons. What a rip-roaring birthday party this is going to be, I thought. After I'd deliberated for a few more seconds, I had a brainwave, though.

'Abigail!' I announced resolutely. 'I'd like to invite Chrissy's friend Abigail.'

Nan popped her head in from the scullery, her glasses now completely steamed up.

'Ooh! Are you sweet on her, then, David? She's a nice-looking thing, I suppose. Bit of a tarty piece, mind you.'

Yes, and that's precisely it, Nan, I thought. I couldn't fathom why I hadn't thought of it before, but Abigail would make the most perfectly convincing beard! It could be like an old-fashioned lavender marriage, and Abigail would be the Phyllis Gates to my Rock Hudson. Surely if Dad saw me cosying up to Abigail at my own birthday dinner, he'd swallow hook line and sinker all the hogwash I'd urgently fed him that afternoon after the incident with Maxie: the stuff about being confused, and needing a nice girl to set me straight – perhaps he'd actually believe it. Yes! Perhaps Abigail could even stay over! I could surely put up with that for one lousy night if it meant throwing Eddie off the scent. The scent of pansy!

There was no denying it had been a fairly grim scenario when I'd followed Dad out into the pigeon loft on that grey afternoon last week, and at first I thought he might cry as he stood there tenderly cosseting his favourite bird, Rasputin. Then, on a second look, I decided that the mist in his eyes was born of anger: I'd seen him like that before, with Mum – so passionately furious there were almost tears.

'It wasn't what it looked like, Dad,' I'd said softly.

I'm not really sure why I said that; it was an oft-trotted-out cliché I'd heard on *Crossroads* a thousand times, and it had never once had the desired effect.

'So what was it, then?' Eddie retorted. 'It was quite obvious to me what you'd both been up to. Trousers undone; the look on your faces when I walked in. You weren't playing Mousetrap, were ya?'

'We hadn't actually done anything, Dad,' I said, trying desperately to be humble. 'I don't really know what I was thinking, I just got confused. I expect you can't remember being fifteen, your hormones are racing and you just want to try things out, and they're not always the right things but you do them anyway . . .'

Eddie's face was pallid and stony. I'd hurt him.

'And how often do you try that out?' he said.

'Never!' I shout. 'I never have, and we didn't then . . . honest! We just got a bit carried away talking about sex and stuff and then you came home, and that was all there was to it. Really!'

I wondered for a moment if my nose might be shooting out from my face like Pinocchio. Why the hell didn't I just bite the bullet and fucking tell him – get it over with? Instead I gingerly stroked a nearby pigeon while Eddie put Rasputin back in his little stall, and then rubbed his bristly chin against the palm of his hand.

'I could arrange for you to see someone,' he eventually said, looking directly at me.

Who, I thought, Raquel Welch?

'A psychiatrist or something,' he said, and I suddenly felt sick.

'I don't need that,' I said. 'I think I just need to meet the right girl to go out on a date with, or something. I've not had a girlfriend really, and I think that's why I . . .'

Dad was shaking his head slowly, and looking down, and out of the blue I felt like shouting, 'Oh, for fuck's sake, Eddie, I've not fucking killed anyone – pull yourself together, you soft wanker.'

However, I didn't. I said, 'You won't tell Mum about this, will you?'

'I won't tell your mother,' he said. 'But I warned you. I don't want to catch you doing anything like that again. And it's best if that Maxie boy doesn't come over here any more either. Do you understand?'

I nodded.

'I do understand . . . and thanks, Dad.'

I'm not completely sure what I was thanking him for, to be honest. For not killing me, possibly; certainly for not throwing a mad fucking fit, or tearing down all my posters like he did when I was nine and I'd accidentally set fire to my blue nylon bedspread during 'teddy bears' firework party' – which involved my drag queen of an Action Man, Chrissy's Penny Puppywalker doll and sundry stuffed toys sitting on my bed while me and Chrissy switched the light off and threw lit matches into the air. I suppose I was thanking him for staying calm, really, disconcerting though it was.

* * *

Anyway, here I am on my sixteenth birthday, on the blower to Abigail Henson, all but begging her to come over for my birthday dinner this evening.

'I don't know why I should,' she's saying in a voice that might curdle milk. 'I've told you already that I think you're a sexist pig who uses girls and then chucks them away once they've pleasured you to your satisfaction, David Starr. Give me one good reason why I should bloody come.'

'Well, you know I think a great deal of you, Abigail, don't you?' I lie. 'And my mum said you can stop over if you want.'

As if that might entice her.

'Stop over?' she shrieks. 'In Chrissy's room with that filthy gerbil of hers rummaging about in its fucking cage all night? No ta very much! I don't do rodentia at the best of times: I'd come up in hives – I'm very allergic.'

'No, not in Chrissy's room, in my room,' I gabble. 'We can stay up late and listen to 'Eat to the Beat', I've just got it for my birthday. Come on, it'll be a hoot – we're having a cake, and wine. We can get to know one another better.'

There's a tomblike silence for a while, and then Abigail says, 'In your room?'

'Yes, my room.'

'And there's cake?'

'Yes ... well ... lemon meringue, cos that's my favourite, but we'll most likely jam some candles in it at some point.'

'All right then,' she says grudgingly. 'I suppose I

could put in an appearance if there's a meringue in the offing. What's the dress code?'

'Cocktail chic,' I say off the top of my head.

'So, hot pants all right, then?' she says.

'Fine,' I say. 'I'll see you here about seven.'

I'm a smooth talker, me, when I want to be.

As it pans out, Squirrel hasn't turned up to my birthday dinner anyway – which I'm quite chuffed about, but if I'd known I would have pestered Frances to toddle over after all. I've decided, for the sake of keeping the peace this evening, to tackle Chrissy on the subject of Squirrel afterwards – when we're on our own – and find out just exactly what the hell she thinks she's doing stepping out with the little thug again. Anyway, in the end the assembled motley cast sitting around Mother's brand-new repro Regency dining table this evening turns out to be just our family, including, of course, Nan and Aunt Val – plus my special guest, Abigail, who as we speak is licking Marie Rose sauce off the rather showy bell sleeve of her crochet cardigan. She catches my eye across the table as I finish off my own prawn cocktail, and wipes a smudge of the creamy mixture from the corner of her mouth with her middle finger. Then she brazenly sticks the finger between her lips, which have formed a perfect O, and winks at me. I smile back at her cheesily, but – truth be told – I'm perilously close to vomiting, though I dare not let on as she's doing me a big favour even being here, little does she know, and Dad certainly seems to be going for it too.

'Why don't you go and sit over next to David, Abi?' he says, placing his shrimp fork on the table and supping lager from a can. 'You keep staring at one another – I think David's got the horn by the look on his face.'

'Oh, Eddie!' my nan grimaces, 'for Gawd's sake!'

I'm mortified.

'Ooh, Mr Starr! You'll 'ave me blushing,' Abigail trills.

Jesus Christ! She sounds like Ruby the scullery maid from *Upstairs, Downstairs* might after a surprise tap on the bottom from the young master while she was blacking the parlour grate. Still, I'd best play along.

'Yes, do come and sit here next to me, Abigail,' I say, coming over all Queen Mother. 'You're so far away over there at the other end of the table.'

The other end of Southend pier would be preferable, if you want the truth. Anyway, over she comes, and as soon as she sits down she puts her over-bejewelled paw right between my thighs under the table. She's plainly going for it tonight, and has consequently trowelled on the Max Factor and curled her hair into the most terrifying ringlets this side of Nellie Oleson.

'That's better,' Eddie grins, and Mum gives him a funny look.

I'm smiling through gritted teeth meanwhile.

'What's for main course, Kath? I never did find out,' Nan suddenly says, pushing her barely touched prawn cocktail asunder in evident repugnance. 'I tend to struggle with a crustacean these days. They make me bilious.'

187

'Just a simple roast, Mum, for main,' my mother replies, and she commences clearing the first-course crockery from the table. 'David requested that we have bloody roasted quail wrapped in prosciutto,' she goes on, 'but I hadn't a clue what prosciutto was, and as it turned out, Wallis's didn't run to a quail anyway, so we're 'avin' beef.'

Nan looks mildly intrigued.

'Oh, nice, and is that wrapped in anything?' she says.

'Yes, love, it's wrapped in tinfoil,' says Mum, and then she looks over at Eddie.

'And before you start,' she says to him, 'I've done two separate gravies: one pissy for you, and another one with a bit more substance to it for the rest of us.'

Then she clatters noisily out of the room, balancing a tray piled high with Pyrex, while Dad rolls his eyes at Chrissy, who is clearly sulking about Squirrel's absence because she's wearing her pork-pie hat pulled down over her eyes at the table. Turning his attention back to Abigail, but addressing her breasts rather than her face, Dad says, 'So I hear you're staying over with us tonight, Abi, in David's room.'

Abigail nods eagerly, and then Eddie says, 'I hope you two are not gonna be getting up to anything too dirty up there.'

And he winks at her nauseatingly, and gulps down some more Heineken.

'What, like repotting an azalea?' Nan says. 'What the bloody hell do you think they'll be getting up to, Eddie? They're just kids.'

Eddie lets out a derisory snort, and even I have to suppress a chortle. Bless Nan's heart – if only she knew what had gone on in that bedroom in the last few weeks, it'd make her hair go straight. Aunt Val suddenly sits up, back stiff, and looks all confused.

'What? Are you and her dating then, or something?' she says to me.

'Not properly yet,' Abigail offers, before I can open my mouth. 'But we've definitely laid the ground sheet, so I don't reckon it'll be long now, eh, Dave?'

Ye gods, has she gone mental? I asked her round for dinner, not to peruse the Pronuptia catalogue, for fuck's sake. Now Aunt Val is looking even more confused.

'Really?' she says. 'I'm quite surprised. I wouldn't have thought you were our Dave's cup of tea – no offence – but he generally goes for yer raven-haired types: green eyes, full lips . . .'

'Stubble . . .' Chrissy suggests under her breath, and I shoot her a puzzled look. What does *she* know? Fortunately Dad's oblivious, so I decide to jump in before this line of dialogue can go any further.

'Well, let's just see how things go,' I say grandly, while reaching for the wine across the table. 'And let's not embarrass poor Abigail now, eh?'

Like that would ever be a possibility.

'Well, as long as you watch him, Abi,' Dad chuckles. 'He's a filthy little fucker; he's always nicking my dirty books . . .'

Oh, Christ, no!

'Mind you, he's never in the bathroom that long

wiv' 'em, so I wouldn't count on his staying power.'

Please let me just die now. Just let me die, right now.

'Oh, fucking shut up, Eddie, it's his birthday,' Aunt Val says, coming to my rescue, but Eddie won't let it drop.

'What?' he says, after gulping down yet another can of lager. 'It's natural for boys to masturbate. Nothing wrong with that – he's always at it.'

Oh, Jesus! Why is he torturing me like this? Does he really fucking hate me that much? Is this his insipid way of getting back at me for the incident with Maxie? Nan and Aunt Val are visibly horrified by Eddie's blatant outburst of vulgarity, and Nan puts her hands over her ears, wincing.

'Eddie, put a bloody sock in it,' Aunt Val says. 'That's vile talk!'

But Abigail just giggles and waves a saucy finger at me as if to say 'naughty boy!'

Just then Mum comes back into the room holding aloft the most beautifully cooked and trimmed joint of roast beef on a gargantuan green and gold platter. That, at least, seems to shut Eddie up.

'That looks really great, Mum,' I say, genuinely thrilled, and I clear a space on the table.

She's made it so nice for me, Mum has, and I hadn't even noticed – too bloody busy trying to fend off Abigail and my dad – but it's gorgeous. She's laid out the lace tablecloth she got when she went on a trip to Bruges last year, and she's made the paper napkins into little red fan shapes. She's even got the posh cutlery out of the blue velvet box that's sat in the sideboard for years, and I note that she's borrowed Nan's silver candelabra and has put it right in the centre of the table next to a white china bowl of my grandad's roses. Even Nan and Aunt Val have dolled themselves up to the nines just to pop two doors along. Nan is wearing her best peacock-blue shift dress with her favourite brooch, and Aunt Val has settled on a flared trouser suit in ivory. Mum's in midi-length red chiffon, which some people couldn't get away with – but she can – and they all look divine in the blush of the candles. I suddenly feel very grown up and resolve to push aside my father's malicious attempts to humiliate me.

Things go fair to middling through the beef course, but by the time we get to the meringue and are singing 'Happy Birthday' it's gone ten, and I can tell that Mum and Dad have both, alas, had one over the eight, as per. For a start, Dad's got that sort of wild-eyed stare he gets – it's a bit like an irate African tribal mask – and he's had it fixed right on me for the past two or three minutes: he's clearly not happy. Mum is squinting slightly, which I generally take to be a bad sign, and she keeps brushing her fringe away from her forehead like she's swatting a fly.

'Are you gonna go and see David in the play, Abigail?' she says, oblivious to Dad's burgeoning fetid disposition, and sipping what must be her ninth or tenth glass of Blue Nun. 'He's 'ad me making his dress, you know,' she laughs.

'I expect I shall,' Abi says. 'When is it?'

Dad tuts loudly and lets his pastry fork clang noisily on to his empty pudding dish.

'Only a couple of weeks off,' I say brightly, trying to ignore him. 'I've still got so much of it to learn, though. I've been rehearsing with Maxie on and off for . . .'

Now why did I say that? Why? I chance a look over at Eddie, who is now glaring at me with a face like winter thunder, and I wriggle fearfully in my chair, grinning uneasily.

He leans over the table and drunkenly shouts to Abigail, 'So what's your opinion about David playing a bird's part in the school play, anyway?'

Abigail – who by this time has shunted so perilously close to me that she's virtually on my fucking lap – says, 'I'm not sure I've got one, Mr Starr.'

'Well, I bloody 'ave,' Eddie slurs.

Mum stands up, albeit precariously.

'Oh, don't start on him, Eddie,' she says, waving her empty glass, and she's slurring as much as him. 'You always 'ave to bloody start.'

Chrissy suddenly and judiciously gets up and excuses herself from the table; she knows damn well what's coming, as do I.

'What d'you mean, don't start?' Eddie bawls.

Here we go.

'I'm only saying, why don't you mind your own fuckin' business, Kath?'

Silence. Then Eddie stands up, knocking his chair backwards, and I sit there impotently as Chrissy disappears up the stairs sharpish. Judas!

'You can't say fuck-all in this house – especially

where he's concerned,' Eddie yells, and he gestures at me accusingly. 'Just cos he's a bit clever, nobody thinks he can do any wrong. Well, you don't know the fuckin' half of what he gets up to, Kath.'

Oh dear. OH DEAR.

'Oh, don't talk rubbish, Eddie,' Aunt Val says, jumping in. 'You're determined to ruin his bloody birthday. You've been digging at him all night.'

'I 'aven't been digging at him, Val,' Eddie spits. 'You lot just think the sun shines out of his arse, but you don't know anything. You don't know what a crafty little fucker he is . . . you can't see it!'

Then he spins around and marches towards the lounge door, kicking his upturned chair as he goes.

'Oh, I'm going round the club for the last hour,' he says.

And thank God for that!

'What the bleedin' hell was all that about?' Nan says once the storm has passed and the porch door has slammed.

'Search me,' Mum says, helping herself to a glass of Nan's Emva Cream. 'He's never happy unless he's fucking moaning, and we've got his birthday to get through next week. I suppose he'll expect us all to make a big song and dance about that.'

She polishes off the sherry in one go, and then she says, 'I went to get him a card today, but I couldn't find one with a pig on it.'

And we all scream with laughter – apart from poor Abigail, who clearly doesn't find uproar and near violence at a family birthday party legitimate grounds for merriment.

'Shall we go upstairs, David?' she suggests loudly, as Mum, Val, Nan and me rock back and forth with glee.

'What on earth for?'

'Well, you said . . .' Abigail hesitates, '. . . play some records, stop over . . .'

'Well, that was before,' I say, edging my chair away from her. 'I think I'd rather just go up to my room alone now, if you don't mind.'

Abigail stares at me, blinking. I really don't know what she's looking at me like that for. What does she expect – for me to take her upstairs and fuck her? I should co-co! The plan had fallen flat anyway, and what was the point of having Abigail stay over to throw Eddie off the pansy scent if Eddie wasn't there to witness it? He'd be at the club drinking with Marty till all hours now. I decide I'd best really hammer the point home.

'You might as well get off actually, Abi,' I say. 'I'm a bit tired, to be honest, and you've been ever so clingy tonight – you know how that irritates me. And aren't there any mirrors in your mother's prefab? Your make-up looks like you tossed it into the air and then ran underneath.'

Abigail stands up slowly and buttons her cardigan with pursed lips. Mum and Nan are still giggling, but Aunt Val is eyeballing me rather peculiarly, almost reproachfully, if I'm not mistaken.

'Do you know what you are, David Starr?' Abigail

says, once she's thrown her bunny jacket on, and gathered up her suede patchwork shoulder bag.

'I'm all ears,' I say, looking up at her.

'A self-obsessed little prick,' she says.

Nan gasps.

'Ooh my Gawd! Language, lovey!'

But Abigail is on her way towards the door. As she reaches it, she looks over her shoulder – possibly for dramatic effect – and tosses her ringlets one last time.

'Happy birthday, wank-face,' she says.

Charming!

Fourteen

Fags and Apples

To be honest, I'd felt pretty damned shoddy about my behaviour towards Abigail almost as soon as she'd shot off home earlier tonight. What was I bloody thinking? Aunt Val had grabbed me by the elbow in our passage afterwards and given me what for while Nan was getting her coat.

'You shouldn't treat people that way, David,' she'd said. 'It's mean. If you don't fancy Abigail then you shouldn't be mucking her about like that.'

I knew she was right and I felt frightful about it.

'I thought I was being funny,' I mumbled, looking down at the floor. 'I don't really fancy Abigail. I actually like somebody else but it's all a bit sticky and so I . . .'

Aunt Val had put a finger under my chin and lifted my face up towards hers.

'I think I've figured that out for meself,' she said softly. 'In fact, I think I've known it for a long while. But you wanna start sorting yourself out, David. It's not like you to be spiteful, and it's not that poor girl's fault, is it?'

I'd looked Aunt Val in the eye, only for a moment, and willed her to say something more, to say the words out loud, but she didn't, so I just said, 'No. Sorry.'

After Mum has staggered off to bed, and Aunt Val has escorted Nan home, I trot out into the front garden armed with a packet of Chrissy's Bensons, and I light one up. I sit down on the front-room window ledge and take a long drag, and then tip my head back, blowing the smoke out, slowly and luxuriously, into the night air. It's warmish for October, I think, and extraordinarily clear and starry into the bargain. I sit and ponder Aunt Val's chiding words in the passage. She was right: it is very unlike me to be spiteful, and I do need to sort myself out, and quick smart about it. Suddenly I make a decision: a snap one, you might say. I decide then and there that I'm going to sweep away the debris and disarray of the past weeks and keep things simple from now on. The simple fact is that I am in love with Maxie and that is that. I will apologize to Abigail, yes, and then I'll explain my atrocious actions by telling her the complete and utter truth – surely she'll forgive me then. And as for Dad – well, there is no reason why he has to know bugger-all about anything, is there? As long as I don't bring Maxie round to our house for the next couple of months and dangle him under Eddie's nose, we could sweep the whole tawdry episode under the shagpile. It's all going to be all right. It really is.

Just as I'm about to go back into the house, feeling rather pleased with my resolution, the porch door swings open and Chrissy appears in her cotton nightie and dressing gown, her bleached hair slicked back, wet.

'There's my fags,' she says, and I throw her the packet.

She sits down next to me and starts picking flaky paint off the ledge. Then she sparks up her own cigarette, and I watch in awe as she puffs out three faultless smoke rings in a row. Chrissy always seems so much more grown up than me, I feel, even though she's a year and a bit younger. She seems to have a composure and assurance about her that I long for but never manage to attain. Sure, I'm the clever one, but Chrissy is just so much fucking cooler. Neither of us speak for quite a while, and then finally I say to her, 'Your hair smells of apples.'

'That'll be me VO5 conditioner,' she replies somewhat tersely.

'It's nice,' I say. 'Apple-ish.'

She looks me up and down for a moment, and then she says, 'Why were you such a fucking tosser towards Abi in there earlier? She was crying when she left, you know. I could hear her from all the way upstairs, making that funny noise at the back of her throat, like she does. You're a bloody freak!'

'I don't know why I was like that,' I whine. 'Everything went wrong last week and I just wanted to—'

'What's gone wrong?' Chrissy suddenly snaps. 'Is it something to do with that bloody Maxie? And where was he on your birthday anyway – your new best friend? You're just behaving really weird lately, David, cos you wanna be different. You always have to be fuckin' different.'

Then I bristle and leap up from the windowsill.

'ME? What about you getting back with bloody Rudolf Hess? Nan told me she spied the two of you snogging. It makes me want to vomit after what he did to Frances and Maxie: he hit him in the face!'

'No!' Chrissy shouts.

'No what?'

'He's not a Nazi, he's not!'

'Oh no?' I snipe caustically. 'Well, he does a bloody good impersonation of one then.'

And I spill my guts about what Frances told me about Chrissy's 'dear little Toby'.

When I'm done, Chrissy lights another B&H, and looks altogether horrified.

'But he didn't know those kids were NF,' she spits, desperately puffing out smoke in short sharp bursts, her eyes fiery. 'He thought they were just into the clothes and the music, like him, and now that he does know he's stopped knocking around with them – honest. He told me that he got very, very pissed on strong cider before that party on the Aylesbury, and that's why he behaved like such a dickhead. He didn't know what he was doing. He swore on his little sister's life, and she's got a semi-withered arm. He never meant to hurt Maxie or Frances – he didn't even know that she was your friend, and he certainly wasn't the one shouting out those vile names – that wasn't Squirrel. He's not like that, David, I know him.'

She suddenly has tears in her eyes.

'He's not,' she says softly, and I put my arm around her.

'You need to get him to talk to Frances then,' I say. 'Put things right.'

Chrissy nods solemnly.

'I will.'

'Sometimes nice people do horrible things, don't they?' I smile. 'Like me with Abigail. I was vile to her tonight. I didn't really mean it, though. You just have to put these things right, don't you?'

'Yeah, you do,' Chrissy says, sniffing.

We sit quiet for a while, a police car whizzing along Lordship Lane with its siren going the only sound you could hear, a woman on a late-night stroll with her boxer dog the only sign of life. I consider, for a moment in the lull, mentioning Squirrel's unexplained liaisons with our cleaner, Moira, but it doesn't seem the right time – Chrissy seems too upset – so I decide to let it lie. Then she suddenly flicks her cigarette high in the air and into the kerb, and turns to face me.

'Are you gay, David?' she says. 'Are you?'

I laugh out loud, smashing the near silence of the evening, and then I say, 'Yes. I am.'

'I knew it,' she says.

And when she hugs me tight around the neck I can smell the apples.

Fifteen

Hitting the Fan

When I arrive home a mere five nights later, after *Oliver!* rehearsals, I'm not overly flabbergasted to discover Chrissy on the sofa in the lounge, sprawled out torpidly across a half-dressed Squirrel. His eyes are fixed on the television, and she is lying there a bit like Cleopatra, only with a Caramac and a bottle of lime Corona. All the lamps are switched off and the room is lit only by the glow of *Tomorrow's World*, so I quietly plonk myself down on one of the armchairs in readiness for tonight's *Top of the Pops*, on which Kate Bush is scheduled to appear. I'm very excited about that!

'All right?' Squirrel says to me, his grey Ben Sherman wide open, exposing his lean, ashy upper body.

'All right,' I reply.

Chrissy pops her head up and looks over at me sheepishly as I take off my school blazer.

'How's rehearsal for the school play going, bruv?' she says. 'I can't wait to see you prancin' round in a frock, to be honest. Did you see your mate Maxie today?'

It's dark, but I can tell that she has a preposterous grin on her face.

'It's all fine,' I say cheerily, 'apart from the fact that half of the actors are retarded, and one would just as soon stab our little Oliver through the heart as look at him. But aside from that, I think it'll be quite good.'

Chrissy giggles, but it actually isn't funny. With only a few weeks to go, the show, I feel, is a complete and unqualified shambles. I mean, don't get me wrong, I wasn't expecting the Ziegfeld Follies, scenery-wise, but this is positively *Blue Peter*; and where Miss Jibbs got the idea that London Bridge is, or has ever been, the colour of overcooked asparagus is a complete mystery to me and to everyone else.

'It's teal,' she'd announced proudly this afternoon. 'I thought we needed a splash of pizzazz, and my Auntie Iris had a couple of tins going begging after she'd finished her Jack and Jill bathroom.'

I argued, of course, that during my death scene, which was played out right in the vicinity of London Bridge, the audience might not be able to see me at all, as my Second Act frock was a rather charming peacock taffeta and not a million miles from the colour she'd seen fit to paint the fucking bridge.

'I'll just look like part of the bloody scenery, miss,' I'd lamented to no avail.

She just told me to go for something showy on the glove front and wave my arms about. As for the singing, well, it's hardly the Vienna Boys' Choir –

more like the terraces at Millwall – but I suppose I'll
have to make the best of it. Maxie and me, at least, will
shine as Bill and Nancy, and the sixth-form lad playing
Fagin is very good, if slightly paunchy.

Chrissy is still grilling me.

'It's just that I've not seen him around for a week or
so, that Maxie. Is he all right?' she says, suddenly
sitting up.

'Why are you so interested all of a sudden?' I laugh,
and I can just about make out my sister winking at me.

'I just am,' she says. 'And did you tell Frances what
I said?'

Chrissy leans forward, clearly eager for my answer.

'I did tell her, and I think she'll probably come
around,' I say, 'but Toby will have to talk to her as well.
It has to come from him, not me.'

Squirrel has been fixated on Judith Hann reclining
on the bonnet of a small space-age-looking car that she
reckons could be folded down and packed into a tote
bag. When he hears his name, he tears his eyes away
from the telly.

'Don't call me Toby, for fuck's sake, Dave,' he
mutters, 'and I will make amends to your mate
Frances, I promise.'

Then he's back to the box.

'You see,' Chrissy grins. 'I told you he would. And
you have to apologize to Abigail about your birthday,
David, like *you* promised, right?'

'I will apologize to Abi,' I say. 'I promise I'll do it
tomorrow when she comes over.'

'Excellent!' Chrissy says, and she snuggles back down, her thick blonde hair splayed out across Squirrel's bony torso. I wonder, as I watch them on the couch in the dark, whether I might soon be reclining like that in Maxie's arms, whether Maxie would even feel comfortable lying on the couch like that with me. I mean, what is the etiquette for sitting at home relaxing with a gay lover? I wonder if Maxie will take to it – to any of it? In the last three days at school, and during rehearsals, we have been tighter than ever, if anything, despite the near-ruinous episode in my bedroom and in the face of the glowering disapproval of Bob Lord, whose disdain for our 'friendship' is now practically rabid. We have even managed to steal a few seconds alone, and a couple of mischievous kisses – yes, kisses – when there is no prying eye to find or trap us. Those moments, however, have been few and far between, so the rehearsals for *Oliver!* – with Maxie and me playing ill-fated sweethearts – are as precious as gold, or at least the rare twelve-inch version of Blondie's 'X Offender'.

A third of the way through *Top of the Pops* the front door bangs shut and, without warning, the lights go on. It's Nan at the lounge door balancing three plates of thick mince and mashed potatoes. Aunt Val is hovering behind with cutlery and a copy of *Titbits*.

'I'm feeding you tonight,' Nan announces. 'So if you're going to eat this in here, eat it fast. I don't want him bloody moaning at me for letting you kids eat in the lounge and getting mince all over the three-piece.'

Nan really is a rather fine and laudable woman, and she isn't an elderly or in any way decaying type of nan either. She has just turned sixty-one, and spends most of her waking hours looking after anyone who'll let her – especially since she lost Grandad to the big C. When she isn't tidying up or making a batch of her unparalleled home-cooked chips, she can oft be found sipping her favourite beverage – a pony – with her friend Judith Goodley at the club. Aunt Val, two years Mum's junior at thirty-four, still living with Nan, has not yet married. It's not like there are not enough suitors, mind. Aunt Val has been in a perpetual state of courtship or semi-engagement since the Tokyo Olympics. She's just fussy, that's all. There'd been Ray the plumber, Julian the architect, Cyril the policeman – an endless stream, it seems to me – but there's always something the matter.

'Ray's beard tends to chafe,' I remember her saying after she'd cruelly dumped him outside Timothy Whites.

'I asked Cyril to book a weekend in the Lake District and he took me to a reservoir in Stoke Newington.'

She was never satisfied. Val had, she tells me, been really and truly in love with only one boy during the mid-to-late sixties: Johnny Barber, his name was. But he'd been tragically killed when his scooter had gone under a tram at Blackpool, and Val says she's never got over it. I think she's happy living at Nan's for the time being, if you want the truth.

Chrissy and I tuck into our plates of thick mince,

mine balanced precariously on my knee as I wait for
Kate Bush to come on.

'What is this stuff?' Squirrel whispers, glaring down
at his plate in abject terror. 'I'm not really that peckish,
Chrissy, to be honest!'

'Are you fucking anorexic or what?' my sister yells.
'Give it here, I'll eat yours, you skinny bastard!'

Chrissy and me both crack up laughing, and then
Nan and Aunt Val decide to sit down and join us for
the back end of *Top of the Pops* – which means I'll have
to put up with Nan saying things like, 'Ooh, she
screeches, that Kate Bush – I can't bloody stand 'er.'

But it makes me laugh out loud – Chrissy and
Squirrel too – and for the first time in days, I actually
have the feeling that everything might be all right after
all. But it doesn't last long . . .

'So where have Mum and Dad gone? Is there a darts
match at the club or something?' Chrissy says, licking
mashed potato off her knife.

'No,' Aunt Val says. 'Your father went off in his cab
to pick up some boxes of cheap brandy or something
from someone in Dartford, and your mum jumped in
for the ride. They'll be at the school by now though,
David, for your parents' evening.'

I'd forgotten it was bloody parents' evening. Jesus
Christ, another thing to fret about. I'm all too horribly
aware of the fact that of late, what with the school
musical and my near-constant starry-eyed daydreaming, my once fiercely conscientious schoolwork
ethic has gone right out of the bastard window. While
I'm quietly confident that Mr Peacock and Miss Jibbs

and the like will be fairly benign when chatting to Mum and Dad about my evident lack of progress, other members of staff, perhaps more disgruntled by half a term of my lackadaisical approach, will be out for revenge, and no doubt stick the boot in. That's all I need with Dad in the mood he's been in for the last couple of weeks, I can tell you.

'Oh yes,' I mutter. 'I'd forgotten about that, what with the play an' all.'

'They'll be back in a tick anyway,' Nan says. 'So finish up and let me get rid of those dirty plates.'

By the time Mum and Dad finally do arrive back from parents' evening, we're well into the second half of *News at Ten*, and Nan is snoozing in the armchair. Dad's face is quite white when he walks in, and his lips are pulled in, skinny. Mother's skin seems to bear the same vaporous pallor as she follows him into the living room in her smart pink work suit and drops her handbag. They both look bloody terrible. Surely the reports from my teachers couldn't have been that fucking awful. Something in Dad's uncivilized stare, though, tells me that they must have been. Really awful!

'Chrissy, get upstairs,' Dad barely mumbles. 'You'd better get home, Squirrel.'

Now I'm really worried. What on earth is going on?

'What's wrong, Kath?' Aunt Val says in a rather shrill tone. 'You're sheet-white!'

Nan wakes up with a start.

'It's him again, that's what's up,' Eddie says, glaring at me. 'You stupid little—'

'Eddie, calm down,' Mum interrupts, and I feel my fingers and neck sweating.

'What?' I squeak, jumping up.

'Sit down!'

Dad is somehow screaming through gritted teeth, which, prior to this moment, I would not have thought possible.

'What?' I say again, only quieter this time. 'What have I done?'

'I've had some boy's mother and father calling me all sorts because of you, you little bastard. It was like a fucking circus up at that school tonight.'

'It was bad,' Mum says softly. 'It was really bad.'

All at once, a white horror falls upon me. I thought everything seemed a little too good to be true. I should have recognized it as a dreadful omen earlier this evening when, instead of Kate Bush actually appearing on *Top of the Pops* as advertised, they'd featured the abysmal Legs & Co. dancing to 'Them Heavy People' in cream negligees instead.

'Somebody's mother and father?' I gulp.

Dad opens his mouth to yell again, but Mum holds up her hand with a mad stare like some kind of demented lollipop lady stopping traffic.

'Let me tell him,' she demands. 'You'll fuckin' explode, Eddie, if you're not careful.'

'Chance'd be a fine thing,' I hear Nan mumble from the corner.

I suddenly feel slightly otherworldly, so I sit down next to Aunt Val, with Mum and Dad standing over me. Dad is now almost a faultless shade of beetroot;

and Mum is speaking in a soft but clipped tone.

'We were talking to your drama teacher, Mr McClarnon, and he was telling us how well you're doing in drama and music. He really likes you, David, he does . . .'

I nod, wide-eyed.

'When all of a sudden, this other bald teacher comes over with some other parents: Mr and Mrs Boswell. Your friend Maxie's mum and dad, right?'

I nod again, small pieces of a terrifying jigsaw falling into place.

'What other teacher?' I ask meekly, as if I didn't know.

'Mr Lord!' Dad pipes up, jerking his head forward and spitting the words.

My heart somersaults.

'Oh! And what did *he* say?' I ask, tasting disgust in the back of my throat.

'Not very much, really, at first,' Mum says. 'But this Mrs Boswell, she just stormed straight up to our table and demanded to know if our son was a . . . if you were . . .'

' "Is it true that your son is a homosexual?" That's what she said,' Dad sing-songed, flopping down on to the sofa that Chrissy and Squirrel had swiftly vacated minutes earlier. ' "According to Mr Lord your son is a homosexual, and he is, how shall I put it, trying to lead my son up a bad path." That is what Mrs fucking Boswell said, David.'

Oh fuck. Oh fuck. Fuck!

I look at Mum. I look at Aunt Val. I look at Reginald

Bosanquet, who is animate but mute on the TV screen. Mum continues quietly, as Dad's face falls into his hands.

'Mrs Boswell says that "her little Maxie" has been acting differently in the past few weeks: secretive and distant. He stayed out all night the other Sunday – she's no clue where – and he's started watching cookery shows. Mr Lord says—'

'Oh, that wanker!' I interrupt, snarling.

'Mr Lord says that this boy, your friend Max Boswell, is letting his sports go to rack and ruin: skipping football practice to hang out with you and a coloured girl.'

'Black!' I snap. 'She's not coloured, she's black.'

'Is that Frances?' Aunt Val asks gingerly, putting a hand on mine.

'Yes.'

I'm furious and terrified all at the same time now, but Mum continues calmly.

'Mr Lord reckons that you are influencing Maxie: trying to make him more like you. More . . . more . . .'

'Fashionable?' I suggest. 'Worldly? Unblinkered? Remarkable?'

'Shut up!' Dad warns.

'Why?' I scream.

And then I jump up, probably unwisely, in an attempt to preserve what is left of my apparently fast-waning honour.

'Bob Lord is a fucking bigot, and you are just like him.'

I gesticulate madly towards my father, who

in turn leaps to his feet, teeth still gritted, pointing.

'Shut your fucking mouth! I knew this was coming, didn't I? I fucking knew it!'

'Eddie, Eddie!' Nan joins in now. 'Calm down!'

Dad, however, has misfired with his prodding index finger and jabbed me hard in the eye. With my right eye covered by my hand, and streaming, the flood-gates are open and I find myself yelling and sobbing all at once.

'Just because we're friends! Just because we're fucking friends! Just because Maxie skipped a couple of poxy football games, Bob fucking born-again Lord thinks I'm giving it to him behind the bike shed.'

'Oh my Gawd,' Nan says, with her hand over her mouth.

But I'm really in my stride now: tears, snot, profanity – the lot. Dad is still yelling, but I'm not hearing him any more.

'What makes them think I'm a queer anyway? Who the fuck told them that? Can't two blokes be friends, for fuck's sake? Jesus Christ, we're just friends, Mum, we're friends!'

I'm intent on defiance. No one can prove any of this, anyway. It's merely the speculation of a Christian-cum-Nazi on Bob Lord's part, and overprotective paranoia from Maxie's mum and dad. I can beat this, I can. I pause for a moment to collect myself, and there is a lull in the hysteria.

'I said that,' Mum says softly.

'What?'

'We said that,' Dad confirms in a slightly more

composed tone. 'We said, they're just close mates, David and Maxie: friends.'

'And?'

'And Mr Lord said that he had at first considered that, until he saw you ... and Maxie ... together, yesterday ... in the drama cupboard ... kissing.'

Shit!

'Kissing?' Nan says.

Dad nods and puts his hand over his mouth as though he is about to burst into tears, or perhaps vomit.

'I can't believe my son is really gay,' he says, voice trembling – rather absurdly, I feel. 'I really can't bloody believe it.'

Aunt Val stands up, looking somewhat vexed.

'Of course he's fucking gay, Eddie,' she shouts. 'I've known that since he was knee-high to a tortoise.'

'Did you?' Mum says, surprised. 'Did you know that, Val?'

'Well, how many other six-year-old boys do you know that can do all Dusty's hand movements to "You Don't Have To Say You Love Me", Kath? Be honest!'

Mum nods in defeated concurrence.

'And he knew where to find the eyelash glue,' Nan smiles.

'Jesus fucking Christ!' is all Dad can manage, getting all irate again. 'I'm gonna go round and see Marty at the club, see if he wants a late drink. I can't fucking do this now.'

That's Eddie's answer for everything – a late drink. And off he goes.

* * *

'Then your Mr McClarnon and Mr Lord had a terrible row, right in the middle of the parents' evening,' Mum says. 'Mr McClarnon said that Mr Lord had no right to say the things he said to Mr and Mrs Boswell, and that he was pure evil. Mr Lord said that the Boswells had a right to know that a known homosexual was corrupting their son. A known homosexual! I couldn't believe it; I nearly fucking died.'

There is at least calm now, after Dad has stormed out. Mum has changed out of her work clothes and she, Aunt Val and Nan are all sitting protectively around me on the couch. Aunt Val is holding my hand.

'Anyway, I told her, that Mrs Boswell,' Mum continues. 'Anyone who gets my David as a friend should count himself sodding lucky.'

And she lights up a cigarette, her hands trembling slightly.

'What did she say to that?' Nan asks, handing me a Kleenex from her pinny – I've been a bit sniffy.

'She fainted,' Mum says.

'She never!' Val stifles a chuckle.

'She did. Silly tart!'

It's long past midnight by the time I've finished unburdening my befuddled teenage heart to the three women. I even come clean about that Sunday night at Moira's – despite my nan's now well-worn cry of 'Ooh my good Gawd' – and I attempt to impress upon them how much I love Maxie, and how certain I am that now, more than ever, we are meant to be together.

213

'Well,' Mum sighs at the end of my starry-eyed discourse. 'If Mr and Mrs Boswell insist you give their precious Maxie a wide berth, then that's what you're gonna have to do, love.'

'I won't!'

'Yes, David, you will!' Mum stands up, and she seems a little annoyed. 'Or you'll be expelled. That's what Mr Lord said, expelled! He's already had words with the headmaster and you know what a fucking nutty Bible-basher he is. There's nothing else you can do; just leave the boy alone, David. Do you hear me?'

The world swirls about me as Nan and Aunt Val gather up their cardigans and head back to their house. Surely life cannot be this ghastly. Surely the gods could not permit me to taste that sweet nectar from a golden chalice, only to seize it away from me not a jiffy later, replacing it with a brass bucket of cold piss. Could they?

Mum appears again, drinking Blue Nun and smoking another fag.

'What about the play?' I mutter.

'Oh! Yes . . . I forgot,' Mum says, sitting beside me. 'I heard Mrs Boswell tell Mr McClarnon that Maxie can only take part in the production if he's in the chorus. He's not allowed to play Bill Sikes any more, David. He can't have any scenes with you. That way he'll have more time for his football practice. Sorry, love.'

'But who'll play Bill?'

'I don't know, do I?' Mum says. 'I'm just saying what I heard, now let it go.'

Now I'm really distraught; this is really happening.

'But the chorus are all the orphans, Mum. They're all first-year boys: Maxie is nearly sixteen!'

'Well, he'll play a fuckin' tall orphan, then, I expect,' Mum says jadedly, and she sips her wine as demurely as one can from a pewter tankard.

'Now let it drop, David. I don't really want to talk about it any more tonight.'

We both sit quietly for a very long time, staring at the television, but there's nothing on except a fuzzy white screen, because ITV has finished for the night, national anthem an' all. Mum looks terribly sad, though.

'Your dad told me,' she eventually says, and she's shaking her head slowly. 'In the car on the way home from parents' evening, he told me what happened the other week.'

'What?'

'You know,' she says, 'when he came home from work early and almost caught you and Maxie . . .'

'Oh.'

'And now I find out you've been stopping over at Moira's flat with him as well,' she says, still hypnotized by the dancing white snow of the TV. 'I didn't peg you for deceitful, David, I must say.'

I let my head drop, and I can't look at her. I adore my mum and I can't stand to see her like this, she looks broken by it all.

'I'm sorry, Mum. I was scared to tell you.'

'Scared?' she says.

'I didn't know what you'd think . . . about me being gay. What do you think, Mum?'

She stands up and switches off the TV, and her heavy charm bracelet bangs against the coffee table as she picks up her cigarette packet and her lighter, and then heads for the door. When she reaches it she turns back to me.

'I don't know what I think, David,' she says. 'I just don't know.'

Sixteen

Go Up West, Young Man

I seem to be out on the wily, windy moors. It's black-board dark and sleet slams on me in gusts every few seconds. Thank heavens I've got my duffle on.

'Take my hand, David,' Kate Bush whispers to me with a marvellous puffy pout. 'We'll go down together.'

I grasp Kate's hand and peer at the lit windows of the tiny house down the hill, far below us. She'll never make it down there, I'm thinking: no shoes and not so much as a poncho. Kate Bush will surely be dead from cold by the time we reach the house.

'Will he be there?' I ask her as we drive ourselves bravely against the gale that's tearing across the peaks and furrows of the moor.

'He will be there, David. He will,' says Kate.

'But how can you be sure?' I say. 'How can you know for certain after all that's happened?'

It appears, however, that Kate Bush is a creature of rather meagre banter, and she just waves her arm across her face dramatically, letting the long draping sleeve of her white dress brush over my frozen nose.

When we reach the stone cottage, with its old walls strangled in the clutches of thick twisting ivy, Kate Bush leads me to the big window.

'Here!' she says.

And rubbing frost from the windowpane with her hand, she peers in momentarily, and then steps away slowly.

'Is he there?' I ask.

Kate Bush points at the window and nods, rather like the ghost of Christmas yet to come, and says, 'He is here, David.'

I move forward delicately, and stand on tiptoe so I might reach the clear pane, but inside all I see is blood. Blood. Everywhere blood – crimson and disgusting: the bed, the walls, the floor all covered and awash. I turn to Kate in panic.

'He is here,' she says grimly, 'but you are too late, David.'

I spin around, terrified, glaring back into the room, and it is then that I see him: Maxie, lying at the foot of the bed, throat slashed and open. Dead!

After last night's hideous confrontation with Mum and Dad and the unqualified catastrophe that had been parents' evening, I'd been utterly shaken, and my nightmare of a ripped and slaughtered Maxie hadn't exactly helped matters, either. The thing that was irking – nay, distressing me – the most was the reaction of Mum. I had been so very certain, perhaps overly so, that she of all people would superbly and deftly rise to the occasion when the truth about my sexuality came tumbling out, that her vagueness and diffidence last night had completely knocked me for six. I wasn't expecting it. My alarm was compounded further this morning when, at breakfast time, Mum scarcely uttered a word to me, unless you count 'We've run out of Frosties', which I don't, as it happens, but that's by the by. The main thing is that, as unprepared for this truly vile turn of events and my mother's evident confusion as I was, what happened next astonished me even more.

It began this morning with a ring on the doorbell after Mum had left for work just after half past eight. A rather dazed Chrissy had opened the door to discover Maxie wringing his hands in our porch, sans school uniform and dressed in grey Farahs and a baby-blue V-neck. As soon as I saw him, I dashed up the passage towards the front door.

'Maxie!'

'Hi, David,' he said solemnly.

He looked wonderfully handsome, but cheerless and fatigued too.

'I need to talk to you,' he said. 'Your mum and dad ain't in, are they?'

'No, they've left already, why?'

Chrissy was hovering with intent, so I shooed her back down the passage and then went out front with Maxie, pulling the porch door to behind me.

'Why aren't you in your uniform?' was the first thing I said. 'Aren't you going to school?'

Maxie shook his head.

'After what happened last night?' he said. 'Are you fucking nuts – no way! Oh, I fuckin' hate Mr Lord. How could he do that to me? He's supposed to like me, ain't he? What an evil bastard. What a fucking mess.'

He was quite hysterical and it was then that I noticed the Gola bag sitting at his feet, and my heart jumped into my mouth.

'You're not running away from home, are you?' I whispered urgently. 'Did your parents go mad? They didn't thrash you, did they?'

'Of course they didn't bloody thrash me,' Maxie said. 'The only thing my mother ever beats is her precious Chinese rugs.'

And he sat himself down on the window ledge, so I followed suit.

'I can't face it today, though, David,' he said with quiet pain in his eyes. 'I can't face school with Mr Lord looking at me, and the other kids. There must have been other mums and dads there when all that shit kicked off at parents' evening last night: they will have told their kids . . . those kids will tell other kids . . . do you see what I'm saying?'

I nodded in simultaneous realization and horror.

'I guess I do,' I said. 'So you are running away?'

'No, silly,' he smiled. 'Well . . . not quite running away.'

And he put his hand on my shoulder, causing my breath to quicken.

'But I think we ought to get away for a day, together, to see if we can fix all this. Just us.'

'What, and not go to school?'

'No, fuck school,' Maxie said. 'Let's go up west and fuck everybody else off. Come on! We can get a Red Bus Rover and go wherever we want. Let's just do it, David!'

I thought about it for a moment as I stared into his perfectly open face: at his uneven smile, and his pleading eyes. It did sound violently romantic, I have to say: the two of us – fugitives from school, from our parents, from the world – just to be together for one day ... perhaps our very last! It was at once both spectacularly defiant and dangerously passionate. I decided I would do it.

'I need to get changed out of my uniform,' I told him. 'But I can't let Chrissy see me or she'll cotton on something's up, so you just wait out here, all right? I'll be ten minutes.'

He nodded keenly and I dashed up to my room, three stairs at a time, to change into something that more befitted the sheer unadulterated drama of it all.

Of course, when Maxie and me got to the end of Chesterfield Street, there stood Frances Bassey, hands on hips, outside Wallis'. She didn't look best pleased, as well she mightn't: with all that had gone on in the past eighteen hours, I'd completely forgotten that I'd promised to meet her there. She was banging her heel against the wall and pouting, her hair combed out into a huge Afro, and she looked quite beautiful: livid, but beautiful, nonetheless.

'You're late!' she sniped. 'Eight forty-five, you said, and what's Maxie doing here? Don't tell me he stayed over at yours?' Her mouth dropped open in pseudo-shock, and she leaned back against the window of the supermarket.

'No, of course he didn't stay over, you dozy tart,' I said. 'After what happened the other week Eddie would have a shit fit! Don't be so soft. Maxie turned up this morning, and we're not going to school today.'

Maxie nodded firmly in concurrence.

'We're getting a Red Bus Rover,' he said.

'What do you mean, you're not going to school?' Frances said with no small amount of intrigue. 'What's going on?'

'Well,' I said, linking arms with her and semi-dragging her along Lordship Lane towards the bus stop. 'Let me first fill you in on last night's lovely little episode . . .'

And off we trailed along the main road, with me giving a perhaps slightly over-theatrical description of the previous night's tumultuous events. Frances was practically hyperventilating by the time I'd finished, as was I.

'Oh, Christ! No wonder you don't wanna go to school – that's fucking awful,' she cried. 'Bob fucking Lord! What a wanker! What a knob!'

And then she came over all pensive for a few seconds.

'Right,' she suddenly said, waving a finger at me as

we crossed Matham Road. 'First thing Monday you boys have to go and see Mr McClarnon. He can help you, surely: tell you what to do next. He might even be able to get you back into the play, Maxie, don't you reckon?'

Maxie shrugged his shoulders.

'I don't think my mother is going to let me back into any school play, Frances,' he said. 'Not after what Mr Lord said.'

Frances stopped suddenly and looked at us both, wide-eyed.

'But surely he can't just get away with saying those things to your parents, Maxie,' she said in disbelief. 'It's just pure bloody evil!'

'It is evil,' I agreed, 'but it's also true up to a point, I suppose, and that's why you, my dear Fran, have to go into school today and report back to us all that's going on . . . everything that's being said about us . . . like a spy. The spy who loved me!'

Frances looked me up and down, her brow deeply furrowed. Then she prodded me, hard, in the ribs.

'Come out, bwoy!' she said. 'It'll be da spy who slapped you upside de head if you're not careful. I'm not playin' flippin' James Bond for no one, and I'm not going into school today now anyway! I'm getting a damn Red Bus Rover wiv yous two batty boys – see it deh?'

And she relinked arms with me, and then in turn with Maxie, and hauled us along the street towards an approaching 176 bus headed for Trafalgar Square.

'Besides,' she went on, 'I'm in the sixth form and I can pretty much do as I please, timetable-wise, so I'm coming with you, and that's all there bloody well is to it!'

We headed first for Carnaby Street, and by the time we got there – at around ten thirty – shopkeepers and traders were busy dragging up their shutters and erecting rails and racks of alluring shirts, hats, shoes, scarves and garish costume jewellery outside their shops. Frances, typically, was famished, only having had a bag of dry roasted peanuts for breakfast, and decided that egg and chips were mandatory before she could even contemplate venturing any further.

'Who has cash?' she demanded and she held her hand out flat.

'Well, I've only got a fiver for the whole day,' Maxie said as we headed into what looked like the most reasonably priced greasy spoon. It was then that I made my dramatic declaration.

'I have funds,' I said.

'Groovy,' Frances beamed. 'How much?'

'I'm not sure,' I said as we shuffled into a brown-leather-seated booth at the back of the café. 'But it's bloody heavy!'

And I went about emptying the contents of my school satchel, which was wholly bereft of books, biros and the like, but at least a good quarter-full of glittering fifty-pence pieces.

'Jesus!' Maxie said as I poured a large pile of them out on to the gravy-spotted yellow Formica table. 'Where did they come from?'

'Shhhh! I nicked them out of Eddie's bottle. He won't notice, he's got loads – he fiddles it out of the fruit machine at the club and shares it with my boss, Marty.'

I had felt the teensiest paroxysm of guilt as I'd half emptied the coin-filled sawn-off whisky bottle out on to the lounge carpet, and then scooped up handfuls of fifty-pence pieces and jammed them into my satchel before dashing to rejoin Maxie outside my front door earlier this morning – but it was just the teensiest. Not enough to actually stop me!

Frances spread the money out on the table with the flat of her hand and started counting it into piles of ten coins – five pounds in a pile.

'There's got to be fifty-odd quid here,' she said, eyes all globular. 'Possibly more.'

I, meanwhile, was chewing my lip.

'Do you think I'm perfectly awful for thieving?' I said.

But Frances had started to giggle, so she clearly didn't, and she continued totting up the plunder while Maxie kept watch to make sure no prying eyes were upon us.

'Sixty-eight quid,' she concluded seriously. 'Sixty-eight fucking quid! We can have an absolutely out-of-this-world day out on that, boys. What shall we do first?'

What we did first, once we'd wolfed down our rather unsatisfying fry-ups, was head along Carnaby Street, weaving in and out of the shops and indoor markets, trying on all the garments and attire we could lay our eager little paws on. I donned mohair jumpers and skinny suits, winkle-pickers and pork-pie hats, while Maxie tried on a Gary Numan-style plastic jumpsuit and a bright-pink trilby. Frances stumbled upon a hippy store, which stank of patchouli oil and where everything but the shop cat was tie-dyed to within an inch of its life. She came out of the curtained dressing area at one point wearing the most beastly grey and dirty-peach maxi-frock, and we all squealed in astonished hilarity as she stomped around the store farcically, until the owner made her take it off and shooed us away down the street. After that, we happened upon the Badge Shop, which was in a dingy basement and according to Frances was where Mr McClarnon found all his political badges and buttons. I, however, bought a nice little Blondie badge there, and another with Agnetha and Anni-Frid from Abba on it, singing in blue catsuits and sticking their bottoms out. Maxie bought a sew-on patch with 'The Jam' on it, and Frances bought two badges: one which she said was a surprise gift for me, and one with a cartoon of a smiling Rasta smoking a huge spliff. We paid, of course, in fifty-pence pieces.

When we wandered through a little park in Soho later in the afternoon, a group of about ten or twelve French kids our age were listening to a noisy radio, and so we went and sat with them, drinking Fresca and eating the latkes we'd bought at Gaby's Deli in the Charing Cross Road. These kids seemed so much cooler than the ones at our school: smoking Gauloises in their chic, coloured denim jackets and punky slogan-emblazoned T-shirts. One quite stunning boy wore the most incredible Debbie Harry shirt, and I was sick with jealousy. Maybe Maxie and I should run away to Paris – it must surely be better there, I thought.

Anyway, after five or so minutes chatting and laughing with a couple of extraordinarily glamorous girls from Biarritz, I noticed two boys amongst the group – perhaps a year or two older than me, but no more than that – sitting with their arms unashamedly about one another. I clocked them for a while, transfixed, as one played with the other's thick dark curls, and then touched his lips tenderly. I found myself smiling, and then almost teary with joy. How unabashed and wondrous these boys were to me. Clearly in love, they didn't give two fucks what anyone else in the park, or indeed the world at large, thought. When they eventually kissed, sweetly, and then smiled so knowingly at one another, my tears spilled over with the beauty of it, and I had to wipe my eyes before anyone noticed. I turned and looked towards Maxie, and sure enough he, too, was mesmerized by the pair. But on Maxie's face I saw something unreservedly different, something I really hadn't wanted to see at all, and it was quite plain. It was a look of trepidation – fear, even. Then he moved over, nearer to me on the grass, and put his hand on mine, smiling. It was a trifle half-hearted, I suppose, but the thought was there, so I grinned back, and even chanced a little wink.

'We've not even talked about any of this, really, have we?' I said quietly to him, and he looked straight at me.

'What?' he said.

'Well, we've been so busy enjoying ourselves we've forgotten why the hell we've cut school and done a bunk in the first place.'

'Oh.'

'We've still got to go back home and face all that other shit. We probably won't even be able to speak to one another tomorrow – even my mum said I should keep away from you. You're not in the play any more; it's just a fucking disaster from start to finish.'

'I know,' he said, looking down. 'But I don't want to talk about it, or think about it, David. It's all too bloody much. One minute I'm this normal kid who plays football and likes acting, and the next I'm branded a fucking queer in front of the whole school and me mum and dad. I can't take it.'

I didn't really know what to say, so I glanced over at Frances, who was at that point flirting, rather disgracefully, with the beautiful French boy in the Debbie Harry T-shirt. Then I turned back to Maxie.

'We'll have to go home soon,' I said miserably, 'and we'll probably be in even deeper shit now we've bunked off school.'

'I know,' Maxie said. 'I suppose it's been worth it, though, hasn't it?'

I semi-shrugged, and then he smiled at me and said, 'You're worth it, David.'

He rummaged around in his pocket and

dragged out a folded-up page from a magazine.

'Look at this,' he said, and he handed it me. 'I tore it out of a free magazine in one of the shops in Carnaby Street.'

I read aloud from the crumpled page.

' "Scandals Discotheque, Oxford Street. Friday night, 9 p.m. – 2 a.m. DJ Big Phil, plus cabaret." '

And there was a printed drawing of two men with moustaches dancing underneath a disco ball, with a pink triangle at the top. I stared at Maxie, somewhat bemused. What on earth was he showing me this leaflet for?

'We should go,' he said eagerly.

'What – to this? But it's late tonight.'

'We've got money,' Maxie reasoned. 'Why not? We're already in the shit. Might as well be hung for a sheep an' all that.'

My mouth fell open and I must have looked fairly ridiculous because Maxie suddenly grabbed me roughly and shook me by the shoulders.

'Come on!' he said. 'Where's your fuckin' renegade spirit?'

'I think it's in the cupboard under the stairs at home,' I laughed. 'Do you think we'd get in? Surely we wouldn't.'

'We can try,' he said.

I looked hard into Maxie's eyes. They were dazzling and effervescent, and I was all of a sudden both gripped and heartened by his unexpected rally to the call.

'All right,' I nodded. 'All fucking right, we'll give it a go.'

'Give what a go?' Frances asked, brusquely aban-doning the pretty French kid and leaning over.

She snatched the magazine page from me.

'You've got to be kidding!' she shouted, scanning it. 'No way! I've got to go home soon.'

Maxie snatched the page back.

'Well, we'll see that you get on the bus OK, Frances,' he said. 'We're going, though!'

'You're insane!' Frances snorted. 'Your parents will fucking murder you if you go to this and stay out till all hours. You'll just be making things ten times worse.'

'They can't get any worse, Fran,' I said. 'We'll be fine. We need to go – just to see if . . . well, we just need to go.'

It was getting on for dusk by then, and folk were shutting up shop and pouring out of their offices into the crisp autumn evening all around the little park. Some of the French kids had got little squat bottles of beer, and they gave some to Maxie, Frances and me. Frances even had a crack at one of their cigarettes, but she hacked and coughed half to death on the first taste of it, and all the kids laughed at her. Then the hand-some boy with the Debbie Harry shirt spoke to her softly, in his sensual native tongue.

'Vous êtes une belle princesse noire,' he said. 'Je voudrais vraiment vous baiser.'

Frances grinned toothily at the boy and touched his face, ever so gently, as Maxie and I looked on, some-what bemused.

'*Dans vos rêves, connard,*' she said. 'I came top in French, you know.'

And then all the French kids laughed at him instead.

Just after that, The Pretenders came on the radio – one of Frances's favourites, and mine, so we started singing along, no doubt livened up by the beer. The French kids knew all the words as well and they joined in with us, singing across the park rowdily with the radio blasting.

'Kid what changed your mood?
You've gone all sad, so I feel sad too
I think I know some things we never outgrow
You think it's wrong – I can tell you do
How can I explain, when you don't want me to?'

We bundled Frances on to the 176 bus on Oxford Street at about six o'clock; she didn't look too thrilled about it, but what could she do?

'I can't stay out much past teatime,' she said as the bus approached. 'My mum'd have kittens. I wish I could – cos I think somebody needs to keep an eye on you two – but I can't, so please be careful if you go to this club, and get a bloody taxi home; you've got the money.'

'Yes, Mum,' Maxie saluted as she hopped aboard.

And she waved sadly as the conductor sharply yanked the bell cord twice before the bus pulled away, leaving Maxie and me to head off in search of a decent hamburger and a bottle of Coke. After we'd eaten, and then wandered around a bit more, we ventured into some public loos near Argyll Street to wash our hands and faces, then we changed into the shirts we'd bought in Carnaby Street – they'd make us look distinctly older and therefore augment, considerably, our chances of getting into the Scandals discotheque. Maxie had bought a plain black shirt, which made him look exceedingly sexy and mature, whereas I had plumped for something blousy in a purply sort of colour that I felt was dead sophisticated and definitely something somebody over the age of twenty-one might be seen to wear. After that we were pretty much ready, I suppose, but by that stage, shoulder aching, I had started to regret not having popped to a bank at some point during the day to change all those weighty fifty-pence pieces from the heist into a lighter denomination. Still, at least we had money, and we were all set to disco.

Seventeen

Love Story – without the Cancer

Outside the club's tiny entrance, though, which was in a side road off Oxford Street, Maxie didn't seem quite as cocky as he had earlier.

'What do you think?' he said, peering at the forbiddingly drawn thick blue velvet curtain inside the club's doorway. 'It looks quite quiet, doesn't it? What time is it?'

'It's twenty past nine,' I said, glancing at my Timex. 'It's definitely open but I've only seen one or two people go in. Perhaps we're too early, and there's no sign above the door, is there?'

Maxie shook his head.

'People must just know,' he suggested.

Then, after another five or ten minutes of us standing on the kerb like lemons, he suddenly took a bold step towards the door and poked his head through the curtain. Traffic whizzed and buzzed about me, and it was getting quite chilly – I wasn't sure how much longer I wanted to stand there if we weren't going to at least try getting in.

'What's it like?' I asked as Maxie reappeared, but he was none the wiser.

'All I can see is a fat lady behind a booth reading a really, really big book,' he said.

'Oh.' I felt slightly disenchanted. 'So what do you think?'

'I think it's *War and Peace*,' he said. 'It's very big.'

'I mean, should we go in? Are we going to risk it? We need to make a decision, cos I'm not standing out here all fucking night.'

I fished around in my satchel for a stray cigarette, to no avail, and as I did I noticed a few young men gathering around the door and then stepping inside. I felt envious.

'I know what we'll do,' Maxie said, suddenly sounding vaguely self-possessed. 'We'll wait till a largish crowd of people go in, and then we'll sort of tail along in behind them – how does that sound?'

'Mildly feasible,' I said flatly.

Then a voice from behind us made us both jump.

'Hello, my dears, and what do we have here?'

We turned around quick and discovered a slight man in a pastel-green pants suit with a sequin-trimmed collar that had clearly seen better days – as had the gentleman himself. Fifty-ish, I'd have said he was, with a greying, coiffured barnet and a kind smile. He was carrying a small metal briefcase in one hand and a pair of burgundy slingbacks in the other, and his fingernails were painted to complement the colour of said shoes.

'And what are you two divine young men doing outside a place like this of a Friday night, might I enquire?' he said. 'You'll not get through that door, that's for a positive – look at you, you're mere chickens, and it's more than the boss's life's worth to let you in – he'd lose his licence.'

Then the man stepped forward and presented us with his hand as if we might kiss it. There was at least one fancy ring on each of his dainty fingers and his nails were manicured to unqualified perfection. I noticed his violet eyes: just like Elizabeth Taylor's, I thought, though these were jewels in a rather tarnished crown, set above his slightly mottled, jowly cheeks, and the kind of lines around the mouth that smokers get after forty years of dragging on ciggies.

'I'm Jeanette,' he said delicately. 'And you two are?'

I stepped forward and smiled bravely.

'I'm David,' I said, 'and this is Maxie. Is your name really Jeanette?'

The man laughed, and pinched my cheek softly.

'No, silly,' he chuckled. 'My mother named me Arthur McDonald but to everyone else I'm Jeanette. Anyway, enough about me, what are you two handsome young fellas doing out here? You're not rent, are you? Cos if you are, you'll get nothing coming out of here till gone midnight at least, and even then I should imagine it'll be fairly slim pickings. You'd be better off staking out the 'Dilly.'

Then he studied us both absorbedly for about fifteen seconds, while we just stood there, mouths half open.

'You don't look much like rent boys,' Jeanette finally

said, his voice crisp and well presented. 'Where do you come from?'

'East Dulwich,' I blurted proudly.

Jeanette smiled.

'I thought you had a whiff of the provinces about you, dear,' he said. 'And what brought you both up to London?'

'We got the 176,' Maxie said. 'We've just come up to town for the day, and we saw this place in a magazine, so we thought we'd try it out.'

'We like to dance,' I added as more and more people filed past us into the club.

'Do you now?' Jeanette said, putting down his brief-case. 'Well, you've got to be twenty-one to come in here, boys, and besides that, do you know what sort of a club this is?'

Then he nodded towards me.

'I bet you do,' he said. 'But your pal here looks reasonably innocent – does he know what he's likely to be up against in there?'

'It's a gay club,' Maxie said with authority.

Jeanette laughed.

'Is it now, my darling? And you two want to go in and see what it's all about, do you?'

Maxie and I both nodded ardently.

'Are you going in, Jeanette?' I asked.

'Yes, of course,' Jeanette said. 'I work here, don't I? But—'

'Doing what?' Maxie interrupted. 'Are you a barman?'

'No, I'm not a barman,' Jeanette laughed. 'I'm an entertainer!'

And he gestured histrionically with both arms.

'I pop on a few records sometimes, if Philip the disc jockey moseys up to the office for a wank, and I do the cabaret at eleven – any more questions?'

'Take us in,' I said. 'Take us in with you.'

'What?'

'Go on. We'll be no trouble, Jeanette,' I pleaded, and I helpfully scooped up his briefcase from the pavement. 'We could be your assistants, and carry your bits and pieces. Just for half an hour. We both look a lot older than we are.'

Jeanette shook his head slowly and chuckled to himself.

'Do you know what? Just for brass neck I think I might. I think you boys need to know what you're letting yourselves in for – how old *are* you, by the by?'

'We're eighteen,' I said.

Jeanette, however, didn't look especially persuaded, and he waved a finger at me.

'It's not that long since I've seen an eighteen-year-old boy, dear heart,' he said. 'How old?'

'Sixteen!' Maxie confessed haughtily. 'We're sixteen, actually.'

'Hmm,' Jeanette said, looking Maxie up and down. 'I know your type as well: more inches on the cock than miles on the clock.'

And he handed Maxie the slingbacks and pushed past him.

'Follow me, the pair of you.'

So as Jeanette breezed in through the door of the

club, Maxie and I followed him swiftly and with our heads down.

'These two chicks are with me, Lil,' Jeanette shouted to the large rosy lady in the booth behind the curtain – and she never even glanced up from her Tolstoy. We were in!

Behind that blue velvet curtain, as it turned out, lay a supernatural and exquisite world that I'd hardly dared believe could ever exist. Red-carpeted stairs drew us down towards a swirling throng of dancing, thrusting men of every size and silhouette, the piquant smell of their varied colognes rising up around us as we descended further and further until we were finally swallowed up in the dancing crowd. Pastel lights flashed on–off–on, lustrous and bright against the white shirts and tanned skins of the beauteous men that encircled us. Maxie and I gawped and glared around and about us as Jeanette marshalled us through the near-rapturous multitude who, hands in the air, were chanting along with the sweet and glorious mantra that was soaring out of the speakers.

'Am I ever gonna fall in love in New York City?
Will I ever find a home so far from Tennessee?
There's no future in the single bars, nothing but the one-
    night stars,
Am I ever gonna fall in love in New York City?'

I stopped for a moment in the middle of the floor, in quiet disbelief beneath the spinning disco ball. This place was spectacular.

'Fuck me, this is amazing,' I said to no one in particular. 'Where did they all come from?'

A striking blond in a black vest, with collar-length hair and a moustache, danced past me languidly and brushed my face with his hand.

'Paradise, baby,' he said with the longest of Southern drawls. 'That's where they all came from, Paradise!'

Then he put his arm around my waist and encircled me, before spinning me around and pulling me close to him from behind, rocking me back and forth to the music.

'What is this music?' I said, half enchanted, half terrified, and looking around for Maxie and Jeanette, who were by now all the way across the other side of the dance floor.

'Grace Jones, baby!' he said. 'She's a fuckin' goddess!'

Then he turned me around to face him, kissed me softly on the mouth and evaporated in the crowd.

When I finally caught up with Maxie he was following Jeanette towards a door by the side of the stage, which was at the far end of the room.

'Come in, darlings,' Jeanette commanded.

And we wandered into a petite but gorgeously bedecked room.

'This is my domain, dears.'

The room was festooned with paper and silk flowers in yellows and reds, and Chinese lanterns hung from its low ceilings. There were boxes everywhere, and a table to one side below a square mirror surrounded by light bulbs, only three of which were currently functioning; atop the table sat an old-fashioned mannequin's head that was wearing a larger-than-life Marilyn Monroe-style wig. The walls above the mirror were adorned with snaps and Polaroids of Jeanette with various luminaries from the world of show business.

'Here's me with Kenny Williams and Babs Windsor,' Jeanette said, pointing. 'And this one's a bit blurry, but it's actually me with the Aga Khan at Windsor Safari Park.'

He suddenly looked forlorn. 'I think we might have had a real future together if he hadn't taken up with that fashion model.'

Then he turned to us and smiled, sitting with his hands in his lap in front of the mirror.

'I've wined and dined with all the greats over the years, boys,' he said. 'Dorothy Squires, Bob Monkhouse, him off *Stars on Sunday* – all of 'em. Judy Garland once told me I had the cheekbones of Garbo.'

'Who?' Maxie said, and Jeanette rolled his eyes.

'Oh, so young, so young,' he cried.

Then he snatched the wig from the mannequin head and started brushing it through, vigorously.

'Now, I've got to tong this before I go on and I've not had any sort of a beverage yet. There's a bottle of Campari lurking about in one of those cupboards with some tumblers. Why don't you boys see if you can lay hands on that, and pour us all a glass? Then you can pull up a box each and tell Auntie Jeanette what the hell it is you're both doing roaming around London this late on a Friday night.'

I parked myself on one of the boxes, which appeared to be full of shoes and frocks, and looked directly into Jeanette's eyes, wondering if I might trust him.

'It's a bit of a long story, actually,' I said, while Maxie poked around in the cupboard.

'I'm not going anywhere,' Jeanette said. 'Not until I go on at eleven, anyway. Spill!'

Well, by the time I'd finished, Jeanette was quite ashen, and he stuck his glass out for Maxie to replenish.

'I need another drink, dear,' he said, so Maxie did the honours.

'I can scarcely believe it,' he went on, knocking back the ruby-red liquid. 'What a story! This Mr Lord sounds like a complete monster, doing everything in his power to stifle and cut down a young, fragile love as it starts to bloom. He's most likely a bitter old queen himself if you ask me – how perfectly frightful! And what with your dad catching you in flagrante delicto! Well, it's like the gay diary of Anne Frank, my darlings, or *Love Story* without the cancer.'

Maxie and I both nodded silently in agreement, and I sipped at my drink, which was tepid and quite disgusting.

'And are you in love, my darlings?' Jeanette asked pleadingly. 'Do you ache to be together whatever the cost? Is that why you've run away to London?'

Maxie poured him yet another full glass of Campari with a dash of flat lemonade.

'We've not exactly run away,' Maxie said. 'We just came up to town for the day to get away from it all. And we do actually live in London, so we couldn't have really run away to it anyway, could we?'

'But we are in love,' I jumped in, eager not to throw cold water on Jeanette's rather agreeable Mills & Boon take on our story. 'Aren't we, Maxie?'

Maxie nodded nervously, and then said, 'It's just all been a bit much really.'

His voice was shaking slightly, and he gulped down a glass of the foul-tasting Campari.

'My mum and dad went nuts. I expect they'll be even angrier now I've disappeared. Do you think I should phone them?'

He looked at Jeanette dolefully, and then at me, and it suddenly dawned on me how much shit we would both almost certainly be in now. Jeanette put a painted fingernail up to his lips and looked thoughtful for a moment. Then he stood up, taking first my hand and then Maxie's.

'I'll tell you what,' he said. 'I'm off at half eleven. Why don't you two boys go watch my tired old act, have a little disco dance and enjoy yourselves, and then take a black taxi over to my place in Pimlico. Nothing untoward, mind, I've got a spare room and I'll be home by half past midnight. But that way you could spend a nice night together before going back home to face the music tomorrow. You could even phone your parents from my flat, though I'm sure they won't be best pleased, but at least they'd know you were safe. Tell them you're at a friend's or something.'

Maxie and I stared at one another, bemused.

'You're going to be in trouble, come what may, boys,' Jeanette smiled, 'but this way you could have some time together. What do you think?'

When we exited the little room and went back out into the vast resplendency of the disco, there was yet another euphoric disco record playing that I'd never heard, and the beautiful people were spinning wildly.

So Maxie and me dashed into the throng to join them . . . and we danced our arses off!

'Did you see that?' Maxie panted as we fell sweating against the bar afterwards.

'What?'

'It's him that reads the regional news on the telly, and he was kissing another man – it really was him!'

'Who?'

'Right there, look!'

'Where?'

I peered through the cigarette smoke back to where Maxie was pointing: a booth table just to one side of the dance floor.

'Shit, you're right,' I said. 'Well, I never knew.'

'Well, you don't, do you?' Maxie said. 'Nobody says it out loud, do they?'

'No,' I said. 'They don't, but they should. It would be a damn sight easier if people did say it out loud. Like Hamish.'

'What do you mean, easier?' Maxie said, and he turned to face me and he put his arms around me, pulling me closer to him, his face and hair gleaming with sweat.

'Well, you've got a choice, haven't you?' I said gravely. 'You can be some kind of fucking wonderful . . . like Hamish, or . . . Jeanette, or you can be scared and sad like my old French teacher Farrah Fawcett-Majors, or a closeted lunchtime newsreader.'

Maxie blinked at me, and I knew he didn't truly understand, so I moved in closer to him, as close as I could get.

'Farrah Fawcett-Majors was your French teacher?' he said, swallowing hard.

And I shrugged and nodded, unable to explain properly with him pressed up against me. Then he leaned towards me and we kissed, and he tasted like Campari, but I liked the taste now. Loved it, in fact.

'Shall we go to Jeanette's?' he said after he'd kissed me for a very long time.

'Yes,' I said. 'We shall.'

Eighteen

Au Fait with Pimlico

So now I'm banging, seemingly to no avail, on the exceedingly dusty door of an apartment up on the third floor of a huge and relatively shabby Victorian house ... in Pimlico ... at half past midnight, for God's sake!

When I bang once more and much harder, it swings open at last. Maxie's looking somewhat fretful so I squeeze his elbow, and then I smile at him in the most reassuring manner I can manage, given the circumstances.

'You found it all right, then,' Jeanette says in a soft voice. 'This end of Lupus Street can be a bit of a bitch to negotiate if you're not au fait with Pimlico.'

He's wearing a sea-green, floor-length silk kimono that's billowing in the breeze from an old-fashioned tabletop fan set on a chest of drawers behind him, and he is puffing on a bright-blue cigarette set in a Holly Golightly cigarette holder.

'Well, do come in, boys,' he says, grandly sweeping

his arm out into the room before us. 'I've made it nice for you.'

When Jeanette swings the door shut behind us, Maxie and I shuffle shyly into the centre of the room, which is lit by a red bulb set in a pretty art deco glass lamp.

'I wasn't sure if you'd be here already, Jeanette,' I gush. 'We loved your act, by the way, especially the Andrews Sisters section; it was terribly clever how you did all three of them just by switching wigs. Anyway, then we danced a bit more – for about half an hour – and then we got a taxi like you said. The driver wasn't very pleased that we paid him all in coins, though, but I suppose money's money, isn't it?'

Jeanette surges forward and gathers us both in his arms.

'Now, darlings,' he says, clearly sensing my apprehension. 'I don't want you to feel uneasy or uncomfortable about coming here. Auntie Jeanette is going to make herself scarce, and you won't hear a peep from me. As I said, you can phone your parents from here, and I've made the sitting room all nice for you. There's a lovely comfy divan over in that corner where I usually sleep, but I'll be in the boudoir on the lilo – truth be told it's more of a walk-in wardrobe than a boudoir – but I'll be quite cosy in there, so you two just enjoy yourselves.'

'Thank you, Jeanette, you've been really kind,' I say softly. 'Why have you been so good to us?'

Jeanette steps back and throws her arms open spectacularly, taking in the sight of Maxie and me with a toothy 'Miss World' smile.

'Dear things,' he says, tilting his head to one side and clasping his hands to his chin as if in prayer. 'You've had an odious time of late – *très difficile* – that much is clear to me. I just want to give you two boys one unforgettable and beautiful night of *l'amour*. That much, you deserve.'

Then he glides towards a door, which I assume leads to the other bedroom, snatching his cigarette holder from the ashtray as he goes.

'I'm going to get off to bed and let you two . . . get on with it, so to speak,' he says, 'and I shall cook you a nice full English in the morning. *Bonne nuit!*'

'Good night, Jeanette,' I say.

We cross the room and sink down on the divan with its ridiculous gold lamé headboard and black silk sheets. Above it are even more framed snaps of Jeanette partying with the glamorous and purportedly famous, though I only manage to identify one actual famous person, that being Danny La Rue, who is posed – rather awkwardly – next to Jeanette, and is wearing a more expensive-looking wig. The room, as I said, is suffused in a reddish glow, and the dimness of it seems to camouflage a multitude of sins, decor-wise: threadbare faux-Persian rugs and a pair of stern 1940s utility armchairs, one of which is piled high with dusty back issues of *Harpers & Queen* and *Vogue*. But Jeanette has sweetly gone to the trouble of lighting some little candles and putting them on the cabinet next to the bed, and he has garnished the bed's two pillows with a few red rose petals. I turn to Maxie – who has been ever so quiet since we got out of the taxi – and smile, giggling nervously like I imagine one of the girls at school might, when about to lose her virginity.

'Look how romantic it all is,' I say. 'Our first proper night together as . . .'

'As what?' Maxie whispers.

He is staring at me in the flush of the candles, but it is not a stare that I especially welcome. It is not the gaze, for instance, of a yearning lover, nor is it even that of a horny football captain. No. It is the cheerless glower of a confused and terrified adolescent, and I know the look well. I had seen it in our bathroom mirror at home, on my own face, just a few short weeks back.

'What?' I say softly to him, and I notice that there are tears in both his eyes.

'All this,' Maxie says.

'All what?'

'The room, the candles, the rose petals,' he says, 'all of it. I'm not sure it's right. I'm not sure it's for me . . . no . . . I am sure. It's not for me, David.'

I suddenly have a tennis-ball-sized lump in my throat.

'You're different to me,' Maxie goes on. 'You're brave and sorted and properly gay and . . .'

'And what?'

Maxie's eyes drift downwards to his lap, in which his hands are clasped tight.

'My mum is a very tidy lady,' he says. 'Everything 'as to go in its proper place as far as Vi's concerned; in its rightful and designated space or little nook. The ironing board 'as to go in the utility cupboard in the kitchen, but the iron goes under the sink. The books have to go in the posh bookcase, but not all of them: the cookery books have to go in the larder, and God help you if she finds an A–Z or a car manual in the posh bookcase – that sort of literature goes in the garage with Dad's things. I'm surprised, actually, that she doesn't make Dad stay in the fuckin' garage as well; she always says he makes the place look untidy.'

I'm not entirely sure where Maxie is headed with this little family-themed discourse, but he looks so very solemn that I'll stick with it and keep mum anyway.

'Mum's a bit like that with people, too,' he goes on. 'My sister Jessica was the clever one, so she was always pegged to go to university – it was never even discussed whether I would go or not, no. I was the sporty one. I would do football or swimming or athletics or all fuckin' three at the same time if she 'ad her way.'

And he laughs, but only fleetingly.

'Anyway, a few years ago, when my sister decided she wasn't going to go to the uni that Vi had picked out for her – that in fact she wasn't going to any bloody uni at all, and was actually going to move out of home and live over the brush, as Vi would say, with her boyfriend, who was a panel-beater from Billericay – Vi started buying things.'

'Buying things?' I say, glancing at the carriage clock on the bedside cabinet – it's pushing one by now.

'Buying things,' Maxie says again, slightly dreamily.

'It started with an electric kettle, and some new net curtains for the upstairs landing. Then she had another row with my sister and she bought herself the same velour tracksuit in four different colours and a set of Carmen heated rollers, followed the next day by a rotisserie and a four-berth tent, even though she hates camping. Over one weekend, just before Jess was due to leave home, Mum bought a cine-camera with projector, a nest of tables, a music centre – even though there was nothing wrong with the one we had – and a full set of Osmond dolls, including little Jimmy. It was like a fucking episode of *Sale of the Century* in our sitting room most of the time. Geoff – that's me dad – reckoned it was best not to mention it, and as she had just bought him a Black & Decker Workmate and me a Raleigh Tomahawk we decided to keep shtum and not look a gift horse in the mouth.'

Maxie is now looking me directly in the face.

'On the Sunday after Jessica actually moved out,' he says, 'my dad went into the garage and found 147 pairs of American tan tights in his screw drawer, and seventy-six packets of cotton buds stuffed in the glove compartment of his car. And then on the Monday when Dad got his Access bill it turns out that Vi had spent three and a half fuckin' grand in less than a month. She'd even booked a fuckin' Mediterranean cruise without tellin' poor old Geoff.'

'But why?' I ask. 'Why did she? And what's all this got to do with you and me?'

'Doctor Krol said that it was a mild nervous collapse,' Maxie says distantly, 'but she just did it because things weren't in their proper place and she couldn't take it. My sister was supposed to go to university, and then meet a nice man and get married with a lovely posh wedding at St John's; she wasn't meant to fuck off to Billericay with a panel-beater called Derek, and Mum just couldn't stand the untidiness of it. Jessica was just like the A–Z in the posh bookcase as far as me mum was concerned, but the difference was you can take the A–Z out of the bookcase and put it where it belongs, in the garage. You can't do that with people, David.'

'No,' I say. 'You can't.'

'I'm meant to be the sporty one,' Maxie says firmly. 'Not the gay one. There isn't a gay one. It would just fuckin' kill her.'

And then he stands up and kisses me on the top of the head.

'You are fantastic, David,' he says. 'But I've got to go 'ome. I'm gonna get the night bus.'

He walks towards the front door and I stand up quickly, as if on springs.

'All right,' I say, and he turns around. 'We'll go home.'

As I pull on my bomber jacket and head towards the door behind him, a bleary-eyed Jeanette appears from the bedroom with chaotic hair and a cigarette – not in a glamorous holder this time. Maxie disappears down the stairs and I turn to face Jeanette, who is leaning in the doorway blowing smoke out in tidy rings.

'Are you off, then?' he asks, sounding mildly surprised.

'We have to,' I tell him. 'We weren't in the right place, apparently.'

'Oh,' Jeanette says matter-of-factly, and he crosses the room to his sink and starts rinsing out some mugs that have been sitting on the draining board.

'And shall I see you boys again?' he says, looking down into the washing-up bowl and scrubbing hard.

'I shouldn't think so,' I reply gently. 'As you say, we're not really all that au fait with Pimlico. Anyway, thanks and all that . . .'

But Jeanette doesn't look round. So I close the door quietly behind me.

Nineteen

Unravelling

I don't see Maxie at all the following week as it's half bloody term and he doesn't even phone me. Then on the first Monday back I find that he's been mysteriously kept at home – what the hell's going on? Now it's Wednesday and still no sign, so when I stride into the drama room after second period I'm all ready to shed my woes at Mr McClarnon's feet and have him anoint me with some munificent and tremendously wise words, but he's somewhat distracted. I discover him limp-wristedly running a duster over the blackboard at a snail's pace, and with a faraway look in his eye.

'Mr McClarnon?'

I announce my presence but to no avail. Hamish appears completely diverted from the world around him and fails even to acknowledge my presence. Then all of a sudden Frances totters into the room behind me eating a bag of salt 'n' shake crisps.

'What's going on?' she says.

'Search me. I just came in to talk to Hamish but he seems to be on another astral plane for the time being.'

The drama room is empty but for us and so Frances and me head for two of the old-fashioned desks at the front of the class and sit down. Eventually Hamish turns around and spots us, blinking as if he's been abruptly woken from a Rip Van Winkle-length slumber.

'Och! It's you two,' he says vaguely.

Frances screws up her empty crisp packet and jams it into the inkwell.

'Yes, sir,' she says. 'It's us. What on earth is the matter?'

'Nothing,' Hamish says, still in a veritable dream state. 'I was just . . .'

And then he drifts off again.

'SIR!' I call out, and he finally snaps back into the here and now with a frown.

'What is it, David? I'm busy.'

'I need to speak to you, Hamish,' I say, getting up, 'about what happened at parents' evening and about what's happened since, and my mum and dad and everything, sir!'

Hamish sits down at his desk and puts his head in his hands.

'Not now, eh, David?' he says, but I lean over the desk and thrust my face pleadingly towards his.

'But you said yesterday that you'd talk to me today, and I'm going nuts here. I don't know what to do about Maxie, he still isn't at school, and I don't know if he's ever coming back, and it's hideous, sir, hideous!'

Hamish lifts his head and shakes it slowly, almost annoyed.

'We've gone over it, David. I told ye yesterday what I thought was going on wi' Maxie, didn't I? I don't know what else te tell y', David.'

The ghastly truth was that, because of our little flit up to London, Maxie was being kept away from school and away from me, and I was beginning to unravel. Mr McClarnon had indeed assured me yesterday that Maxie would almost certainly be coming back to school, and would still be involved in the school production if he was inclined to – as props manager – but at the moment his wretchedly overprotective parents, Vi and Geoff Boswell, had decided that Maxie needed to lie low until the proverbial fairy dust had settled, and that's all there was to it. Hamish firmly believed that Maxie would be back at school next Monday, and that the best and safest course of action for me was to work hard and keep my head down until everyone had calmed down over the whole ludicrous debacle of parents' evening and its aftermath. Easier said than done. Three teachers had hauled me over the coals already this week for not completing any of the assignments I'd been set over the half-term, and that was in subjects I actually like.

Even nice Mr Peacock had shaken his head mournfully at me when I handed in a flimsy few paragraphs on the Battle of the Bulge on Monday, but to be honest I wasn't at all fussed about lessons any more. I mean, I used to be an out-and-out sponge for knowledge,

I really did, but quite frankly now I don't give a shit. And having heard nothing from Maxie since all this had blown up has rendered me marginally hysterical and more than a little anxious for some reassurance from him of our love, or at least our connection. How, I thought, could he be just sitting there at home without trying to phone me at the very least? Why hadn't Maxie attempted to scale the walls of my home to tap on my bedroom window and lead me to escape with him? Did he not care about us? Was he not tormented by the same insidious torture that I myself was enduring? By this morning, it seemed to me that he might not be.

'I will sit down with you, David, I promise,' Hamish says. 'I know there's a lot ye need to talk about, I know there is.'

And he leans back in his chair, resting his head against the 'Who killed Blair Peach?' poster behind him and staring out of the skylight in the sloped ceiling above him.

'I've just got a hell of a lot of other shite te deal wi' today, kids, honest I have.'

Frances jumps up and joins me at Hamish's desk, intrigued.

'Why, what's up, Mr McClarnon?' she says, all breathless. 'Is it something to do with the filth being at the school this morning? I saw the meat wagon outside the sixth-form centre – what's cooking?'

'Police?' I ask. I hadn't seen them.

'Yes, yes,' Hamish says, agitated and waving his

arms, 'and o' course it's all landed on ma bloody lap, hasn't it.'

'What has?'

'Two kids in ma form who shall remain nameless,' Hamish says. 'Caught wi' drugs during a technical drawing lesson . . . by Bob Lord, no less. Not only does the man now think I'm the son o' Satan for harbouring underage practising homosexuals, but he also thinks I'm sheltering drug dealers under my lovely left wing as well.'

'No,' Frances gasps.

'Drugs?' I say. 'What sort? Weed?'

'I wish it were only weed,' Hamish says. 'But it's pills: speed, and plenty of 'em. After ma form was searched there was four other boys wi' drugs on 'em too, and we suspect we have a dealer in our midst. Any road, dear old Mr Lord and the headmaster thought it best if the police were informed, and now I've got te head off te the cop shop in a wee while te try te sort the whole mess out. Two o' my lads are in a cell right about now.'

'Shit,' Frances says.

'Exactly!' Hamish nods. 'So you'll excuse me, David, if I'm a bit preoccupied. I promise I'll talk te you tomorrow when I get the chance, OK?'

'OK.'

Frances and me decide to head out to the playing fields and find our usual spot by the goalposts as we've got a free period, and, as ever, we gossip fiendishly as we walk, speculating on who the guilty parties in Mr McClarnon's form might be, narcotics-wise, and who might be dealing within the school grounds.

'I reckon it's Miss Jibbs,' Frances surmises. 'She looks like a coke fiend to me.'

'Or Bob Lord,' I sneer, 'jacking up heroin while he watches the boys in the showers after football.'

And we howl with laughter as we kick through the fallen, brittle, russet leaves that blanket the grass surrounding the footy pitch, and I feel better for a moment.

It's very definitely autumn now, and so the pair of us are bundled up in our duffels and scarves, despite today's blue skies and cheery splash of sun. Frances – never without sustenance of one sort or another – has managed to rustle up a couple of toffee Yo-Yos and a can of Tab to share, and once we've sat down she starts prodding at me as I nibble disconsolately at my half-unwrapped biscuit.

'David,' she trills with a rather pronounced upward inflection, and I turn to face her.

'What?'

She looks shamefaced for some reason, and she won't look me in the eye.

'Don't be cross,' she says, 'will you?'

'About what?' I say thoughtfully. 'Thatcher's fascist regime, or the fact that Abba haven't had a number one since "Take A Chance On Me" in February 1978?'

Frances laughs, and then she says, 'No, neither of those. I mean don't be cross about what I'm about to tell you.'

'Which is?'

Frances stuffs the last half of her Yo-Yo biscuit into her mouth and chews it quickly, rather like some sort of demented rodent.

'Well,' she says, spitting chocolate dust. 'I went to see Maxie during half-term . . .'

And then she swallows hard.

'Went to see him – where?' I shriek, jumping up.

'At his house,' Frances says. 'I was wondering how he was doing, and so I went over there to see him. I was only going to knock for him but his mother invited me into the house for tea, so in I went. It was quite a nice house, actually – a bit too much peach, I thought, but anyway, quite nice . . . Sit down, David, will you, for fuck's sake?'

I throw myself back down on to the grass next to her, then yank her towards me with two of the toggles on her duffle.

'What did he say?' I ask impatiently. 'How was he? Did he say anything about me?'

Frances is chuckling annoyingly.

'Yes, he did,' she says, 'and that's why I'm telling you this now, so you'll stop bloody fretting so much. He said that he cares about you, David . . . very much.'

'Did he?'

'Yes!'

I had wondered, to be honest. After we'd left Jeanette's flat in Pimlico two Friday's ago and made a dash for the night bus, Maxie had hardly said two words all the way home.

His face had looked as though it were wracked with a multiplicity of quandaries, and he kept biting his bottom lip and looking down and shaking his head. When he did speak, as we came round Elephant and Castle roundabout, it was only to say, 'My mum's gonna fucking kill me.'

And try as I might, I couldn't for the life of me come up with any sort of appropriate riposte to that, so I just kept my mouth shut and gazed out of the window at all the many and varied creatures of the night. There were drunks all over the show, more than one could shake a stick at, and I noticed that many of them didn't seem particularly cheerful. Overweight girls tottering along on fiendishly high shoes and hollering foul-mouthed abuse at their theoretical loved ones seemed to be the order of the night, and there were also a fair few underage lads knocking about: skinheads and soul boys who weaved and staggered along the Walworth Road absurdly, before vomiting into a litter bin or a shop doorway. When we finally disembarked at Goose Green, where Maxie and I would be due to go our separate ways, he stopped and looked at me, glassy-eyed.

'It's quarter past two in the fuckin' morning,' he said, and I nodded.

'I had a really great time today, David, I really did. It's just . . .'

'What?'

'I've got a lot to think about, that's all.'

I put my hand up and touched his shoulder, and I said, 'So there's hope for me yet, then?'

But he just smiled and shrugged, then he turned and walked off towards his house, and that was the very last I'd seen of him.

'So what else did he say?' I yell at Frances, still pulling at her toggles.

But now she's shaking her head.

'Nothing,' she says. 'His mum was there most of the time showing me the new vacuum cleaner she'd just bought, and it was only when she went out to fetch the tea that we had a chance to talk properly. The important thing, though, is that Maxie is all right, David, and he says he cares about you – so stop worrying. He'll be back at school soon, I know he will.'

'I suppose,' I sigh, finally releasing Frances from my clutches. 'Hamish did say Maxie would be coming back to do the props for the play, so I guess that's something; but it's not just Maxie, though, is it, Fran? Have you seen how the other kids are with me now since parents' evening? They all know! The ones that don't shout fucking names at me can't bring themselves to look at me without sniggering. I walk around this place like a fucking ghost. I'm like Cathy at the tail end of *Wuthering Heights*.'

Frances is rolling her eyes.

'I just wish Hamish would hurry up and cast another bloody Bill Sikes,' I tell her. 'At least if I could get on with my bit in the sodding play it would take my mind off all this other shit.'

'Your language is getting worse,' Frances smiles.

And then, quite suddenly, her face falls and freezes into a death mask of unequivocal odium.

'Oh, bollocks!' she mutters.

So I spin my head around just in time to catch a glut of fourth-year boys headed towards us, tailgated by a grinning Bob Lord, who is merrily kicking a football along in front of him, and Mr Peacock, who looks utterly inappropriate in a bright-red Adidas tracksuit with a whistle hanging around his neck. The boys themselves just sail past us, but not without one of them, a spotty creature with an erratic bum-fluff moustache, shouting 'Bender!' at me as he does. Mr Lord, however, comes to a sharp halt as he reaches us, and he kicks the ball towards the centre of the pitch, the boys chasing it like puppies. Mr Peacock stops behind him, waving and winking at Frances and me.

'Well, Mr Starr,' Bob Lord smiles. 'Are you happy now, son?'

I look up at him, and Frances grabs my arm as if to stop me saying something I might fast regret.

'Happy, sir?' I say, mirroring his colourless grin. 'What do you mean, sir?'

'I mean, Starr, that we now have a boy – young Maxie Boswell – missing his school and all his friends and his sports because of your selfishness,' Mr Lord says.

'Leave it, Bob,' Mr Peacock interjects softly, but it falls on deaf ears.

'We have a distraught mother and a broken-hearted father, and the reputation of another teacher on the line because of your antics, because you couldn't keep your filthy hands to yourself. And now I don't think he'll be coming back to this school at all, despite what your Mr McClarnon seems to think – I did warn you, Starr.'

'That's not fair, Bob.' Mr Peacock tries again. 'David's not to blame. Now let's get on, shall we?'

But Mr Lord completely ignores him and shakes his head, laughing quietly and smugly. I stand up, slow, to face him and Frances jumps up behind me, still holding my arm protectively.

'You're not a very nice man, are you, Mr Lord,' I say.

'Am I not?' he says, still grinning. 'I think you'll find I just did what was for the best, Starr, despite what you and anyone else might imagine. It's what Jesus would have done.'

I smile and nod in agreement.

'You might be right there, Mr Lord,' I say, sweating slightly but trying desperately not to lose equanimity. '. . . but then look what happened to him.'

And as Bob Lord's face sours to an incensed scowl, Mr Peacock grits his teeth and closes his eyes as if he wishes he might disappear into thin air. Then he blows his whistle loudly to signal the start of the game. Frances and me head back across the field towards the school for our next lessons.

On my way home that evening in the semi-dark, I stop outside the bistro that used to be David Greig's. It's open tonight and I can see the light from the crystal chandeliers bouncing off the emerald tiles.

'You'd know what to do, Grandad,' I say out loud.

But would he? Grandad's answer to almost any problem was to make a hot, sweet cup of tea and pop on a Kathy Kirby record, and I doubt that would help me now. I mean, how am I supposed to keep going back to school to face all this on my own, day after rotten day? Dreaming my way through lessons, dodging Jason and his mob as best I can and, on top of that, Mum and Dad hardly speaking to me when I get home. Even the musical seems ruined now that Maxie can't be in it. It suddenly dawns on me, as I stare at the happy, laughing couples in the bistro, that I'm very, very tired. I need to sleep. I need to go home to bed and sleep. I shan't even bother with *Crossroads* tonight.

When I finally do get off to sleep, I can hear a helicopter, its blades spinning faster and faster, and now I can see it. Agnetha and Anni-Frid are standing beside it in their brilliant-white jumpsuits, beckoning to me with urgency. I have to get on, I'm thinking, I have to get on that helicopter – I can't miss it. But hard as I try, and hard as I run, my bare feet slip and fail on the sodden grass and I don't seem to be getting any closer.

'Wait!' I hear myself calling through the din of the engine, but they're boarding it now, waving sadly at me and closing the door.

'Can't you wait? I've lost my clogs!'

And then it lifts off the ground, swinging gracefully from side to side, then moving up higher . . . faster . . . higher. And then it's gone. Shit.

Twenty

A Slow Fast Train

November 1979

It has not been an especially good day today. For a kick-off, advertising this train as a fast service is possibly one of the great overstatements of the twentieth century. It has lurched unceremoniously to a halt so many times between stations that I firmly believe I could have ridden a pogo stick up the A23, blindfolded, and arrived at my destination more rapidly than this. I also seem to be faced with a jarring fusion of life's unfortunates in this cramped British Rail carriage; a microcosm of hell, one might imagine. An extremely overweight man opposite me is munching his way through his second box of Kentucky Fried Chicken, while his perilously thin female companion is peeling, and nibbling, Dairylea cheese triangles.

'I'm full up!' she announces for the second time in the last ten minutes. He, apparently, isn't.

To my left is a woman in the company of two of the worst-behaved and most putrid-smelling children

I have ever had the misfortune to stumble upon.

'I want my comic,' screeches the snot-covered little boy.

'You're not 'avin' your fuckin' comic,' says the mother, who is wearing a parka with the hood up.

'I want *my* comic an' all!' squeals the little girl, who is porcine and wildly unruly.

'You're not 'avin' *your* fuckin' comic,' says the mother.

I actually want to suggest to 'mum' that she fling these children from the train when it reaches top speed, but I shan't. I also long to recommend that she extinguish her cigarette in this tiny space, before the filthy, matted, fake-fur fringe around her parka hood catches fire and we all go up like a blue light. But of course I don't. Instead, I turn my attention to the ill-advised couture adorning the glaringly evident transsexual in the far corner of the carriage: a skirt in thigh-length puce, with bulky American tan tights and court shoes you could cruise the Med in. I soften slightly though when I consider that, like mine, her chosen path – particularly gender-wise – cannot have been easy with a jaw like Joe Frazier, so I give her a little smile to communicate some sense of kinship or solidarity. She thinks I'm taking the piss, though, and sneers at me maliciously.

No, it is categorically not a good day today.

I put my hand up to my eye and touch it gingerly – Christ, black eyes fucking hurt! I can still feel the ferocious welt on my lip too, taste the blood, and my stomach turns over. I hate violence, and I especially hate it when it's directed at me. How dare he? How dare any of them?

As it happens, I'm running away to Brighton – and why not? There seems to be little to nothing left for me back there in Chesterfield Street, or at the Dog Kennel Road Secondary Modern, or, indeed, at the Lordship Lane Working Men's Club. My parents have all but betrayed me, I'm pretty much certain I've lost Maxie for good, and even Frances Bassey doesn't want to know me any more after today, so it's a done deal. My first port of call will be Hamish McClarnon's flat in Hove. It's like his weekend home, I suppose, and I know exactly where it is because he took Frances and me there once after a school trip, and we had brownies laced with hash and fell about laughing and listening to Linton Kwesi Johnson. He's there now, actually, having taken a day off – backed up with marking – but I'm not entirely sure what I'm going to say to him once I get there. Can I be fearless enough, perhaps, to at last tell someone the truth about what happened last summer? After all, that has reared its ugly head again and led to my getting a good kicking. Could I possibly be brave enough to tell Hamish about what happened . . . today?

The previous twelve hours' events unravel in front of me like a lurid nightmare that did not, could not really have happened. My brain is flickering and blundering around each frightful episode in the day's proceedings, unable to settle on or digest the machinations and consequences of any of them. It did happen though. Today did happen. And it happened like this.

'I don't want to go into school, Moira. How can I? How can I conceivably go in there again, day after hideous, wretched day, with everyone knowing and laughing at me or about me? The teachers, the headmaster and, worse, the other kids? None of them fucking want me there any more, so why should I keep going?'

It was eight thirty on the morning of what was to be the worst day of my life, and Moira was wringing out a J-cloth at the kitchen sink and shaking her head.

'You're gonna 'ave to, love. You're gonna 'ave to keep goin' in, cos it's school and you 'ave to go. You can't hide in 'ere for the rest of your natural, can ya? Feelin' sorry for yourself – upstairs, playin' your LPs: your Abba and your Debbie Harry; sitting there sur-rounded by all your posters. Life's not about that, love. It's about . . . it's about something else other than that, but you've got to go to school and keep on going. If someone's got something to say, then let 'em say it. If someone kicks the shit out of you they'll only do it once. Then they'll get bored.'

Moira attempted to smile benevolently, but her new short-cropped wig afforded her the look of an unyield-ing women's prison guard.

'Oh, great!' I snorted, picking up my blazer and shoving my unfinished Weetabix across the table. 'That's really reassuring, Moira – ta very much! And where's Chrissy? Even she doesn't want to walk to school with me any more. She doesn't want to be seen with me either.'

Moira came over to the table and put a chubby hand on my shoulder.

'Look, Dave, you've been at school for the last few days with everyone knowing and nothin's 'appened yet, has it? You've just got to ride it out. Besides, you've got the musical to look forward to, 'aven't ya? Surely you don't want to let all that bloody 'ard graft go to waste, not to mention all that taffeta your mum used to make your frock.'

'But I'm starting to think he's not coming back, Moira,' I said. 'Maxie, I mean. I think his mum and dad might keep him away for good. And anyway, what use is doing the play without Maxie? And how can I go on stage as Nancy after what's happened? They'll shout things out at me . . . they'll bloody crucify me!'

'They bloody well won't,' she said, and she pulled me close, pressing her breasts up against me absurdly. 'My dad gave me some very sound advice once regardin' ignorant people shouting things at ya. He said to me, "Moira, if you don't want people shouting things at ya, cover your tits up when you walk past the docks." '

And she winked and tickled me under the chin.

'Why did he say that?' I asked.

'He was a pisshead,' Moira said. 'Now get to school with you, you fuckin' drama queen.'

As I reached the kitchen door I stopped in my tracks and turned slowly back. Moira had turned the radio up loud and was singing along to 'Reasons To Be Cheerful'.

'Moira,' I said, but she didn't hear me, so I hollered over the din.

'Moira!'

'What now?'

She swivelled round with a bottle of Squeezy, and looked irritated.

'Haven't you gone yet?'

I looked her square in the face, and I put down my satchel.

'Are you having an affair with Chrissy's Squirrel?' I asked. 'Because if you are . . .'

Moira's almost instantaneous scarlet flush told me that I might have whacked the nail on the head.

'Don't be an arsehole!' was her eventual retort. 'What the fuck makes you think I'd wanna be messing around with a schoolboy? I like my men to be men, darlin'. Who's been tellin' you that, anyway?'

'No one. But I've seen you and him all friendly, and so has Frances – she saw him in your bloody mini-van!'

Moira silently put down the washing-up liquid, and then straightened her wig slightly in the mirror on the kitchen wall.

'I got him some weed, if you must know,' she all but spat.

'Oh!'

'Yes, oh!' Moira said – she was clearly furious. 'Accusing me of all sorts before you know the sodding facts. You wanna sort out your own back alley before you start pokin' around in mine, David Starr!'

'I wasn't accusing,' I shouted in a very high pitched voice. 'I was just asking, and now I know . . . then . . . that's OK.'

'Oh, is it?' Moira laughed acerbically. 'Well, thank you very much, David, I must say. And by the way, I'd like you to keep this quiet, please. I promised Squirrel that I wouldn't tell Chrissy cos she don't like 'im smokin' the stuff, so if you don't mind . . .'

And she stormed back over to the sink, muttering to herself. 'Havin' an affair with Squirrel, for Christ's sake!'

I felt like shit.

'Sorry, Moira,' I mumbled.

Then I gathered up my satchel and trundled off.

I was just dragging myself past the Co-op on my way to school when my employer, Marty Duncombe, shouted at me from across the street.

'Oy! Davey! Davey!'

I wasn't feeling much in the market for his brand of joviality, so I quickened my pace as I shouted back to him.

'What, Marty? I've got to get to school . . . apparently.'

Marty, however, not taking the hint, jogged over the main road towards me in grey track pants and a washed-out burgundy Lacoste shirt.

'I've heard all about your troubles at school an' that, mate. Sorry!' he said, almost genuinely.

'Everyone's heard,' I said with a fixed grin.

'Your dad just needed someone to talk to, I guess,' Marty smiled, popping a Rothman into his mouth and lighting up. 'So he came to me. It can't be easy for him.'

'Can't it?'

I leaned back against the bus stop and Marty held out his cigarette to me, smirking. I snatched it, half laughing, and took a long drag, filling my lungs, and puffing out with a slight cough.

'Didn't know you smoked, Davey boy,' Marty said, also leaning on the bus stop.

'On the odd occasion I do,' I said. 'I might start full-time the way things are panning out lately. Right now though, Marty, I've got to get to school – I'm in enough shit as it is. I'll see you at work tomorrow, eh?'

I passed the cigarette back to him, and he smiled at me with something that for a moment I felt might be approaching compassion.

'Actually,' he said, straightening up and tossing his smoke, 'I've got a bit of a favour to ask you, Davey. The fucking drayman has done his back, so I've got a beer delivery to get down the cellar. You don't fancy comin' over the club and givin' me a hand wiv it, do ya?'

'What, now?'

'Well, you didn't wanna go to school anyway, did ya?' he chuckled playfully. 'Come on, mate, it'll fucking kill me doin' it on me own. It'll take us twenty minutes, tops! And I'll shout you a bacon roll after – how's that sound?'

I stared up at Marty's rather daft, pleading simper. Fuck it, I thought, I didn't have a lesson first period anyway.

'I want extra for this,' I said flatly.

'You'll get it,' Marty said. 'You'll definitely get it.'

'And,' I added, suddenly blessed with a genius idea, 'I need to use the office phone first.'

Marty slapped me on the back, hard.

'Done!'

The club was empty when we got there but for a solitary cleaner who was mopping out the Gents, which was precisely as I'd hoped it would be. While Marty toddled off to converse with the semi-invalided drayman, I tore into the office and grabbed the telephone, dialling Maxie's home number so fast I nearly broke my fucking finger. This was the best thing to do, I told myself. I'd call him at home from the club office where nobody could hear me, and finally get to speak to him properly: tell him how much I love him, tell him how terrible it all is without him, tell him . . .

'Hello.'

When Maxie answered the telephone – after thirteen and a half rings – his tone was dull and wintry.

'Maxie, it's David.'

'Oh!'

'I'm so glad I finally got to speak to you, it's been fucking awful this last week – bloody torture!'

Maxie's silence was unsettling.

'Is somebody there: your mum?'

'No.'

'Well then, can you try and manage more than one syllable?' I laughed. 'I've been absolutely dying to talk to you. They're all trying to stop us from seeing one another, you know, for ever. Your mum and dad, mine

273

. . . all of them. Mr Lord has kicked up such a fucking fuss at school, the evil bastard. Apparently half the teachers in the staffroom aren't even talking to him any more. It's OK though, Maxie, I'm not going to let them fucking scare me off. You don't have to worry about that.'

Maxie was quiet for so long that I wasn't altogether sure if he was still there. Then he mumbled, 'I think it's best . . . don't you?'

'What?' I snapped. 'What do you think is best?'

'Us not seeing each other,' he virtually whispered.

'But . . .'

'I think that when I come back to school I reckon we should just cool it: stay away from one another. My mum is all stressed and broken up with it, so is my dad, and they don't even know the half of it. I don't want them digging any deeper – finding out what happened . . . you know . . . at Moira's place.'

Jesus Christ! What did he mean – finding out what happened? What did he mean – it's for the best? What had happened to my brave, bold Maxie, the boy who threatened to flatten Jason Lancaster and single-handedly take on the National Front? Who was this muttering, gibbering article on the other end of the line?

'But you told Frances that you cared about me,' I said urgently. 'She told me what you said to her.'

'I do care about you, David,' Maxie said, 'but maybe just not in the way you want me to. I told you, mate, it's too much for me, I . . .'

Mate? Had he actually called me mate? There was

silence again for a few unbearably long seconds. Then Maxie said, 'Maybe we can be friends again one day, when this shit has all blown over.'

'Great!' I laughed caustically. 'That sounds absolutely fucking . . . great!'

More silence.

'I'd best go now, David,' he eventually muttered. 'I can see me mum coming up the front path with another tapestry footstool. It's the second this week. I'll see ya.'

And then he was gone. He was actually fucking gone.

As I rolled the final Watney's Bitter keg into its allotted space in the club's cavernous, ill-lit cellar, I was on the brink of tears, and trying to hide it from Marty who was busy whistling 'Ride of the Valkyries'. I felt completely unable to grasp or make any sense of Maxie's abrupt and violent turn away from me. I was an idiot, a sucker, an idealistic, romantic loser who should have spotted this cantering towards me a mile off. How on earth could I have been such a ludicrous love-fool?

'I'm done,' I yelled over at Marty, who was stacking some crates in the other corner. 'Can I go now?'

'Hang on,' he shouted back, so I plonked myself down on a barrel and seethed quietly while Marty finished what he was doing.

OK then! OK! Fuck you, Maxie, I told myself. Fuck you and your cheeky grin, and your football, and your freakishly big penis. I don't need your 'perhaps we can be mates one day' bollocks. You're a gutless tosser and there are plenty of other blokes out there who'll fancy me – other men who will fill my dance card and fall in love with me, gallantly and fearlessly. You wait and see! Then you'll know; then you'll realize and you'll regret what you've done, and you'll want me back again – well, you can just PISS OFF!

Marty, who was by this time sitting on a barrel opposite me, eyed me across the dark cellar.

'What's the matter with you?'

I collected myself as best I could, wiping my face with the sleeve of my shirt.

'Fuck all!' I shouted, and then I began to cry and laugh at the same time. Marty said nothing until I'd hauled myself back together.

'Are you really, truly queer, Davey boy?' he asked finally.

'Bent as a nine-bob note,' I sniffed.

'Huh! Funny. I always thought you were. I know I take the piss sometimes, Davey, but there's nothing wrong with it, you know.'

'Isn't there?' I said. 'You could have fooled me!'

He leaned forward and stared at me in the half-light, and he looked quite sexy in an uncouth sort of a fashion. I actually had thought about Marty in that way on a number of occasions but, to be honest, his personality was so god-awful most of the time that it completely obliterated any appealing qualities he might otherwise have had.

'You're a nice kid,' he said.

'Am I?'

'Well, my Denise loves ya, and you're a sexy little thing as well, ain't ya? Sort of . . . girlish.'

He stood up and sauntered nonchalantly two steps towards me, grinning foolishly.

'Like . . . if you were a bird . . .' he said.

'A parrot?' I quipped, endeavouring to flirt, as I suspected that was where Marty was headed.

'A woman,' he said. 'If you were a woman . . .'

'You'd what?' I whispered, standing up straight to meet his murky stare. 'And what difference would it make to you anyway whether I was a woman or not? A blow job's a blow job isn't it, Marty? That's what you always say.'

And then I laughed, rather too loudly and rather too laboriously.

'I told you I would . . . one day,' Marty smiled with a forged cockiness. Then he took another small but explicit step closer to me.

'Fuck off!' I said quietly, incredulous. 'Told me you'd do what?'

He wouldn't dare. He wouldn't . . .

Marty chanced another move forward, and I felt the backs of my legs come to rest against a Kronenberg barrel. There was a weird, hypnotic lust in his eyes, and it was at this juncture that moderate amusement on my part suddenly morphed into a considerably more potent cocktail of panic and arousal. I was stiffer downstairs than I could ever remember, and I felt ever so slightly like I was going to throw up.

Marty semi-lunged suddenly, kissing me on the mouth and shoving his hand under my shirt. My stomach felt slippery with sweat and Marty's hand glided across it, finding first my chest, then nipples, navel and groin.

'I thought you weren't going to,' I gulped, my mouth against his. 'What was it you said the other week, you'd fuck me but you'd never kiss me – didn't you say that?'

Marty, however, was heedless of any chit-chat; he was well and truly occupied grappling to liberate his dick from his pants with his one free hand, and he appeared to be doing a reasonably good job. In what seemed like no time at all my shirt was open, and pulled around and off my shoulders, then tossed over the salt-and-vinegar-crisp boxes. Marty's jogging pants and underwear were pushed below his knees, and this sudden nakedness and vulnerability made me feel dirty and somewhat appalled.

I giggled slightly and tried to straighten up, but Marty seemed to be guiding me to the ground and, sure enough, in due course I felt the grey chill of the cellar floor against me. Marty was on top of me now – raging hard – and I felt one shoe slip from my foot as his sturdy legs pinned me down. He swallowed nervously and looked down at me, as if he were making quite certain that this was something approaching what I'd wanted. Foolishly I smiled diffidently up at him, perhaps reassuring him that it actually was. I did want it, didn't I? If I couldn't have Maxie then I wanted a man – not a boy like myself, or the other inept fools at school. I tensed against the fingers that were on me, determined to chase away the image of my dad and Marty a few nights before, drinking Jameson's whiskey together at the lock-in at the club, but the picture was going nowhere fast.

'Go on – touch me, Davey,' Marty said, breathing hard into my neck, but his hands were coming at me more roughly and I was abruptly out of my depth.

'That's enough now, isn't it Mart?' I said. 'I'm not sure I really . . .'

Marty was groaning in a slow rhythm now, gripping my wrist so tightly it burned, pulling my hand to him, to where *he* wanted it.

'Marty, you're hurting me a bit . . . I don't want to . . .'

'Shh!' Marty whispered. 'It's all right! Just touch me, mate . . . go on, do it for me, Davey.'

And so I did.

It was the sound of his wife, Denise, singing along to 'Secret Love' and cleaning the ashtrays in the bar upstairs that sent Marty Duncombe over the falls, his semen firing untidily all over my thigh, apart from one solitary athletic spurt that reached my shoulder. I didn't come.

'You dirty little sod,' Marty sniggered conspiratorially, as he got up. 'What would your old man say?'

'What would Denise say?' I answered dourly, dragging myself up from the cellar floor and looking around for my missing shoe.

Marty sniffed and shrugged, yanking up his pants.

'Are you down in that cellar, Marty?' Denise's

279

braying shriek echoed from above us. 'There's a leak in the ladies' lavvy cistern.'

Marty tossed a damp bar towel at me and then rubbed his head vigorously with both hands. He suddenly seemed uncomfortable, couldn't look at me.

'Yeah ... I'm down 'ere, love,' he shouted up through the hatch that led to the bar – he sounded like a little boy. 'I'm just coming.'

'You've just come,' I said.

But I didn't smile, and Marty stared at me for a moment as I picked up my shirt from behind the crisp boxes. Then he said, 'Come on, fly-boy, clean yourself up. You'd better get yourself off to school.'

Twenty-one

Parfait!

The train's just pulling out of Haywards Heath now, and some other unfortunates have boarded: a disconcerting man, who's sitting opposite me and who keeps twitching and laughing out loud at nothing in particular, plus two ceaselessly gossiping middle-aged women in pleated skirts and A-line rain macs who got on at Redhill and haven't come up for air since.

'I got up eight times during the night last night,' the much skinnier of the two women was saying as we passed Three Bridges. 'Had fourteen cups of tea.'

'Ooh!' the other, frizzy-grey-haired one, said. 'All that tannin!'

I must have drifted off after that, but as the train lurches to yet another halt between stations, I've woken with a start and they're still going at it hammer and tongs.

'I said to him,' the skinny and clearly more talkative one is cackling, 'I know what you're gonna say to me, Bob . . . pork chop!'

I glance wearily over at the man opposite me, who twitches three times in succession – and well he might, I think, having to listen to these two idiots. I'm not sure that they're ever going to let up. I decide then and there that I must blot their voices out of my sore, bruised head or go completely insane – one of the two – so I take a crack at gazing out of the window at the leaden skies and let my thoughts drift back to the grisly events of the day again. I would dearly love to say that it had improved after the incident in the cellar with Marty, but that wasn't the case. As I'd stumbled up the steps of the cellar and into the day-lit yard – I couldn't possibly have gone out through the bar and waved cheerily to Denise with her old man's muck all over me as she emptied out the slops trays – I felt giddy, as if I were drunk.

I began to weave slightly along Lordship Lane, like the time Frances Bassey and I had drunk my nan's Southern Comfort from the sideboard and then set off to get saveloy and chips from Elvis's Chip Shop: Frances had, that evening, nearly come a cropper in front of a 185 bus headed for Catford Garage, but I'd grabbed her culottes and yanked her back on the pavement in the nick of time.

As I crossed the road, I feared I might be staring death in the eye myself as traffic whizzed and buzzed around me. I felt entirely unable to navigate my way across: the swish of every passing vehicle became a jet engine, causing me to flinch and start until eventually I just stood solid, like some kind of human traffic island.

'Get out the fuckin' way, you prat,' someone yelled at me from a Mini, and I snapped out of it for a moment and finished crossing, shakily. When I reached the other side of the road I was outside the bistro and I stopped again, only this time in an attempt to pull myself together. I closed my eyes and squeezed my left hand shut, tight, as if I was holding on to my grandad's hand.

'Right! What are we havin' for lunch today?' he'd say. 'Some of that nice cold meat pie with a bit of piccalilli while me and your nan watch the racing? That sounds good, eh, Melksham? And when we've got that, we'll go up the betting shop and you can pick me out a pony in the four forty-five. There's one called Kathy's Clown – named after your mum. P'raps we should put two bob each way on that one, eh?'

Yes, Grandad, let's do that. Please, let's do that.

When I got a bit closer to school I felt no better, as the drunken, woozy sensation was fast replaced by a waterfall of repugnance poured upon me from somewhere above. As I passed the small bit of green that housed the big advertising hoarding, I caught the smell of Marty on me, and I stopped and vomited with as much poise as one might on a busy main road at nine thirty in the morning. There was only a cup of tea and half a sugared Weetabix to behold, but it was abundant and grim nonetheless. I was disgusted, and disgusting. What the fuck had I done? Looking up at the Marlboro man, I took several deep breaths and turned back towards the school, only to discover

Frances tearing towards me in some sort of semi-hysterical flap.

'David! Where the bugger have you been? I've got something to tell you; you're not gonna believe it.'

Oh, Christ, not now, Frances, I thought, please! And I lurched on in the direction of the school gates, barely acknowledging my friend and her overexcited blether.

'You'll never guess in three million yonks what's happened – you won't! Mr McClarnon has given Maxie's part in the play to none other than Jason Lancaster! Jason is playing Bill Sikes – Mr McClarnon says he's got less than a week to learn the part properly, and he has to be on his absolute best behaviour. Can you fucking believe it?'

I looked at her fleetingly, and shrugged. I could believe just about anything.

'Did you hear me, David? Don't you fucking care?' Frances screeched. 'Jason Lancaster! Nazi boy is playing Bill . . . your Bill. He's got to kill you in the second act. It wouldn't surprise me if he did it for real. David!'

I stopped suddenly, whipping my head around.

'What the fuck do I care about the poxy school play now? I don't give a shit: my whole world's falling apart – crumbling around my fucking ears!'

Frances did the West Indian whoop that I'd heard her mother do.

'Lisun to yaself, bwoy!' she mocked. 'Such a feisty likkle drama queen!'

Then, in her regular voice – but fuming and hurt – she said, 'Don't you ever speak like that to me, David

Starr. I've been the one that's been your friend, I've been the one that's—'

'Yeah, Frances, whatever you say, lovey,' I snarled back. 'Now, why don't you run along and be someone else's friend, eh?'

Frances grabbed my arm, pinching it hard through my blazer.

'Well, maybe I should,' she yelled through tears and teeth. 'You obviously don't give a shit that your sister is back with that NF Squirrel freak after what he did to me. All chummy-chummy with him now, are you? Some fucking friend!'

I yanked myself free of her and headed across the playground, saying nothing. When I reached the centre of the playground I suddenly felt dreadful, and I turned to look behind me. Frances had gone.

What actually proved to be the straw that broke the camel's back, as they say, came at the end of second period as I hurried along the corridor on the top floor towards the drama room, in the fraught hope of locating Hamish McClarnon. I had struggled valiantly through my first lesson, but I now felt as though I could not possibly go on for another minute without talking to him. He alone would understand and offer me safe harbour – help me make sense of this morbid twist of events: he'd help me turn it around, help me to find myself again ... help me find a way to get Maxie back. But just a few short yards from my destination, and sanctuary, Jason Lancaster stepped out in front of me, emerging from the boys' washroom like one of Doctor Who's arch-enemies in the final scene of the penultimate episode.

'Hello, my little darlin',' he beamed. 'Have you been avoiding me? I've not seen you around much since you and your little mate got rumbled at parents' evening – what a fucking palaver.'

And then he howled like a dog. I tried to pass him but he stepped efficiently to one side, blocking my path.

''Ang on, 'ang on,' he said. ''Aven't you 'eard the good news? We're gonna be sweethearts; you've been promised to me, darlin'!'

He shook gently with a cocky and nauseating chuckle, and I wanted to grab hold of the ludicrously fat knot in his tie and pull it tight until he turned blue and stopped breathing.

'I might just have to use a real club in the scene where I beat the shit out of you and kill you, though,' he went on, not smiling any more. 'I want it to look realistic. I'm a bit of a method actor, me.'

'Oh, get lost, Lancaster,' I snapped.

And I shoved past him, forging purposefully on towards the door at the end of the hallway; but then, quite suddenly – and I have no idea why the hell I did it – I shouted back at him over my shoulder.

'You'll like that, anyway, won't you?' I called out spitefully and, as it turned out, injudiciously. 'Playing my boyfriend. It'll probably stir some old memories for you: make your cock hard for the first time in a year, eh, Jason?'

The unwelcome note Sellotaped to the small glass

window in the locked drama-room door sent my stomach into freefall.

Mr McClarnon is away till Monday to catch up on some marking. Miss Jibbs will be taking his classes in Room 3g.

Oh Jesus fucking H. Christ!

As I turned and lumbered, slow and zombie-like, back along the corridor, Jason was upon me again, but this time there was no escape. This time he was seething, his face a furious burgundy.

'Don't you ever fucking say shit like that to me again, Starr,' he hollered, punching me full and fast in the face. 'You fucking bent cunt – don't you EVER!' A blow to my belly, felling me like a dry tree, my knees hitting wood with a thud, Jason's finger prodding at my throat.

'You better watch yourself from now on, Starr. One of these days you're gonna turn down the wrong street on the wrong night and get your queer arse raped. I know people. I seen it done.'

A kick in the mouth left me slumped outside the French room, and there ended a delightful morning. *Parfait!*

At long last my train slows into Brighton, and now it is dark. The twitching, laughing man has got off somewhere without me noticing – or perhaps he in fact threw himself from the moving train in despair at the sustained babbling from the two cartoonish middle-aged women who are, of course, still rattling on as we draw into the station.

I grab my Gola bag from the rack above me and

shuffle past them, then stepping off the train and eventually on to a rainy street, I realize that my plan of 'having a little wander' before heading for Mr McClarnon's flat mightn't have been a wise one. It is teeming down, and I'm all confused about directions now it's turned dark. I am also both ravenous and dehydrated, not to mention drained from the day's cataclysmic events and the excessively lengthy and exasperating train journey. And, of course, I'm sporting a singularly unfetching fat lip, courtesy of the lovely Jason. So instead I start to trudge in what I believe is the general direction towards Mr McClarnon's place, face smarting as the fat raindrops slap my war wounds.

I can smell the sea air now, and it takes me back to the beanos we went on with the club when I was a kid: a coachload of us there'd be – all the grown-ups drinking and singing and telling filthy jokes along the way to whichever seaside town we were about to invade. We'd actually come here to Brighton a fair few times – it would be of a Sunday or a bank holiday – and my grandad would take me on the rides along the pier and on the front. Mum and Aunt Val were always dressed up really nice, and they'd take Chrissy and me to buy chips while Dad and his mates played on the machines in the arcade. Then, if we behaved, and it was warm enough, we'd sit and eat our chips on the beach and then we'd go for a paddle, with Nan and Grandad holding Chrissy's hand cos she was scared of the waves.

There was never any rain then, I don't think, or at

least there hadn't seemed to be, looking back – I think it was always sunny. Different today. When we'd go back home on the coach, there'd be a gang of us kids who would all sit together on the back seat, singing along to my tape recorder and the songs I'd recorded off the Top Twenty on a Sunday evening: The Sweet, Gary Glitter or The Bay City Rollers. How the weather's changed now.

I turn, utterly drenched, into another street, and as I walk I attempt to map out in my mind how I'm going to lay this all out to Hamish when I get there – all this new stuff, and the old; where I'm going to actually start with it all. But the more I think about it, the more mixed up and disorderly it all becomes in my head, so I just give up and plough forward up a rather steep and unfamiliar street, and wonder what on earth Hamish will say when he sees me at his front door. I can't smell the sea any more.

Twenty-two

Spilling the Beans

'Are you shittin' me wi' this?' is what Hamish actually says as he swings open his apartment door, dressed in what I would, in all probability, describe as a polyester-knit muumuu. 'What the hell are ye doin' here, David? And what in God's name have ye done te ye face?'

I step boldly through the door and into the hall.

'It's all over for me there,' I say, affording him my very best Sarah Bernhardt: lifting up my bruised chin and closing my eyes. 'Those people are dead to me now.'

When I open my eyes again, Hamish is glowering at me, his brow furrowed in several profound trenches.

'Do your parents know you're here?'

He ushers me further into the hallway and then straight up the stairs.

'It's eight o'clock at night, will they not be expecting you for ye tea?'

'I wanted to get some food when I got to Brighton,

but I hadn't really got enough money,' I blurt breathlessly, reaching the top of the stairs and stepping into the small living room to the right of me. 'And then I got lost. I thought you lived over a betting shop, sir, but I couldn't find it.'

'Bookies has closed ages back,' Hamish says, relieving me of my bomber jacket and then shaking the rain off it and hanging it over the partly open door. 'It's a hairdresser's now. And don't call me sir outside school – it's Hamish.'

'Well, I knocked on about fourteen doors, Hamish,' I laugh, flopping down on to a beanbag. 'Then I finally found you.'

'Yes . . . you have, and what I want te know is, why? Why are ye here, David?'

Hamish is peering at me hard, and I'm still not sure quite how to begin.

'Well, let me get ye somethin' te drink, anyway,' he says. 'A glass o' Sainsbury's red do ya, will it?'

And he finally smiles, cracking his frown.

'It will,' I say.

Hamish trots off to the kitchen and I sink into my beanbag, contemplating the lyric to 'Sing If You're Glad To Be Gay', which is currently playing on the stereo, and perusing the posters of Che Guevara and Barbara Cook on the wall above the undersized dining table. A poster heralding the opening of a 1971 university production of Bertolt Brecht's *Life of Galileo* takes pride of place above the comfy-looking but down-at-heel sofa; directed by Hamish McClarnon, it affirms modestly at the bottom. The room is lit with a soft, orange-coloured bulb and a couple of orange candles, and it feels warm and out of harm's reach. When Hamish reappears, he is carrying two plates of spaghetti bolognese and two large tumblers of red wine on a tray.

'Here, ye said ye was hungry. I made it maself.'

'Thanks, I'm really starving!'

And I eat quickly and greedily, nourishing and refuelling my drained carcass, preparing to impart to Mr McClarnon every last thought and feeling – the whole confused cauldron – everything, in fact, about my eventful and desolately putrid day . . . and perhaps even more besides . . . perhaps . . . Oh, what the hell, here goes . . .

One of the orange candles has burned almost completely down, and Hamish is looking at me from the sofa with a strange otherworldly gaze as I conclude my heart-rending diatribe. He lifts his glass slowly to his mouth and sips at his wine, then he rests it on the low, dark-wood coffee table.

'This Marty character: he could be in a lot of trouble if this came out. He could go te prison for that, ye know. You're well under twenty-one and he's . . .'

'Twenty-seven,' I whisper.

'Is that what you want?' Hamish says softly.

'What?'

'Do ye want to report this, or tell ye parents?'

'No!' I say, suddenly shocked at the implication. 'I don't want that, sir – I mean Hamish. Marty's an idiot, but it wasn't his entire fault. I did kind of fancy him, and he didn't exactly force me. If I'd wanted to stop I could have . . . I guess.'

'You don't sound so positive,' Hamish says. 'And anyway, he should know better, David; he's an adult. Mind you, what am I goin' on about? Think of the deep crevice o' crap I'd be in if the school found out I'd been encouragin' the two o' you – Maxie and yourself – in a relationship of the sort you've been havin': two barely sixteen-year-old boys, for Christ's sake – ma pupils. It doesn't even bear thinkin' about. I guess we should all know better.'

'No!' I shout, jumping up from the beanbag and slopping red wine everywhere. 'It's *them* that should know better – everyone else! Fucking hell, Hamish! Half the boys in my class are shagging their girlfriends but no one gives a shit about that. No one bleats on about corruption or innocent boys not knowing their own mind then, do they? No, they get a pat on the back from their dads while people like me get sent to a fucking shrink.'

Hamish is nodding.

'It would be funny if it weren't so sick,' he says. 'But at your age the law isn't on your side, pet. It just isn't.'

'I don't want to report Marty, anyway,' I say, sitting back down. 'I don't care about Marty. I don't care two fucks about Marty. I only care about Maxie . . . and Frances too. I've been such a cunt to her.'

Hamish pours me another half-glass of wine.

'Yes, well, that's a very sexist term, David, appropriate though it may sometimes feel, so can we not use that particular word?'

'Sorry!'

'You'll make it up with Frances,' he says. 'That's the easy part, but what about Jason Lancaster? What te do wi' him?' He looks sickened as he speaks. 'I thought that boy was turnin' over a new leaf – he promised me he was – hence me givin' him the part in the play. Surely we have te do somethin' about that. I'll not have that sort of anti-gay violent shit go on in any school I teach at.'

'I'd rather you just let that go too, Hamish,' I say, looking down. 'Really I would.'

Hamish looks bewildered, and he shrugs and holds out his hands like a comedy Jewish mother.

'But why? Why leave it? And why does the boy hate ye so much?'

I let out a small but sufficiently ironic chortle, and I smile at Hamish over the glow of the remaining candle.

'It's not me he hates, Hamish,' I say, 'it's himself. When he looks at me – batty boy David Starr – he sees himself, sees what he might well turn out to be.'

'Go on,' Hamish says, intrigued and leaning forward.

And so at long, long last I spill the beans.

On a winter's evening the previous year, when my mother and father were ensconced at the Lordship Lane Working Men's Club, I'd answered a knock at our back gate. It was reasonably dark, and when I drew back the big bolt and peered outside I was some-what taken aback to discover Jason Lancaster there, grinning and apprehensive, that immorally beautiful face lustrous and cherry-red.

'I need a favour, Starr,' he'd snapped austerely, shoving his way into the alley that led to our back garden, and I fell back against the wall with the force of him.

'A favour?'

I was on full alert. What on earth could Jason possibly want from me? He barely spoke to me unless it was to communicate some sort of slur or abuse. This was just weird!

Jason continued softly, but with exigency. 'Remember when you snogged Sonia Barker outside the mini-mart a couple of months back?' he said.

I did remember – how could I not? It had been the day after my fifteenth birthday, and long before love, and Maxie, and coming out. There'd been a group of us, including Jason, and I'd been dared and goaded into kissing a girl, namely Sonia (who, though re-nowned for putting it about, was not one of the world's top beauties) for a full minute – with tongues.

'Go on, prove you're not a queer,' Jason had said at the time. 'Kiss her, and stick your finger inside her knickers – 'ave a good feel.'

My sister Chrissy and Abigail Henson had also been present, and I remember, even then, Abigail suggest-ing that it be *her* I snogged and not Sonia, who according to Abigail had communicable mouth ulcers and terribly grubby fingernails, which, she felt, put the girl out of the running. But Jason had insisted.

'No, it 'as to be Sonia.'

And as Sonia herself didn't really seem to have any sort of chunter about the proposal at hand, then Sonia it was. I must confess that I didn't, for the most part, enjoy it, but after I'd politely enquired what was in it for me, it turned out there was a yellow vinyl copy of Blondie's 'Picture This' up for grabs, and an opportunity, at least, I supposed, to institute some impression of masculinity amongst my peers, which at the time seemed de rigueur. Frances Bassey, also present, had subsequently described the whole incident as freakish beyond credence, but there it was.

'Yes, Jason, I remember kissing Sonia. What about it?' I enquired, justly cautious, as he leaned against our fence.

Jason's cigarette glowed as he drew on it nervously, allowing me a fleeting shufti of coffee eyes and sandy, close-shaved hair.

'You looked like you knew what you was doing,' he said.

'Did I?'

He nodded slowly, and then he looked me up and down as if I might be something from another world.

'I need you to show me how to do it properly, Starr,' he said.

'What?'

'I'm taking Sonia ice-skating tomorrow and she's dead experienced, ain't she? And she said you were an all right kisser, and I don't wanna look a twat, do I? I mean . . . I don't . . . I haven't ever . . . I haven't really ever . . .'

Jason trailed off as I frantically tried to absorb and collate the connotations of his proposition and, indeed, ascertain what precisely he was asking of me.

'You want us to kiss?' I finally suggested uneasily, hoping against hope that he wasn't about to smash me in the face. 'You want me to give you some sort of tonsil-hockey tutorial?'

He blinked at me, twice. I said, 'Is this a joke?'

'If you fucking tell anyone, I'll break your arms,' Jason said.

And with very little further ado, he dropped his cigarette and moved so perilously close to me that there was nothing to do *but* kiss him. I did it fast – because I thought I might faint if I didn't – and I had no clue at the time why I wanted to kiss him anyway – he was a boy, for God's sake – but I did . . . I really did. I stumbled upon his mouth: it was hot and sweet, and eager. I felt somewhat confused because he smelled and tasted like something I'd been waiting for, and there was none of the expected inelegance in his kiss: it was tender, no fumbling. Jason sent his hands over my back until he held me firm – kissed me deep. In turn, I slipped my arms under the back of his blazer and shirt and on to his warm skin, pulling him closer. He let out a tiny gasp. And we kissed, and we kissed, and I felt . . . significant.

I remember my cheeks on that chilly evening, damp with tears by the time the penny dropped, by the time it had all fallen, finally, into place. A lifetime's conundrum packed with years of random sensations, emotions and events suddenly unravelled to reveal a blindingly flawless truth. Yes – Billy Blue from *The High Chaparral* who always gave me butterflies; the lads, wet from swimming; my Aunt Val shouting out from the landing, 'David, are you wearin' my bleedin' amber necklace again?' Even my grandad's Kathy Kirby LPs seemed to make perfect sense at last. Turns out I hadn't wanted to fuck Lindsay Wagner after all – I'd just wanted to be The Bionic Woman. It was all there, really, plain as day – aligned with that moment, and that kiss: a true and bona fide awakening, if you will. As I held Jason in my arms against the bricks of our alleyway, I thought about this revelation, what it might mean, and I resolved then and there to lock it tightly away in the box whence it came, terrified in the knowledge that sooner rather than later the box would almost certainly come flying open again, sending its volatile and clandestine contents tumbling about me for all humanity to witness. And I wasn't ready for that. Not then.

'I think I'll be able to handle Sonia Barker now,' Jason had smiled afterwards, pausing superciliously before a parting consideration. 'And there really is no point in blabbing, cos no one would believe you, Starr, you know that, don't you. I matter at school, you see. You don't matter at all.'

'He never really spoke to me again,' I tell Hamish forlornly. 'Unless you count bender or shirt-lifter.'

Hamish's mouth is wide open.

'And so you knew then?' he said, and I nodded.

'When I first saw Maxie that day in the hall,' I said, 'it just sort of compounded it, I suppose. I thought I was confused, but I really already knew. I knew thanks to Jason bloody Lancaster, and that is why he hates me so much – because of one stupid kiss, and Jason said I didn't matter anyway, so I . . .'

There's suddenly an awful lot going on in my head and, though I try to foil them, I can feel tears falling, unexpectedly, unwanted and swift.

'If you don't mind, Hamish,' I say through soft sobs, 'I'd rather not unearth any of this stuff. I can deal with a couple of bruises and a fat lip – I just want to forget it all.'

'Oh, David!' Hamish says quietly. 'You do matter, you know. You matter very much; don't ever let anyone tell you that you don't. Just remember – the rest of the world's wrong and we're right, OK?'

I'm nodding.

'I must say,' he laughs gently, 'I wasn't expecting all this tonight, but I'm glad ye finally got it off ye chest. Now, have a wee drop o' wine and I'll fetch ye a Kleenex . . . man-size.'

I throw back what's left in my glass like a bar-room connoisseur, and suddenly I feel like someone has lifted a small rhinoceros from the top of my head. Hamish is back and holding out a tissue with one hand and the telephone receiver with the other.

'Who am I calling?' I ask, knowing the answer.

'You're calling your parents to tell them where ye are; then tomorrow I'm drivin' ye back te London. We've got a show te put on.'

'OK!'

'And then,' Hamish says, rubbing his hands together excitedly, 'we're gonna stay up late and watch some Bette Davis on BBC2 – have you seen any Bette Davis films, David?'

'I don't think so, no.'

'Och! Well, you're in for a real treat. It's a double bill: *All About Eve* and *The Man Who Came to Dinner*. She's the greatest actress that's ever lived, David. I think you're gonna love her!'

'Cool!' I smile, and I feel genuinely brighter. I mean, let's face it, if Hamish McClarnon can be as wise and as brilliant a gay man as he clearly is, and manage to promenade through life having a damn good time – then so can bloody well I!

'Oh, and one more thing, David?' Hamish says.

He is smiling mischievously as I gather myself and dial home.

'What, Hamish?'

'Do you know how te roll a decent joint?'

I'm seated beneath a hairdryer in a 1960s-style hair salon full of middle-aged women and pensioners with hair rinses of blue, emerald and mauve. Most are reading magazines, and a couple of them are sipping hot beverages. There is a ghostly carpet of dry ice covering every inch of the floor. As I lean forward in my chair and look to my right, there seems to be an unending line of hairdryer-adorned ladies, all cross-legged, and all reading the same issue of *Woman's Realm*, and I can hear the eerie sound of organ chords along with the thumping heartbeat of tom-toms coming from nowhere in particular. Anyway, sitting next to me on my left is Debbie Harry, which hardly surprises me any more, to be honest. She flips up the front of her hairdryer, emerging with a huge magenta beehive and a dress made completely from mirrors, which, when the light hits it, blinds me completely, causing me to recoil violently and squint.

'Hello, David!' Debbie says, stretching her hand out regally, like some sort of half-barmy fuchsia-crowned empress.

'Hello again!' I say.

'You did good, David,' she says, pointing at me. 'Real good: got all that shit outta there, and now you can move on with your life.'

'I guess!' I shout over the noise of the hairdryers and the music, which I now recognize as the intro to 'Fade Away And Radiate'. 'I guess I did good.'

'Listen, there will be other boys, other times: trust me. You got a whole lot of life to live, baby; now get out there and live it.'

I pull up the front of my dryer and stand up as the tom-toms thump still, tall and proud amongst the billowing dry ice, gazing into the baroque gold mirror in front of me. My hair is a gargantuan, aquamarine, Jackie O, ratted and flipped bob. Turning slowly to Debbie, I ask, 'With this hair?'

Twenty-three

Pod People

It was a bit like a fucking madhouse today at twenty-two Chesterfield Street, especially given it was a Sunday and I'm quite thankful to have got out of there alive and come to work at the club. Yes, I have actually come to work behind the bar at the Lordship Lane Working Men's Club tonight, and I've looked Marty Duncombe in the eye and smiled very sweetly, and I've said absolutely nothing. He did turn a peculiar salmony colour when I saw him, it has to be said, and he didn't say very much, but then again it was only the day before yesterday that he was proudly standing in front of me with his trousers round his ankles in the beer cellar. I suppose I never really expected him to acknowledge the event, to be honest, and although the entire state of affairs is all a bit fucking weird, it *has* been that sort of day. I mean, for a start I'm fairly certain that my mum, and in particular my dad, have been replaced during the night by people or beings that look and sound very much like they do, but aren't them! You know, like *Invasion of the Body Snatchers* – pod people, I think one would call them.

During the last few weeks Kath has been very offish with me indeed – ever since parents' evening – and that's been painful, to be frank, because when the chips are down – and let's face it, my chips have been well and truly down – a boy needs his mother. She's not been mean, no, or especially angry – not at all – but our banter had disappeared, and her soft smile and swift wit had vanished along with it. I'd missed her. When I'd phoned her from Hamish's late on Friday night after to all intents and purposes running away from home, you'd have thought she might have been somewhat distraught, but she was actually terribly cross with me.

'What do you mean you're in Brighton?' she said. 'How the bloody 'ell did you get there? Eddie, did you hear that, this little sod's in Brighton! Well, you can come straight home tomorrow, son, do you hear? I'm not sure how many more surprises I can take off you, David. It's been one thing after another lately . . .'

Et cetera, et cetera . . .

Today, though – and this is what I mean about pod people – she breezed in from somewhere or other with a huge plastic Arding & Hobbs bag and swooped towards me, beaming a smile.

'Guess what's in here?' she cooed, as I leafed through my *Smash Hits*.

'Well, I don't imagine for one minute it's the Crown jewels, Mother,' I'd said, 'but apart from that, I'm at a loss.'

'It's your First Act dress,' she said excitedly.

'Nancy's First Act dress – all finished for the dress rehearsal this week.'

'Oh!'

She ceremoniously peeled it out of the bag, and I must say it was magnificent: emerald cheesecloth with a laced bodice in lemon satin.

'And look at the eyelet detail around the bust,' Mum whooped. 'I'm a genius!'

She held it up against me, and then she gave me a little hug. After she'd pulled away from me, she suddenly surged forth again and hugged me once more, this time more tightly, with her face against mine, and she wouldn't let me go.

'I don't want you to run away,' she said in a whisper. 'I never want that.'

Before I knew it, Eddie – who'd been down the road at my nan's demolishing the old outside lavvy – had appeared at the kitchen door in filthy overalls, and it was the first time I'd clocked his face in weeks without 'murder' written across it.

'Sit down at the table, David,' he said seriously and without warning. 'You an' all, Kath.'

And so we obeyed expectantly, Mum draping the dress over the back of one of the kitchen chairs. Dad sat down in between Mum and me, his hair covered in what looked like brick dust, and he clearly had something of great magnitude to impart as he was fiddling madly with the sovereign ring on his finger, and perspiring slightly.

'Right,' he said, over the distant clatter of Moira rejigging the shoe cupboard in the hall. 'I've got sommin' to say.'

Mum and me afforded one another quick sideways glances and then looked back at Eddie, who was rapping on the glass top of the table anxiously.

'David, in the last couple of weeks you've stolen money off me, played hooky from school, stayed out half the night and then run away to Christ knows where, and come home 'ere Saturday morning lookin' like you've just done ten rounds with Henry Cooper.'

'Dad, I'm really—'

'Wait!' Eddie said. 'Now, I'm not 'appy about any of this, and I don't really understand what the fuck it is you're goin' through, or why it is you've chosen the path you seem to 'ave chosen, but you have to promise us, and I mean promise us, son, that you won't do a runner like that again – whatever 'appens.'

They both fixed stares on me then, and I shuffled fretfully in my chair.

'I won't.'

Then Eddie let out a chuckle, but it was a vague, faraway chuckle, and he said, 'When you phoned us Friday night from Brighton, Dave . . . I hadn't even noticed you weren't here. I hadn't even noticed that me own son was missing, for fuck's sake.'

'We hadn't,' Mum said, and she looked down. 'I felt terrible.'

'Oh.'

With some hesitancy, Eddie lifted up a dust-caked hand and touched my face, which was now spectacularly black and blue, and he tutted and shook his head.

'You come to your mum and me from now on,' he said. 'Do you 'ear? It doesn't matter what it is, you come to us.'

Then he put his hand on my arm. I wasn't used to him actually touching me.

'I don't really understand all this gay stuff: gay pride, whatever, I don't fucking know. When I was a teenager if you were a queer you were a queer and that was that. And there was some decent ones an' all, don't get me wrong, and some hard nuts too. Reggie Kray, apparently: he was one. Anyway, you're basically a good kid, David, and that's the main thing. And no little bastard thug is gonna do this to my boy again, whatever he is.'

And I sat there in a stunned sort of quiet, the pair of them staring at me peculiarly, Mum nodding and smiling. Then they both got up and went about the rest of their afternoon as if nothing had been said. Pod people, I tell you!

At around four thirty there were more fun and games to be had when the doorbell went and I galloped down the stairs to answer it, thinking, nay hoping, it might be Frances – I'd left three ludicrously repentant messages for her with her mother, which seemed to have fallen on deaf ears – but it wasn't her at all, it was the bloody police.

'Oh, hello!' I said, taking in the two men on the porch, one in uniform and the other not.

'Can I help you?'

The plain-clothed and taller of the two men was

reedy with bulging eyes, and didn't look especially jovial.

'Might I find Miss Moira Doyle here?' he enquired politely, and I nodded.

'You might,' I said. 'Why, what's she done?'

And I actually started to giggle.

'Can we come in?' the one in uniform said affably. He was actually very handsome, with a lovely square jaw and sandy five o'clock shadow.

'Yes,' I said, now ever so slightly alarmed. 'Come in.'

And into the passage they came, stopping halfway down it outside the lounge door. Mum and Dad were on the scene in seconds – they'd been upstairs having one of their Sunday afternoon 'lie-downs', and Dad could evidently spot a copper's voice from two floors up.

'What's the matter, mate?' he said to the nice-looking one.

'He's looking for Moira,' I announced. 'She was in the shoe cupboard earlier.'

'Hiding, was she?' the taller policeman barked.

'No,' Mum said, buttoning up her blouse, 'pairing up the flip-flops. Why?'

Then Moira herself materialized from the lounge with a chamois leather, her eyes narrowed, cheeks ablaze with colour, and she stood with her hands defiantly on her hips and tossed her head back, sending her wig slightly skew-whiff.

'I'm Moira Doyle,' she said.

'Yes, I'm fully alert to that fact,' the taller man smiled smugly. 'And what are you doing at this particular address?'

'I'm cleaning,' she said flatly. 'I'm the cleaner.'

'Of a Sunday?' the man said. 'That's a tad out-landish, isn't it?'

Moira stepped forward and Eddie flanked her like a bodyguard.

'I can't do me shift tomorrow like I usually do,' Moira sneered at the man. 'I've got some other business to attend to.'

'Like what?' the handsome copper said softly.

'Dentist,' Moira spat, and then she apparently noticed his strong jaw, and the chunky bulge in his trousers that I, too, had made a mental note of only seconds earlier.

'Dentist,' she said again, only this time in a voice that sounded as though it might have come from Marilyn Monroe's slightly more slutty auntie.

'Dentist, is it, love?' the tall policeman said, chuckling. 'Not selling speed outside Dog Kennel Road School like you were seen doing twice last week, then?'

'What?'

My mother's voice almost burst my eardrum.

'Don't be so fuckin' ridiculous, she's our cleaner!'

'You got any proof?' Eddie demanded.

But Moira just stood there with her mouth wide open, and the next thing you know it was 'You have the right to remain silent' and 'Would you mind popping on these handcuffs, please, love?'

Out-and-out pandemonium ensued next. Chrissy burst through the porch door, barely able to breathe and in buckets of tears, announcing that pretty much the same fate had befallen Squirrel at the bottom of our road just now as they walked home from the Wimpy. The tall policeman nodded gravely, as if he might know something about this, and then he and his much sexier counterpart led a dazed Moira out of our front door in handcuffs.

'What are you talking about?' Mum was screeching over Chrissy's ear-splitting and inconsolable lament. 'I can't understand what you're saying, Chrissy, calm down!'

But she was plainly hysterical, so I slapped her like they do on *Crossroads*, and that seemed to do the trick.

'What do you mean, Squirrel's been arrested?' Mum asked confusedly, while Chrissy held her hand up to her cheek in a sudden, stunned silence. 'Moira's been arrested an' all – what's goin' on? Is everybody being arrested?'

I watched as Dad chased Benny Hill-style after Moira and the two policemen down the front path, and then I turned back to Chrissy, who had slid down the passage wall and was slumped hopelessly on the floor at the bottom of the stairs. Mum knelt down next to her and brushed the sweaty hair out of her mascara-smeared eyes, and then Chrissy began to cry all over again, her sobs soft and sharp.

'He's been nicked, Mum,' she said. 'He's been selling drugs, him and Moira – outside schools, for fuck's sake!'

'No!'

'Yes!' I hollered. 'It all makes sense now – I knew there was something funny going on with them two. Fuck me! Why didn't I figure it out?'

To be honest I think I was just thrilled and relieved to have another drama taking some of the attention away from me!

'What do you mean, selling drugs with Moira?'

Mum is completely incredulous.

'I didn't know they even bloody knew one another.'

'They used to live on the same estate,' Chrissy sniffed. 'That's all I fucking know.'

Mum put her hand up to her mouth in utter disbelief, and then she closed her eyes and shook her head slowly.

'Oh, Chrissy! Christ al-bastard-mighty,' she said. 'Are you tellin' me that our cleaner's actually been dealing drugs to kids? D'you know – I knew I should 'ave gone to an agency.'

I sat down beside Chrissy and put my arm around her, drawing her to me – it was the brotherly thing to do, I felt.

'I knew he was bad news, love,' I said as compassionately as I possibly could, but she turned on me like a snake.

'Oh, fuck off, you!' she spat at me. 'What the fuck do you care, anyway? You think everything's about you, you do – you make me sick!'

And she screamed the word 'sick' so loudly, and banged the floor so hard, that Mum's Elvis clock came away from the wall above us and smashed against the stair banister.

By the time Eddie arrives at the club tonight I'm busy bottling up, and he virtually falls against the snug bar. He looks done in.

'Give me a Scotch, Davey, for fuck's sake,' he says, rolling his eyes to the heavens.

Marty and Denise come tearing out of the office when they hear his voice.

'Jesus Christ, mate,' Marty says. 'You look bloody awful.'

He does as well. Still in his overalls, and now filthy with the sweat-smeared brick dust of my nan's partially demolished outside khazi, Dad looks fit to drop.

'I've been at the fuckin' cop shop all afternoon trying to find out what's goin' on with Moira and get 'er a solicitor,' he says.

'Oh, I know, Davey told us,' Denise says, relieving Dad of his already empty whisky glass and refilling it with a double. 'What *is* going on with her? Did she do it?'

She was relishing the scandal of it.

'Looks like it,' Dad says, defeated. 'I managed to get five minutes with Squirrel – silly little bastard – and he came clean to me and his mum about what they'd been up to – cried his eyes out.'

'Your Chrissy's fella?' Marty says, surprised. 'I always thought he was a lovely little chap.'

Yes, I bet you did, Marty.

'What's gonna happen to them, Dad?' I say. 'Will they go to prison?'

'I don't know, David, do I?' he says, wiping dust away from his mouth before he downs another drink. 'Squirrel's only fifteen, so they might go easier on him, but Moira's been providin' him with bloody pills to sell to his mates – boys at your school, especially. Christ knows where she's been getting 'em from. She says they're fuckin' slimming pills.'

Then he leans on the bar and puts his dirty face into his even dirtier hands.

'What a bloody weekend,' he sighs. 'Get me another Scotch will ya, Denise?'

What a very strange day it's been.

The club is extra quiet tonight, probably after all the frenzied excitement of last night's darts trophy presentation dinner dance, and after it's all cleared out at a quarter to eleven Eddie is still here, propping up the bar. He's at least washed his face now, but twelve or thirteen whiskies along, he's not looking too clever; in fact, it's a wonder he's still standing.

'Have you eaten, Dad?' I ask him.

'Nah!' he mumbles. 'I'm not 'ungry: I'll 'ave another drink, though.'

Marty has also been knocking them back, and he's standing next to Dad on the other side of the bar with his red tracksuit top unzipped to the waist, showing off his neat, hairy chest. The two of them have been getting right up my nose for the last hour – putting the world to rights, as they saw it: what a marvellous bloody job Mrs Thatcher is doing, and what was the point of women being liberated when they spent most of their free time looking through catalogues at saucepans. It was only a matter of time, it seemed, before Dad drunkenly trotted out the subject of my sexuality, and as I furnish him with his umpteenth whisky of the night, he grabs my wrist and turns to Marty, pie-eyed.

'I don't care if my boy *is* gay, Marty,' he slurs. 'It don't make no fuckin' difference to me, mate, I've seen it all before.'

Oh God, no!

'I was inside for receiving stolen goods, ye know, Marty – four months,' Dad shouts, pointing at Marty, and then falling forward against him.

'I know you was, mate,' an equally pissed Marty says. 'I know!'

'You see all fuckin' sorts in there, mate – trust me – all sorts.'

'I'll bet,' Marty says, swaying. 'I bet you fuckin' do!'

'You never know what two geezers will get up to when there's not a bird around for months on end,' Eddie says, and I watch as Marty's jaw drops farcically.

'I'm tellin' ya!' Dad says.

I laugh out loud as I wipe down the bar, wondering if anyone I'd ever clapped eyes on was truly and completely straight, and then I turn to Marty, who is looking on in quiet terror. So I wink at him and pour myself a double Baileys.

On the way home from the club I feel a little bit otherworldly as I pass the Co-op, and I'm not really sure whether I'm experiencing the end of something or the beginning of it. It's as if the whole world has changed again in one single weekend. Tomorrow, for sure, I would have to face up to school and all the bloody work I've missed, and Frances, and to Mr Lord and Jason Lancaster, and, perhaps scariest of all, to myself. I'm not sure how I feel about that. I suppose, looking at it one way, at least I don't really need to be afraid of Jason any more, do I? And Mr Lord has done his worst now, surely. In fact, after parents' evening, everyone in the entire school knows full well I'm a fucking fairy, so what else is there to say or do about it? Perhaps that's what's scaring me, though. Perhaps now all the exhilarating drama of it is played out I just have to get on with it.

Hamish had informed me that Maxie would almost certainly be making an appearance at school to-morrow, and that's unsettling me too, after the things he'd said to me on the phone when we last spoke. I mean, how will he be with me now? He might hate me for ruining his life, but I didn't mean to, did I? I suppose that's something else I'll have to live with. What was far more crucial to me, immediately, was making up with Frances tomorrow, and being the most fabulous Nancy that I could possibly be in the musical next week – not to mention getting through the rest of the school year without getting the shit kicked out of me every other day.

The eleven o'clock Sunday streets are reasonably hushed, and it's nippy, so people are not hanging about outside the pubs like they tend to in the summer; but as I cross the road by the bus stop I spot Chrissy and Abigail Henson outside the bistro, so I head over. Chrissy's got her pork-pie hat on, and the brand-new grey Crombie overcoat that Squirrel bought her last week – quite possibly with his cut of the filthy lucre – and she's puffing on a fag as per; but she smiles at me, which is a good sign, and then she offers me one.

'Ta,' I say, accepting the nicotine-laced olive branch.

'All right,' she says and then she smiles.

'You know, Grandad used to bring me here every Saturday when this was David Greig's,' I say, leaning back on the dark window.

She nods and smiles.

'I know, I remember. He was mad about you.'

She looks at me for a moment with a softness I'd forgotten she even had, and I say, 'What are you two doing out here this late, anyway?'

'Filling Abi in on my fuckin' nutcase drug-dealer of a boyfriend,' Chrissy says, taking a deep drag on her ciggie.

'I'm sorry,' I tell her. And I was.

'It's all right,' she says, exhaling smoke. 'What with that and the NF connections, he wasn't much of a catch, was he? His cock was a bit on the small side, to be honest, as well – that's why I wasn't that fussed giving up me cherry.'

'Well, there you are, then,' I chuckle.

We stand quiet for a minute, and then I say, 'There's loads of blokes I know fancy you, anyway, Chris – you too, Abigail.'

'Are there?' Abigail jumps in.

As usual, she's practically nothing on to speak of, even in virtual sub-zero temperatures, and she's halfway through a bag of sauce-slathered chips from the Wimpy.

'Yes! Boys at my school,' I say. 'They'd go nuts for you. I told you, you look like Debbie Harry in the right light.'

'A coal cellar?' Chrissy says, and we all laugh.

Then I have a flash of inspiration.

'Why don't you come and see me in the play next week, Abi,' I suggest. 'As my personal guest. I'll introduce you to some boys with twinkly eyes and big dicks.'

Abigail screams.

'How do you know which ones have got big dicks, David Starr?'

And I give her a wink.

'I've been checking them out in the showers for years,' I say.

Twenty-four

Becoming Nancy

I'm fairly convinced that I've applied far too much of the Twilight Blush panstick and that I should have plumped for the Nouveau Beige, or, perhaps, Forever Porcelain, but then again I am supposed to be a whore, so one assumes that one would pile on the make-up, doesn't one? I'm not altogether sure, either, that they'd actually refined, or even invented, eyeshadow with glitter in back then, or, indeed, any eyeshadow at all; and my wig's slightly frizzier than I'd have liked, but it's a look, I suppose, come what may. Stepping back, and taking in the full picture, I reckon I'd be a dead ringer for Marsha Hunt if it weren't for the ringlets and the pox scab, and I do feel very strongly that given some of the other poor showings, costume-wise, mine is nothing short of a small triumph. Behind me in the mirror, out of the corner of my heavily made-up eye, I catch Maxie looking at me piteously as he dashes across the dressing room – well, school library, actually – with Mr Sowerberry's staff and a bunch of

Fagin's handkerchiefs, and I flinch all of a sudden and want to turn around. I won't, though: I couldn't stand to look in those guilty hazel eyes – not for a single second; and as it's been two weeks or so since we've even spoken, managing somehow to wholly evade one another during the last few days of play rehearsals, there's no point. It's very painful, no denying. But what else can one do?

'Oh my God – you are an absolute freak!' Frances Bassey whoops as she lays eyes on me. 'You look absolutely grisly! Boys cannot do make-up.'

Then she whispers, 'Even gay ones!'

We'd been emotively reunited, Frances and I, on Monday morning outside the Co-op: me beseeching her forgiveness, and her settling for a cream horn from Broomfields as apt atonement for my former despicability. I told her about Moira and Squirrel's incarceration, and I thought she'd actually become semi-melancholic at first.

'Poor likkle Toby,' she'd said. 'He was such a nice bwoy when him small, den 'im go bad!'

But after that she screamed with malicious delight as I recounted the actual events adjacent to poor Moira's arrest at our house the previous afternoon, and Chrissy's resultant hysteria.

'I suppose it serve dem right,' she said in her mother's voice. 'Selling drugs to kids!' And I nodded solemnly.

When we got closer to school, by the big Marlboro man, she stopped me and said, 'I've got something for you, David.'

So I turned to face her, curious, as she fished around at the bottom of her satchel.

'Remember when we went to the badge shop that afternoon?' she said. 'Well, I got you a surprise gift – remember I told you?'

'Oh yes!'

'Only I forgot to give it to you, and then last night I suddenly remembered it, and . . . well . . . here! I hope you like it!'

And she handed me a badge, a pink badge with a black arrow on it, and a bold slogan: Gays Against Nazis.

'Oh!'

'Do you like it?' she said expectantly.

I stared down at it in the palm of my hand for five or six seconds, and then I said, 'Yeah, I do. I really like it.'

'I thought you could wear it,' she said, 'to school.'

'Today?' I said. 'You mean right this minute?'

And she nodded, smiling.

'They all know,' she said. 'Why not be the one to say it first?'

So I gingerly pinned the badge on to my blazer lapel, and then grinned at Frances apprehensively, and grabbed her hand.

'Brilliant!' she said. 'Now let's see them call you queer.'

And we'd giggled and walked arm in arm through the school gates.

'Now, why don't you come up to Chorus' dressing room and I'll do your make-up properly?' Frances suggests. 'You look like you're auditioning for the Black and White Minstrels! We're just up on the next floor in Class D6.'

She's right! My vision of Nancy is looking more and more like a cheap disco act that's been shopping at Oxfam.

'OK, then.'

And I gather up my stuff.

'And mind you don't trip over your bloody frock, dear,' she laughs, as she dances back out of the library in front of me.

Inside Class D6, a host of Fagin's orphans, various black-toothed street vendors and sundry members of the ensemble are all buzzing about wildly under the tentative supervision of a slouching and somewhat dispassionate Miss Jibbs, who must – me and Frances have always imagined – have some sort of bovine lineage. She is currently flaccid in an armchair, smoking, and attempting to ignore the screaming accumulation of students surrounding her.

'The play's been extended to a three-night run,' squeaks one excitable nineteenth-century pallbearer. 'The auditorium is packed.'

By auditorium, this diminutive coffin-carrier had meant the lower assembly hall, currently rammed to the rafters with our collective families and friends: mine, Frances's and, indeed, Maxie Boswell's. Even my dad has shown his face, with an enthusiasm that has floored me. And Moira – full of remorse, and with the cheek of Old Nick – has, rather staggeringly, turned up too, having been charged and released on Monday morning. She is, however, incognito and sporting a brand-new hairpiece and dark sunglasses for the occasion.

'Isn't that Myra Hindley sitting next to your mum?' Sonia Barker had said to me on spotting her. 'I didn't know she was out.'

Frances is now hurriedly getting into her own First Act costume, and I'm staring into the mirror feeling much more contented with my overall manifestation – she's done a superb job, has Frances.

'That looks a million times better, David,' she says, as she adds a few finishing touches to my rehabilitated maquillage. 'You look like a proper Nancy now.'

'Good! Now I need to warm up my voice before the show. Have you got that Kate Bush cassette?'

And we head back out into the corridor excitedly. As we reach the top of the stairs to come down, a devilishly handsome but authentically evil Bill Sikes – aka Jason Lancaster – is leaning against the wall, flanked by two of his shorter, plainer cronies with the same style of cropped hair as him. My stomach flips, and I involuntarily put my hand up to my lip, to the very place where one of the vicious cuts administered by Jason only a week or so before had been. Frances shakes her head at him in disgust.

'Well, look who it is,' she says. 'Stinkin' up d' hallway.'

But Jason doesn't even look at her, and just flicks the brim of his top hat cockily.

'I've seen it all now,' he laughs, tugging at my wig. 'Jesus, could you be any more of a queer, Starr?'

And at first I falter, edging back away from him; but then, out of the blue, something comes over me and I lift the bottom of my gown and step forward, oddly unafraid, shoving my face at Jason's.

'Listen to me, you fucking brainless moron, it really doesn't matter to me what you or any of your miniature brownshirts call me now. Yes, I'm gay, yes, I like boys, yes, I'm all the things you and your little pals say I am: bender, poofter, batty boy, pansy, a fucking fully fledged cocksucking – chance would be a fine thing – queer! So why don't you run along and taunt somebody that's vaguely interested in and/or intimidated by your wretched and ever-shrinking repertoire of hate?'

Jason blinked three times.

'What?'

'Shall I simplify it for you, dear? Fuck off!'

And I smile agreeably.

Frances is giggling into her pelerine collar, and Jason looks entirely bewildered for a second. It is bewilderment, though, that fast turns to fury, and he whirls around to finally acknowledge her sniggers.

'And what are you laughing at?' he spits at her, yanking her dress down at the neck.

'Did they even have darkies in frocks those days? I don't think they did ... they were all fucking slaves, weren't they?'

Frances stops laughing fast, and catches her breath, turning to me, eyes wide. I look back at her for what seems an age and then, with one nippy jerk, she yanks up her petticoats and lets fly with a laced-up, calf-length, dangerously pointed boot: a trenchant kick to Jason Lancaster's soft and unshielded bollocks.

'Nazi,' she says quietly.

We both step back, suddenly drenched in a melange of astonishment, fear and utter hilarity, as Jason shrieks an inhuman cry, doubling up in pain and dropping to his knees. When he vomits uncontrollably on to the shoes of his horrified captains, Frances and I turn and saunter, leisurely and somewhat in-differently, down the stairs and back to the library.

Hamish McClarnon is in mid-pre-performance pep lecture as we waft elatedly through the library door, swinging our skirts, with the mood in the room at fever pitch. All around us kids are rushing about singing songs and reciting lines, chased by wild-eyed teachers brandishing mob caps and frock coats, and Hamish seems to be fighting a losing battle as he bellows over the melee.

'There you are, David,' Hamish interrupts his speech mid-flow. 'We're on in ten and I thought I'd lost ma Nancy and ma Bill.'

'No, I'm right here, sir!' I shout over the din.

Sonia Barker is hot on our heels through the door, panting breathlessly and wearing plunge-necked red and white gingham, which looks more Calamity Jane than Oliver Twist, if you ask me.

'Sir! Sir!' she hollers. 'Jason's been taken sick, he's spewing his ring up in the boys' khazi.'

'What?'

Hamish squints, slightly disbelieving, and I toss Frances a worried glance, biting my bottom lip. Frances just shrugs her shoulders, though.

'He's absolutely fucked, sir!' Sonia goes on, her naturally matted hair generously adding to the facade of a grubby tart from the Old West. 'Absolutely fuckin' fucked!'

'Oh, Jesus, no!' Hamish says, banging his fist on his head. 'Not now, not now!'

Step forward Maxie Boswell, who strides into the middle of the room like Sir Lancelot to face a befuddled Hamish.

'I'll do it!' he says. 'I know Bill Sikes' part backwards and I'm a better actor than Jason Lancaster ever was. Let me do it!'

My heart does a couple of full and fast flips as Hamish glares down at him.

'I don't know about that, Maxie – are ye parents not here?' he says. 'They didne want you in the play at all, lad; I don't want te cause a rumpus wi' them.'

But Maxie is unwavering.

'What if I go and ask them, sir?' he pleads. 'They won't say no if I explain that we'll have to cancel the play otherwise – they'd be too embarrassed.'

Hamish chews his bottom lip and looks around the room, which erupts into cries of 'Oh go on, sir!' and 'Let Maxie do it, sir!'

Nobody wants to cancel the show.

'Run and ask, then,' Hamish relents. 'And if they say it's all right, and only then, go and see how much of that costume ye can prise off o' Lancaster. Just make sure it's not covered in sick.'

'Yes, sir!'

Maxie dashes across the library, halting in his tracks as he reaches Frances and me.

'Are you OK with this?' he says with a delicate but panicky smile.

And then he puts his hands in his pockets and looks down at the carpet like a little boy, so I nod.

'I'm OK with it.'

'Right!' Hamish commands, clapping his hands together. 'Overture and beginners! Go round up the orphans, Sonia, and then everyone in Act One go down the stairs quietly . . . I said quietly!'

I'm standing at the top of the stairs now, gathering myself . . . focusing . . . becoming Nancy, as her buoyant but ultimately tragic spirit seeps through my every sinew. I descend, as the orchestra strikes up, all set for my too-long-awaited debut. All set to show them what I'm made of. Here I go . . .

The first act whizzes past in a blur, and goes fairly swimmingly, I think, though I'm unpleasantly aware that nobody can fathom a damn word that our particular Mr Bumble – who boasts a stutter and a fairly thick Zimbabwean accent – is saying. What with that and Oliver's lisp I start to think that subtitles projected on to a screen at the side of the stage mightn't have been a bad idea. In the crowd, though the lights are in my eyes, I spot Mum, Dad, Nan and Aunt Val, all

grinning with enthusiasm during my stirring inter-
pretation of 'It's A Fine Life'. Sonia Barker is of very
little use, though, as my sidekick, Bet, so I snatch back
most of the song lines that Hamish has charitably and
imprudently donated to her, and watch as her mouth
opens and closes like a dying flounder while my voice
soars across the Three Cripples Tavern over the top of
hers.

There is one slightly disconcerting episode just after
the start of Act Two, when one of the flower-sellers
totters violently backwards into the scenery during
'Who Will Buy This Wonderful Morning?', but I don't
think most of the audience even twig, and there's very
little blood to speak of.

Maxie, as Bill Sikes, has, betwixt all the grimacing
and snarling, given me several gentle, almost pining
looks during our scenes together, but I am far too
swathed in my role to crumble under the weight of
those doe eyes at the present time. I am a tour de force
– charming the pants off the audience with 'I'd Do
Anything'; inciting them to a vigorous singalong with
'Oom Pah Pah'; and then, finally, tearing their hearts
asunder with 'As Long As He Needs Me' (Judy
Garland version).

'You're doing great, love, absolutely fantastic,' Mum
had enthused when she, plus Nan and Aunt Val, came
backstage during the interval, all dolled up. 'I'm
really proud of you, Davey, especially after all the stuff
that's gone on in the last couple of weeks. Really
proud!'

'Fucking fabulous!' Aunt Val concurred. 'You're

easily the best one in it; even your father's singing along, silly bastard.'

And Nan gave me a big wet kiss on the cheek to seal the deal. I was a hit at last!

As the string section of the orchestra – a group of snotty but reasonably capable sixth-formers from Dulwich College – meander around a sinister refrain, I am discovered under a single white spotlight on a somewhat rickety London Bridge. I am clutching dear, runny-nosed Oliver, ready to deliver him selflessly into the safe arms of Mr Brownlow at the expense of my own life. As I cast my eyes across the hall, packed with enthralled spectators, I spot Bob Lord sitting stiffly next to Vi and Geoff Boswell, who are wriggling uncomfortably in their seats in the third row. Oh, God! I take a deep breath and turn my attention back to the action. I am, after all, about to be murdered, destroyed by Maxie Boswell – for the second time in two weeks.

'Let 'im go, Bill,' I cry as Maxie accosts me viciously and convincingly. 'Let the boy go!'

But Bill Sikes is having none of it, dragging sweet, sweaty little Oliver from me and brutally casting him to the ground.

'No, Bill . . . no . . . you wouldn't!' I wail.

And I'm convinced I hear terrified gasps from the audience, so I ad lib slightly and switch the Cockney twang up a gear to realize full dramatic effect.

'Not tha' boy, Biwl! Please dunt 'urt the boy!'

Bill, née Maxie, grabs my arm, driving me forcefully against the shuddering, teal-painted hardboard of

London Bridge and putting his hands around my throat.

'I'll pay you back!' he roars. 'I'll pay you back!'

Now, in most other productions of the play, Nancy is beaten mercilessly to death with Bill Sikes' staff, but our headmaster had deemed this excessively bloodthirsty, so I was to be asphyxiated, i.e. choked to death, by my malevolent lover while his faithful and ferocious dog, Bullseye – in this event, Miss Jibbs' bichon frise, Tilly – looks on. I let out one last, strangled scream as Bill's hands tighten around my neck, and I look pleadingly into his cruel, unforgiving eyes.

'NAAW!!!!'

It is at that moment that Maxie stops dead, his grip loosening: what the hell is he doing? Why doesn't he kill me? He's supposed to kill me. He stares at me, instead, an almost puzzled gaze – deep into my eyes – for several very long, conspicuous seconds, and does not move or make a sound. I can see Hamish gesticulating frantically from the wings, mouthing 'What's going on' and 'Get on with it', but Maxie has his back to him so is completely oblivious. The audience are starting to mutter uneasily now, so I decide that the most pragmatic course of action is to ignore Maxie altogether and drop down dead of my own accord. Before I can actually wriggle free and accomplish this, though, Maxie lifts his hand, touching my face softly, and then he leans in – closer and closer towards me – until he is kissing me lovingly on the mouth for exactly five seconds, and to a soundtrack of gasps from the

cast and audience in the lower assembly hall. I suspect
that Bob Lord and Vi Boswell might have actually died
right then and there, not to mention my own father,
but I care nothing about any of that, or for anyone else
in that moment under the spotlight on London Bridge
– and neither, it seems, does Maxie.

When he is done his eyes are bright and his face full
of devilment, and I grin back at him. Then, clearing his
throat and composing himself, he places his hands
back around my neck and finishes off the dirty,
murderous deed he's there to do. I finally slump to the
ground. Dead. And smiling.

When we stand in rows to take our bows at the end,
the crowd exalts us rowdily. Mum, Nan and Moira,
still in her dark glasses, are up on their feet in the
second row, cheering, as are Chrissy and Abigail. Dad
is clapping, but sitting, and Aunt Val is projecting loud
wolf whistles across the hall. As the principals trot forward for a final bow, this time with Hamish – our
director – I notice that the Boswells and Bob Lord are
nowhere to be seen in the appreciative throng, so I
turn to Maxie, next to me, offering a concerned, if not
terribly sad, smile. He merely shrugs and winks at me,
just at the moment when Frances Bassey roughly
shoves her way to the front through a line of orphans,
sending them scattering. The crowd lets go with one
ultimate cheer, and the orchestra erupts into a rousing
reprise of 'It's A Fine Life'. Everybody sings along as
Maxie, Frances and I suddenly surge forward together
in a line, laughing and singing louder than everybody

else . . . then, holding hands very, very tight, we curtsy.

In my dream, now, Agnetha, Anni-Frid and I are running towards the helicopter in slow motion, just as the chopper's strident engines start, and its blades begin to circle, flattening the long, thick grass all around it. The air is salt and brittle and I sense water nearby, but only see green and sky, and I feel invigorated beyond anything I've ever experienced. As we reach the awaiting bird-machine in our white jumpsuits and clogs, the girls and I turn and wave regally, but there is nobody there and I'm suddenly baffled.

'It's time to go, David,' Anni-Frid says with a dark Scandinavian lilt. 'Are you ready?'

I nod but I'm not terribly convinced; Agnetha touches my epaulette reassuringly.

'Let's go.'

We clamber aboard and there, rather unsurprisingly, I discover the boys from Abba, too, Benny and Björn, and sitting beside them, rather more surprisingly, Debbie Harry dressed in a black plastic bin-liner and pixie boots.

'Where are we going?' I shout, hauling myself in.

'That's the thing, baby,' Debbie smiles. 'You can go anywhere you want from here. You just have to decide.'

'We can take you any place you wanna go,' adds Björn.

Hmmm . . . well, this is something that clearly warrants careful deliberation then, surely. Where *do* I want to go? What do I want to see? In a second I have whispered my chosen destination to Anni-Frid and she, in turn, leans over and informs the pilot.

'Buckle up, David,' Benny instructs over the engine's din, and I settle down between the ladies as we tear away from the ground, hovering momentarily like an eagle riding on the breeze, and then shooting into the white sky.

Epilogue

I am tantamount to wetting myself with excitement, despite our really crappy seats, as I leaf through my concert programme. Wembley Arena is positively glittering tonight, and much, much bigger than anywhere I have ever been to see a show of any sort – but then again . . . this is Abba!

Frances's face is glowing next to me as she unravels her shabby homemade fan-scarf and waves it above her head, screaming, 'Come on!'

I giggle to myself and wonder what the Jason Lancasters of this world might make of Frances and me – whooping and hollering for our Swedish idols with glitter on our faces and scarves around our wrists. They were all still out there – those unapprised fuckers – but tonight we cared not. Tonight, just like Jason, crumpled hopelessly on the school stairwell outside Class D6, they were voiceless.

'I want it to start!' Frances says, turning to me.

'Maxie would have loved it – wouldn't Maxie have loved it, David?'

I'm not convinced that Maxie even liked Abba, to be honest, but I'm certain he'd have got a kick out of the buzzing crowd, and the electric atmosphere, were he here. But he wasn't.

On the afternoon before our opening-night triumph, Geoff Boswell, Maxie's dad, had apparently announced to his family that he'd been relocated, after a vehement reshuffle at Stationery Universe had left the company wanting in one of their smaller concerns just outside Lytham St Annes. Evidently Vi Boswell had scarcely waited for her old man to peruse the letter before she'd packed up her bits and pieces, alerted the estate agent and enrolled poor Maxie in a high-achieving mixed comprehensive in Ormskirk. They'd put their house up for rent and vacated it within about two weeks and, according to Maxie, had been so wildly keen to do so that Vi had not even given her recently lain and hitherto much cherished peach shagpile a second glance backward.

Anyway, the long and the short of it was – Maxie was gone, and, after a certain amount of lip service implying unwavering devotion and a few desultory phone calls, so was Maxie's apparent zeal for our so-called romance. It had stung at first, and for a short while, as having one's heart ripped out might tend to. Then, on the night I threw Frances a glam-rock-themed birthday party and sleepover at number twenty-two Chesterfield Street, her dashing next-door neighbour, Warren, boldly invited himself to stay, sharing my bed in the shortage.

A boy of mixed race, Warren boasted glossy, poker-straight black hair and lips with a trampoline bounce, and he had behaved unexpectedly and gloriously improperly for a blindside flanker during the night, and well into the hours of dawn. He then cheerily reported to me, as he pulled on his Farrahs that morning, that I had definitely – and I might be paraphrasing here – brought him off better than his bird ever had. This was quite an accolade, I felt, and served to bring me notion and hope of pastures new, boyfriend-wise: onwards and upwards, I thought.

That very same bright week, there had been splendid reports of the downfall of Bob Lord at the Board of Teacher Governors' extraordinary meeting to determine the new Head of Fifth Year, Miss Jibbs having point-blank refused to return from her auntie Iris' chalet in the Vale of Glamorgan after a stress-related depression that led to Bell's palsy. Mr Lord had attempted to convince all and sundry that he would be taking over from the afflicted Miss Jibbs, insisting that he was the only man for the job. Bob came unstuck, however, when facing the board – which, chaired by the headmaster, also consisted of Hamish McClarnon, Mr Peacock and a couple of the more left-wing members of staff, who felt that he might not possess the nurturing disposition required to handle the gaping array of teenage issues that he could well be called upon to deal with.

'I'm afraid that as a unanimous vote of the board is required,' Hamish had seemingly told a crestfallen Mr Lord, 'you'll not be offered the position you've applied for in this school.'

Word has it that Bob Lord's resignation was on the head's desk that afternoon.

Things are ticking over favourably on the home front, too, on the whole. Mum and Aunt Val are no different than they were before my coming out, apart from the fact that now they try to get me to admit that I do, in fact, lust after Paul Michael Glaser and hadn't just wanted to get my hands on the knitting pattern for the cardigan after all. Even Dad seems to have resigned himself to the inevitable, this highlighted by an incident at the Lordship Lane Working Men's Club last Thursday night, on my shift during the ladies' darts match. I was enthusing to Denise about a well-endowed French acrobat I'd spotted on *The Generation Game*, when an unfamiliar man waiting to be served – a thickset and rather puffy individual with an unruly tone – turned to my dad, who was also propping up the bar, and snorted, 'Who's the fuckin' faggot serving behind the jump?'

An older woman standing next to my dad and holding a barley wine turned and met the man's eye with a toxic stare.

'That's my grandson,' Nan said.

'Yeah, so fuck off!' Dad supplemented.

And he did.

* * *

'Wooooooooooh!'

Frances is shrieking and making a complete show of herself as synthesizer swells build and then suddenly consume the arena before melting into a spectacular refrain, the crowd's ovation duly rapturous.

'I can't believe we're here, about to watch Abba, can you?' Frances says, almost tearfully.

'No, I can't! I really can't.'

Now drums . . . now bass . . . now guitars . . . everyone is on their feet, except for me – I'm strangely frozen. Now lights . . . now screams!

'Get up!' Frances hollers. 'It's starting – they're on! They're on!'

And I leap out of my seat, and then there they are . . .

'People everywhere, sense of expectation hanging in the air . . .'

And we're off!